True
HEART'S
DESIRE

Center Point
Large Print

Also by Caroline Fyffe and available from Center Point Large Print:

Heart of Eden

This Large Print Book carries the Seal of Approval of N.A.V.H.

True HEART'S DESIRE

A Colorado Hearts Novel

Caroline Fyffe

CENTER POINT LARGE PRINT
THORNDIKE, MAINE

This Center Point Large Print edition
is published in the year 2018 by arrangement with
Amazon Publishing, www.apub.com.

Originally published in the United States by
Amazon Publishing, 2018.

The text of this Large Print edition is unabridged.
In other aspects, this book may vary
from the original edition.
Printed in the United States of America
on permanent paper.
Set in 16-point Times New Roman type.

ISBN: 978-1-68324-924-5

Library of Congress Cataloging-in-Publication Data

Names: Fyffe, Caroline, author.
Title: True heart's desire : a Colorado hearts novel / Caroline Fyffe.
Description: Center Point Large Print edition. | Thorndike, Maine :
    Center Point Large Print, 2018.
Identifiers: LCCN 2018023382 | ISBN 9781683249245
    (hardcover : large print)
Subjects: LCSH: Large type books. | GSAFD: Love stories.
Classification: LCC PS3606.Y44 T78 2018 | DDC 813/.6—dc23
LC record available at https://lccn.loc.gov/2018023382

For Rachel Brown, a beautiful, delightful,
and inspirational young woman
who brings much love, light, and joy
into our lives.

True
HEART'S
DESIRE

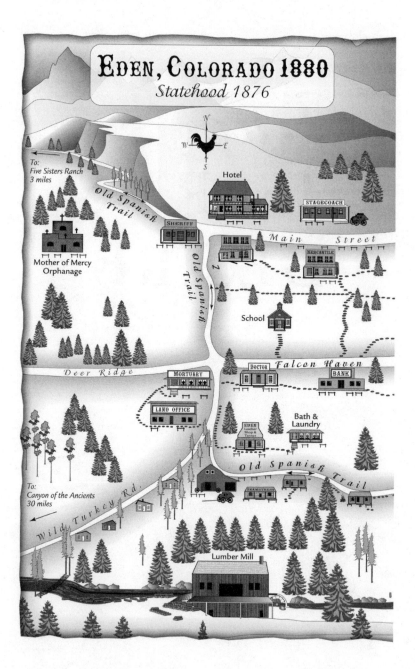

CHAPTER ONE

San Francisco, California, February 1881

O ne ticket to Eden, Colorado."
The grizzled ticket agent scratched his oily hair with a trembling hand. "One-way or round-trip, young man?"

Rhett Laughlin heaved a deep sigh. He hardly felt young, but compared with the slow-moving old-timer, one might call him that. "One-way."

A line had formed behind Rhett. When a baby shrieked in his ear, he glanced over his shoulder to see a red-faced boy in the arms of threadbare parents.

The woman gave an apologetic smile.

Rhett reached into his pocket and pulled out a small wooden ship. He placed the toy into the tiny hand of the child, who looked to be about one year old. "This might help," he said, nodding to the baby's mother. His gaze lingered on the old toy that had been his brother's when they were boys.

"We couldn't," she demurred.

"Sure you can. See, he's already quieted."

With a small smile, he turned back as a welcome silence settled over his agitated shoulders.

The ticket agent was waiting. "Cantal Pacific Union will take ya into southern Wyoming Territory where you'll have ta take a stage south, iffin you don't want ta buy a horse."

By the man's tone, he'd said those words a million times. As if to punctuate his sentence, he rolled his lips over his teeth and then spit behind the counter—into a spittoon, Rhett hoped. Lifting his arm, the agent wiped a wrinkled sleeve across his mouth.

Uncertainty tried to muddle Rhett's resolve. Tried to jumble his thoughts. *No. I've finally made a decision.* He shoved forward the fare, the folded newspaper clasped beneath his arm feeling heavy. Not in weight, but for the part the paper played in his decision to leave San Francisco and his father.

The old-timer slowly counted Rhett's cash, arranging the money properly in his drawer, unmindful of everyone waiting. He pushed back a large ticket printed in red ink. "Don't be late. Train runs on time. She'll pull out not caring if you're on or off."

The deed done, Rhett left the cramped office and strode down the busy San Francisco street, the view of the bay easing his spirits. He'd miss the mist on his face and the sound of the fog-horns. The large white gulls always looking for a handout. The city was in his blood. He'd been born and raised here.

Scents of fish, steam pots, and refuse assaulted his senses—the hustle and bustle a blessing that kept him from thinking, remembering. Rita and Lucy, two women he knew from his time spent at the bars, waved from the opposite side of the road. Lucy called his name and smiled suggestively. After his relationship with Margery, his sweetheart of three years, came to an abrupt end, he'd spent time with both saloon girls, easing his broken heart. But the days of whiling his time away in taverns and card rooms were in the past. He had something else, something important, to accomplish. All he had to do was to stay on track.

It's time to make some changes. Not for me, but for Shawn.

He smiled and nodded at the women but didn't cross the street to talk. Instead, he turned sharply and entered a two-story boardinghouse.

Dallas, sitting by the front window, bolted toward Rhett in welcome.

Rhett leaned down and rubbed the dusty-brown-haired mix on the neck, thankful the dog hadn't been lost along with his brother.

"You're going, then?" Elmer, another boarder, called from a small table where he played solitaire.

"I am. On tomorrow's train. But first, I'm

13

going to visit my father. Say goodbye." He'd lost his father just as much as he'd lost Margery and Shawn. His father would never say so, but Rhett had seen the truth in his eyes: *If not for me, Shawn would still be here.*

Elmer smiled at Dallas waiting at Rhett's heels. "He's been hounding all day to get out. I'm glad you're finally back."

"Thanks for keeping him. He runs to the dock every chance he gets." Rhett hunkered down and put an arm around Dallas's neck, a wave of emotion rocking his resolve. "Shawn's not coming back, boy. I'm sorry."

"The dog going with you?"

Rhett stood. "He is."

Elmer nodded as he dealt out a new hand. "I'm glad fer ya then. Ever since your brother read those stories about those sisters, things changed with him. I hope you find what you're looking for."

Rhett only smiled and ascended the stairs, Dallas's toenails clicking softly beside. He wouldn't miss this old place. Having a direction, a purpose, would actually feel good. *If I don't buckle down, I'll end up like Elmer downstairs. Wasting away my life.*

Once he arrived in Eden, he'd make his brother proud, if the doing took every bit of hard work he had left inside him. The plan was already in motion. Rhett had sent an inquiring telegram to Colorado a few weeks ago but hadn't made a final decision about whether he was actually going or not until this morning.

Slipping his room key into the lock, he twisted it, then shoved the unwilling door with his shoulder. He'd be more than glad to leave this place. Moving to Eden had been Shawn's idea, but now that his brother was dead, he planned to fulfill Shawn's dream. And after that?

His own future had yet to be determined.

CHAPTER TWO

~✻~

Eden, Colorado, March 1881

Lavinia Brinkman steeled herself against the coming pain, her heartbreak more than she could bear. She levered her upper body off the hotel bed and onto her elbow, being careful to keep her eyes closed. Even so, a stinging jab cut through her left eye and pierced inside her head, making her gasp.

What are the chances?

And today of all days.

She peeked at the clock. Everyone else was already at the church. Tears leaked from behind her closed eyelids, the thought of missing her sister's wedding adding a deep, throbbing ache. Each day since their arrival in Eden last September had been building to this day . . .

Oh, Belle . . . Her chest quivered. *We've been through so much—all of us, and always together. I want to hear you say your vows. Only a miracle can help me now . . .*

Drawing in a shaky breath, she thought of their father loving them from almost two thousand miles away. For eighteen years he sent support, unbeknownst to them. The tragic story was never far from her thoughts. When he died and they'd been summoned to Eden, she and her sisters had left behind a soot-filled Philadelphia for lofty mountain peaks and fresh, clean air. And that had only been the beginning.

Unable to keep them in check, Lavinia let the tears scorch her cheeks. She reached blindly toward the nightstand, where a lantern burned in the dim room, and patted around until her fingers closed on the handkerchief Mavis had placed there for her use. By now, the ushers would have seated the guests and Blake would be waiting at the altar. Belle, their other sisters, and their good friend Lara Marsh, who'd traveled all the way from Pennsylvania to be in attendance for the event, would be atwitter with excitement in the entry of the church, safely away from curious eyes.

Dearest Belle, I'm sending you my love. Can you feel it? I'm with you in my heart.

This morning, when Lavinia had been putting the finishing touches on the veil she'd created for Belle, a tiny stem fragment from one of the blossoms she'd been attaching to the crown had splintered off and flicked into her eye. The pain had been excruciating, dropping her to her knees. Her sisters had laid her on the bed and then set out to help. Rinsing, crying, and even examining her eye with a magnifying glass. Soon, there was nothing for them to do but dress and go to the church. Her sisters hadn't wanted to leave her behind, but she'd insisted. She'd not let her accident ruin Belle's wedding day.

A knock came at her door. "Lavinia, it's me, Karen. May I come in?"

"Of course."

Karen Forester, waitress in the hotel café and now Lavinia's employee, hurried inside. When they'd first arrived in Eden, the middle-aged woman had taken her and her sisters under her protective wing. Looking out for them, introducing them around, and being the mother they'd all lost fifteen years before. Today was no different.

She heard Karen quietly enter and close the door behind her.

"You must hurry or you'll miss the wedding," Lavinia said softly. She forced a smile, knowing all too well Karen was watching her every expression. Karen, in her generosity, would stay behind in a heartbeat.

"I'm about to set off, but I've warmed a little oil and brought a medicine dropper. There's a possibility whatever was in your eye is now gone but left a scratch, and that's what's causing the pain. Perhaps the liquid will help soothe the discomfort. Do you want to try?"

"Even if what you say is true, I'd still have to

18

finish dressing. I'd never arrive in time. And now I fear you won't either. Hurry now, please. Belle needs to see you there."

The rumble of the afternoon stagecoach jerked and rattled outside. Lavinia listened as Karen went to the window. She heard the sound of Karen pushing back the curtain.

"Lavinia?"

There was a note of wonder in Karen's voice.

"Today's the fifth of March. In the madness leading up to the wedding, we all forgot the new doctor is scheduled to arrive. A man I've never seen before has just stepped out of the stagecoach and is coming into the hotel. He's carrying a small black case . . ."

Hope surged into Lavinia's throat. What were the chances? "Oh!"

"He's tall and broad, but . . . ah, well, unkempt for any doctor I've seen."

Karen gasped in what sounded like surprise.

"A large dog has jumped out of the stage as well."

Lavinia clapped her hands with excitement. "My miracle has arrived! The question is, Can he help me in time? Could you please run down and bring him up?"

"Right away."

"Wait! Even if he *can* extract the object, if we don't let Belle know I'm on my way, ask her to hold off for a few minutes, I'll still miss the ceremony. If you can help me to my feet, I'll manage the doctor and you run to the church."

"Wonderful idea!"

Carefully, so as not to inflict more pain, Karen helped Lavinia, clad only in her corset and pantaloons, to her feet and held wide her robe so she could shrug inside. After a few fumbles, Lavinia cinched the garment tight.

"I must hurry," Lavinia breathed, each passing second seeming more urgent. "The side exit will save you a few steps."

Once Karen had left for the church, Lavinia navigated the empty hallway as quickly as her infirmity would allow. For the occasion, she had closed the café downstairs so Karen and the other help could attend the long-awaited nuptials between the second-oldest Brinkman daughter and Blake Harding, the man who would become their partner in the Five Sisters Ranch in a few short weeks.

Lavinia carefully descended the stairs in the silent building. She peeked from her good eye every few steps to be sure she wasn't going off course, while keeping her left eye closed as best she could. With one hand firmly on the banister, and the other clenching together the lapels of her robe, she arrived on the last step and could see the shadowy figure of a man standing in the vacant lobby. The small black case in his right hand brought a wave of excitement. Help had arrived!

As she got closer, though, she felt herself shrinking in his large presence. Dark stubble covered his face, as if he hadn't bothered to shave for two or three days. Hatless, his wavy, dark hair suggested his fingers were the only implements to try to tame the mass. Lavinia's gaze dropped to the handle of the black case and the fingers holding the bag. There was no dog in sight.

"Thank heavens you've arrived! Please, I need your assistance right away." When he didn't move or respond, she took hold of his free arm, noticing an elusive scent of pine, dust, and travel.

He pulled back, surely surprised to be accosted by a strange woman wearing a dressing gown. Still filled with hope, she carefully opened her right eye, bracing herself against the pain.

"I have something in my left eye," she explained, "and the pain is just too great for me to open it." She tugged on his arm again, but he stayed rooted to the spot. "Please, we have to hurry. I've a magnifying glass upstairs and—"

"What?"

His deep voice sent a wave of awareness skittering around inside her.

"I'm looking for a meal, but I see the café is closed," he said. "Where is everybody?"

"Oh!" she gushed. "Of course. I'll be more than happy to provide you a meal as thanks for your assistance. I'm sorry, but there's no time now." Her efforts had moved him all of three steps. "I can understand how odd this looks, but Belle," she said more slowly, "my beautiful *sister* Belle is about to get married—*right now!* Everyone is already in the church except me. You've arrived just in time to help me so I can attend as well." She tugged, and he came along a few more steps. "All I need is for you to look into my eye and extract whatever is causing the pain."

He was moving now. With her eyes closed, but peeking every few steps, she pulled him along. "We've tried absolutely everything. Rinsing with water, crying, even blowing—but that really hurt. As soon as you extract the evil object, I'll slip into my bridesmaid's dress and run down the street. My friend has gone ahead to let them know I'm on my way. They're holding the ceremony for my arrival."

During her long oration, she'd dragged him halfway up the stairs, amazing even herself. Karen had been right. The doctor was large, possibly taller than Blake or even Clint. The strange thing was, he seemed reluctant to do his job, or even to speak. Perhaps he was put off by her half-dressed state. Maybe he was a Quaker and she had offended his delicate senses. Or possibly she was his first female patient. Could a doctor really be as shy as a newborn bunny? Frightened or not, she was bound and determined that their new doctor help her. She couldn't miss the wedding!

Tugging his arm the last few steps, she pulled him inside her hotel room, slammed the door, and then flung herself onto the bed. "I await your assistance!"

CHAPTER THREE

*A*nd what am I supposed to do with her?
Irritation seeped through Rhett as he gazed
down at the distraught young woman on the
bed, her eyes clamped closed, and the rapidness
of her pulse at the base of her throat reminding
him of a hummingbird. Her dark hair, done up
in some sort of curled fashion, was a bit untidy.
Was she disturbed in the mind? She had to be
a Brinkman, right here before him on the bed.
Belle Brinkman, the sister she'd mentioned, was
the second oldest. At the time he'd read them, the
papers had said all the sisters were single and the
oldest was a widow. He hadn't been aware of any
upcoming nuptials.

"Doctor?"

*Doctor? Now things are beginning to make
sense.* He wasn't a doctor, but he wasn't a
rogue either. He wouldn't take advantage of the
situation.

Her right eye cracked open, but only for a
second. She'd be steaming mad if he told her
the truth now, and for Shawn's plan to work, it
would behoove him to stay on the Brinkmans'

24

good side. Perhaps he *could* help her make the wedding. "This warm oil?"

"Yes. We were just about to put some in my eye when you arrived. My friend saw you had a dog when you got off the stage. Where is it?"

Setting his bag next to her on the bed, he bent over. "He's waiting on the porch."

"He won't run off?"

"No." *There are no docks to run to and look for Shawn.* "Can you open your eye at all?"

Her right eye opened again, and then her left cracked a tiny bit. Her mouth tightened, most likely caused by pain, and he glanced away. He realized he'd have to lean closer, *much closer,* to see anything. But first, he needed more light.

Straightening, he retrieved a second lantern from the far side of the room and set it next to the lamp already burning on the nightstand. He lit the new addition and gave an encouraging smile in response to Miss Brinkman's wobbly expression. The tracks of her tears made him swallow. He turned both lamps up as far as possible and hunkered down on one knee.

"All right. I'm just going to look first, see if I can see anything. I'll be as gentle as possible."

With the tip of his finger, he lifted her eyelid from just below her brow, and with his other hand gently pulled down below her eye. She bore the pain like a soldier. They were eyeball

25

to eyeball. He couldn't see anything amiss.

He drew back. Nervous now, he rubbed his hands together for a few moments, thinking, and then swiped the back of his wrist across his mouth, realizing with a start that three days had passed since he'd scraped off his whiskers. If he looked frightening, she didn't show it. "Did you say you had a magnifying glass?" he asked as he stood and glanced around.

There, across the room on a chair.

"Never mind." Retrieving the implement, he returned and knelt again.

"At this rate, I'll miss the wedding *and* the reception."

He blinked, and then chuckled when he realized she'd made a joke. "I'll hurry."

"Thank you."

It didn't take a magnifying glass to see her extraordinary beauty. Her heart-shaped face was offset with high cheekbones lightly brushed with peach. Her skin looked incredibly soft. Warmth swished through his veins. In the telescopic glass, her eye, now bloodshot, appeared much larger than normal.

"There," he lied. His father had taught him the mind was a powerful tool. Perhaps if Miss Brinkman thought he'd helped her, the pain might go away. "Hold tight. I think I see what's causing the problem. I'll make the extraction and then put in a few drops of the warm oil to soothe

the sting. After which, we can cover your eye with a patch to keep out the light."

"Thank you. If you could, *please* hurry."

Yes, he could do that.

Using the handkerchief on the nightstand, Rhett quickly twisted the end into a tiny spear. He tried not to be distracted as he again came close, touching the side of her eyeball once, and then another time, lingering a moment or two, just long enough to appear like he was doing something real. Even in an agitated state, her eye was the prettiest one he'd ever seen . . . or had the pleasure of memorizing. Sun-colored flecks, as well as snippets of emerald, filled her fawn-colored iris.

Finished, he drew back.

She blinked once and then waited, staring up at the ceiling.

Working fast, he sucked up a tiny amount of oil into the eyedropper. "Open wide for the oil." When she obeyed, he squeezed two drops into her waiting eye. She didn't flinch but clenched her eyes closed. He placed the handkerchief into her hand. "For the excess."

She nodded and opened her right eye.

"Keep your eyes closed and let the oil do its job. I'll look for something to use as a patch." He stood and glanced around. A lavender dress draped the back of a chair. A pair of tiny, feminine shoes sat close by. "How does that feel?"

"Warm."

"Can you open your eye?"

She lifted a hand, dabbed at both corners, and then blinked several times. "I think the pain is lessening."

"Good. Now let's see what we can use to cover it." He glanced around and saw several hats hanging from the opposite corners of her dresser mirror.

She rose onto her elbow and turned toward his bag. "Don't you carry an eye patch with you?"

He barked out a laugh. "An eye patch? No."

"You might consider one for the future. For any more eye emergencies you might have."

A yellow straw bonnet was decorated with several wide ribbons. *Perfect.* Long as well as wide, the sash would keep movement of her eyelid to a minimum. He lifted the headpiece down and in a swift move removed one long ribbon.

She gasped.

He turned in surprise. She looked like she wanted to protest—maybe it had been her favorite?—but her lips only wobbled.

"W-what do you have in your doctor's case?" she said in an unsteady voice.

He really shouldn't, but the thought of what her reaction might be when she saw what the bag contained was just too tempting. He reached for the satchel and clicked the latch so she could have a look. Three long blades glinted in the light.

At the sight of the knives, she shrank back. "What're those for?"

"Need you ask?"

Color drained from her face. "No. I need not, especially since I must quickly dress. Can you please help me one last time?"

Help her dress? She might be able to come to terms with him assisting her in her need, but she wouldn't appreciate him helping her dress once she found out he was no doctor. The last thing he needed if he valued his life—or the reputation he wanted to establish in this town—was a scandal. Putting up his hands, he took a step back and glanced at the door. "Help you dress? I, well, I've need of—"

"I'm the one who should be shy, Doctor, but I don't have the time." She smiled, sitting up on the bed. "You're a physician. The human anatomy is nothing new to you. Besides, I'm not naked under my robe. Please, I insist."

If she insisted, what could he do?

He crossed the room to her dress and carried the garment over. Miss Brinkman, now standing, stripped off her robe without so much as a by-your-leave. A pretty pink corset encased her slender body, as did a pair of fine silk pantaloons and stockings. He jerked his gaze away from her long, slim legs and anchored his attention to an ant crawling on the wall.

She delicately grasped his forearm for support,

but as she stepped in something caught and jerked.

"I'm sorry but you're going to have to look, Doctor. I almost fell when I caught my toe in the fabric."

He reluctantly turned her way as she tried again, carefully stepping into the gown they held between them. She shimmied the dress up into place, slipping her arms through the delicate arm-holes. Her creamy skin looked as soft as a rose petal. He swallowed.

Grasping the material, she tugged down and to the right, positioning the garment perfectly.

Fascination with her progress warmed his mind. She turned her back to him, an invitation for him to do up the long row of tiny buttons.

She glanced at him over her shoulder. "Thank you from the bottom of my heart. My eye is improving by the minute. Be sure to add a sum to your bill for your assistance in helping me dress, as I'm sure it's not something you normally do." She softly laughed. "Our attorney, Henry Glass, will see you're promptly paid."

Encased in the incredibly soft-looking dress, she again cast him a tempting smile over her shoulder. "Please hurry, if you can. Hopefully, they're holding the ceremony for me. If not, perhaps I'll catch the kiss. In any case, because of you, Doctor, all is not lost. I owe you so much more than money."

Yeah, like a slap in the face.

After a moment's more hesitation, he reached for her. When he was almost finished with the fabric-covered buttons, she spared him another glance and batted her eyes. "My eye still hurts, but nothing like before. You're a miracle worker."

She crossed the room and slipped into her shoes. Standing at the mirror, she wound the yellow ribbon around her head and over one eye, tying it with deft fingers.

Maybe her eye was feeling better, but her sensibilities were going to be shred to tatters when she found out who he was.

And that he was as close to being a doctor as he was to being her brother.

CHAPTER FOUR

~❧❦~

On the sturdy arm of the tall, good-looking doctor, and feeling extremely proud of herself, Lavinia crossed the threshold of the simple church. It was true—his dog had waited patiently at the hotel entrance until his master had called from the side door of the hotel. The dog trotted behind and was now waiting outside the church door.

Her sisters rushed forward in greeting, their concerned expressions mixed with a double dose of surprise and delight. The twin doors between the entry and the sanctuary hid the bride and bridesmaids from the waiting guests. A pair of stained glass windows on opposing walls were the only decorative adornments. They glowed golden and rose in the afternoon light, heightening the beauty of her four sisters.

If the number of buggies and wagons parked outside was any indication of how many friends and townsfolk had shown up for the wedding, the church would be bursting. Lavinia had loathed holding up the ceremony but was so relieved the girls were here instead of up at the altar.

Mavis, always the most conscious of propriety, gently touched the yellow ribbon tied around Lavinia's head, concern softening her wide-set blue eyes. Her wavy, coffee-colored hair, done up on her head, looked soft and refined, a complete contrast to the long ponytail or messy bun she usually wore while working at the livery and blacksmith shop she'd inherited from their father. Lavinia hardly noticed Mavis's wrist-length gloves anymore, the ones used to hide the missing pinkie finger on her left hand.

She smiled even though a small pain pinched her eye. "Most people are used to my homemade hats and adornments," she said, gesturing to the yellow sash. "The townsfolk will just think I got carried away."

Wearing outrageous hats had been her way of getting attention as a child, and young lady, in a sea of outstanding sisters. She wasn't the youngest, to have been doted on like Katie, or the oldest like Mavis, the boldest like Belle, or the most soft-spoken and feminine like Emma. She'd been invisible. Unseen. Those early experiments with simple hand-sewn felt or crocheted beanies had blossomed into a love of making hats and an offer of an apprenticeship as a milliner back in Philadelphia. Something she'd intended to get back to once things settled down for the family in Eden, if only—

"Nonsense," Emma scolded, pulling her away

from her thoughts and running her hand down Lavinia's arm.

Emma's strawberry-blond hair made her emerald eyes pop. Their father had bequeathed her the Toggery, a clothing shop in town, and it fit her determined femininity perfectly. She'd begun bringing in more stylish clothing than the women of the West were used to. She'd even graciously offered to stock a few of Lavinia's hat creations—although, Lavinia thought with an inward frown, none had yet sold.

"You always look beautiful," Emma said confidently. No one would ever guess she was still timid in their new home and needed warm milk to fall asleep. "How's your eye? We hated leaving you behind. Especially in pain. You seem much better."

"I am. Due to Eden's new *doctor*."

She searched out the doctor standing against the sidewall. His gaze caught hers and she smiled, liking his blue eyes as well as the straight white teeth of his smile. He stood tall and comfortable, not asking for anyone's approval. The women of Eden would corral him soon enough, she was sure. His wide shoulders and rugged good looks would attract most. Powerful legs traveled up to a trim waist and extremely broad chest. Even in his disheveled state, he outshone old, dishonest Dr. Dodge by five hundred miles.

Her gaze went to his hands clasped in front, but

she was too far away to see if he was wearing a wedding ring. That thought hadn't entered her mind when she'd been in pain.

"He extracted the offending object and administered warm oil. I'd be lying if I said the pain was completely gone, but I'll get through the day happily. I can't sing his praises enough."

She had to laugh at her sisters' astonished expressions.

Holding her short, simple train over one arm, Belle smiled, excitement deep in her twinkling blue eyes. She had inherited the tannery, which had finally been rebuilt after a devastating explosion several months ago. "Karen came bursting through the doors like a mad mama bear was on her heels. Once she told us you were on your way, there was no way we would go ahead without you."

Pride washed through Lavinia as she took in Belle's veil with its small crown of pink and white alyssum, as well as a scant few early bluebells. Her sister's shimmering tresses of blond, woven through the blossoms, looked magical.

"That reminds me." Lavinia glanced around. "Where's Henry? Shouldn't he be here to give you away?" For all intents and purposes, Henry Glass, their father's attorney, had stepped in as their father after John Brinkman had passed on. They loved Henry—*she* loved him.

Emma beamed. "He'll be right back from

seating Karen next to Elizabeth. He probably got to talking since he knew we were waiting for you. I'll peek in the door and get his attention."

She was back in a heartbeat. "He's on his way. And oh, you should see the groomsmen. They look so handsome in their suits—Moses, Trevor, and Clint. You'd never know they were crusty ol' cowhands."

The doctor cleared his throat and took a step in their direction. "Excuse me, Miss Brinkman, but since you've arrived on time, I'll take my leave." He glanced at their faces and then to the door. "I hope no one will mind if I scrounge around the café kitchen and find something to eat. I noticed the 'Closed' sign right before you whisked me up to your room. I'll pay for anything I consume."

Mortified by her manners, Lavinia rushed over. "Oh no, Doctor, you *must* stay . . . What is your name? I can't believe I never asked. I was so preoccupied with my eye . . ."

The doctor's face actually colored up, and his gaze darted uncomfortably to her watching sisters. Maybe she'd been correct with her initial assumption and she really was his first female patient. He'd have to get over that if he wanted to be a success.

"I couldn't. I'd feel like an intruder. I don't know any of you. Besides, I'm still in my traveling clothes and—" He rubbed a hand over his whiskered chin. "I'm not presentable."

"You look absolutely fine. And you'll know everyone soon enough. The ceremony won't take but a few minutes, and then we're heading over to Mademoiselle de Sells for the reception. I promise you, you'll be sorry if you decline. They serve the finest food in all of Colorado, and that includes my small hotel café."

His eyebrows shot up.

"Besides, what a perfect time for you to meet everyone in Eden."

Emma, Mavis, and Katie nodded in agreement. She thought she caught Emma poking her elbow into Mavis's side.

"Please do," Belle echoed. "As our special guest. To thank you for all you did for Lavinia."

His eyes brightened and he smiled. "That's a generous offer. So hospitable, I feel I'd be a fool to pass. I've heard of Mademoiselle de Sells. Thank you. I'll just slip into the last bench and make myself comfortable. Ladies." He tipped his head.

"Wait," Lavinia called. "Your name?"

He gave a roguish wink, the first action that was out of character with his steadfastness and professionalism. "Rhetten Laughlin. At your service. Everyone calls me Rhett."

Rhetten Laughlin! Such a name suits him. "But you have no Irish accent."

"My father was born in America, but his parents, my grandparents, who came from

37

Ireland, passed soon after his birth. He was raised in an orphanage and didn't hear the Irish language spoken."

Katie touched her arm, behaving like the schoolteacher she'd trained to be. "Lavinia, let him get seated. We need to begin."

Their youngest sister's coloring was much like Belle's, with her blond hair and deep blue eyes. Her baby sister had flourished in Eden as the owner of the lumber mill, surprising them all. In the past, Katie had at times taken to flights of fancy—but it seemed in Colorado she'd settled down.

Henry came through the door just as Dr. Laughlin passed inside. The men nodded at each other, and Henry stopped, turned, and gazed at the door in curiosity after the newcomer disappeared.

Lavinia felt a totally inappropriate blush move through her. "That's the man who rescued me. Our new doctor."

"Ah." Henry beamed. "Well, good, I'm glad for it."

Their friend and attorney looked happier than Lavinia had ever seen him. And why wouldn't he? A wedding between Blake and one of John's daughters had been their father's ardent wish, and no one in Eden had been closer to their father than Henry and Blake.

"Blake's ready and able," Henry said. "And I

believe, if my eyes don't fool me, he's champing at the bit. I don't think I've ever seen such an anxious groom." He clapped his hands together, the way he was fond of doing whenever something important was going his way. "This is your last chance to back out, Belle. Speak now or forever hold your peace."

Belle laughed, her face more sun kissed and freckled than when they'd arrived from Philadelphia. "You know I'm not backing out, Henry. Let the pianist know I'm ready to become Mrs. Blake Harding." She hugged herself with happiness. "Thank you, Father, for bringing us back to Eden. We belong here."

Lavinia heaved a relieved, joyful sigh. *How romantic.* Belle and Blake. Her thoughts strayed to Rhett Laughlin. She'd never thought any man could be as handsome as Blake, but she'd just changed her mind.

CHAPTER FIVE

R hett had no intention of perpetuating the mis-conception of his identity past the wedding ceremony. As soon as that was over, the first person he spoke with, he'd right the wrong, who-ever that person happened to be, and no matter about Miss Brinkman. But now wasn't the time to upset the applecart. Not before the bride and all her sisters walked down the aisle.

Noticing that the last polished-oak bench had some space, he settled next to an old fellow whose hair was slicked back, his tattered suit clean and pressed. Several parishioners turned Rhett's way and eyed him with curiosity.

"Howdy," the old man whispered. "I'm Mr. Little. You new ta town?"

He nodded, not feeling particularly friendly at the moment. All hell was going to break loose over the fact that he'd helped Miss Brinkman dress. He wondered if he'd been born under a dark star. "Rhetten Laughlin," he responded. He nodded at a middle-aged woman halfway up the pews who'd glanced his way. She promptly turned away. Men outnumbered the women five to one. *Just like Shawn thought. And this is only the beginning . . .*

"You come in on the stage?"

"Yep."

The people filling this church were the customers he aimed to entice. The *San Francisco Daily Call* had run a series of human-interest stories about the death of the wealthy rancher John Brinkman and how he'd drawn his daughters back to Eden after eighteen years, turning them into extremely wealthy women in their own right. The articles had run three Sundays in a row. Readers had been spellbound, as had Shawn, waiting each week for the new installment. Rhett had to admit the stories were pretty entertaining.

Shawn had come up with the plan right then. Five—*now four*—young, beautiful, and *rich* women would draw an abundance of men to this small, rustic Colorado town. They'd come rushing in, not for gold or silver but in hope of winning a Brinkman's heart. Rhett smiled to himself. *A gold rush of a different sort.*

And where there were men looking to settle down, women would follow. To Shawn's way of thinking, only five men would be lucky enough to win the hand of a Brinkman. That would leave a good many bachelors in Eden. Spinsters, widows, women down on their luck, all looking to start fresh and in need of suitable mates, would flock to Eden—especially if the paper kept printing stories like the ones that had captured his brother's attention. Eden was on the verge of a population explosion—and Shawn had been willing to bank on it.

Now I am too. From the look of the male-dominated congregation, his brother's calculations had been correct. Rhett aimed to capitalize on these men now, and the ones to come in the future, including the women, and feed their appetites. Everyone had to eat, especially if he was courting.

And I'll fulfill Shawn's dream. That's the least I can do to atone for my hand in his death.

"I'm business partners with the bride-to-be," the old man whispered with pride. He smelled of hair wax and peppermint. The comment garnered a chastising eyebrow from a woman across the way. "Ain't started yet," he grumbled back at her and she turned away.

Rhett smiled but didn't respond, hoping the old man would get the idea now wasn't the time for conversation.

"Plannin' ta stay?"

There was no hope for it. "If things work out," he mumbled.

The double doors opened, and a hush wrapped around the church. The pianist tipped her chin and began to play.

"I used to run the local tannery," Mr. Little went on as if nothing special was about to happen. "Before the place got blowed up last year. New one's just finished, and we're getting everything up and—"

"*Shhhhh.*"

Mr. Little snapped his mouth closed at the sound directed at them. Rhett's face heated, and he focused his attention to the front in hopes the man beside him would stop talking.

"That's Blake, Belle's intended."

Of course that was. The man he gestured to at the front of the church was flanked by four groomsmen.

"That tall fella, two in, is Clint Dawson, the sheriff of Eden. The colored fella, Blake's best man, saved Blake's life during the Civil War, when Blake was just a kid. They's more like brothers than friends. Third fella is Trevor Hill, one of the ranch hands. And Henry Glass, who'll be escorting Belle down the aisle, is the local lawyer. If you need legal advice, he's the one to see."

Rhett nodded, not wanting to be rude, but not wanting to encourage him either. Mr. Little must be hard of hearing, because he wasn't all that quiet.

The woman on the piano changed her tune as the first bridesmaid appeared.

"That's Katie, the baby," Mr. Little said, his whisper only low to himself. "She sure is a pretty little thing."

The old man chuckled and held a gnarled hand over his mouth, leaning toward Rhett as if he had a secret. "And here comes Lavinia. Lookie at that thing on her head. She's fond of making head ornaments of all kinds, but being a pirate at her own sister's wedding is taking her obsession a bit far. That looks downright silly."

Rhett shrugged. He wouldn't say a word, share the story, or expound on anything that had happened behind the hotel door to anyone, least of all his companion. He wanted to live down his part as soon as he could. Still, seeing Miss Brinkman brought an unbidden memory of her long, stocking-clad legs. The creamy, soft skin on the back of her neck that he'd accidentally brushed in the process of buttoning her gown. Angry, he jerked his gaze away and looked out the window and up into the clouds. He'd not gone looking for such a compromising situation with a local young woman the moment he stepped off the stage. He was disappointed trouble had found him so quickly, especially with the sorrow he'd left back in San Francisco. His chance to begin anew was before him. His reckless days were over.

Mr. Little straightened, going serious. "But I'll not laugh at her pot roast. It's as good as any I ever ate. She's done her father proud with that restaurant she inherited. It's a plumb pleasure to eat there. Now here's Emma. The sight of her purty, rose-colored hair always makes me feel like spring. She's a rascal, though, and a tease, but bakes me cookies almost every week." His face pinked up.

He gestured with his chin to the tall, slim young woman standing in the alcove ready to walk down the aisle. "That's Mavis. Quite a distinguished woman." Her calm demeanor mixed with a dash of authority easily marked her as the oldest. The articles had mentioned her several times, noting that she was a new widow. Her face was pretty, but not like the heart shape of her sister Lavinia. That young woman had caught his eye, and why not? He'd more than gazed into the depths of *her* eyes long enough.

Once Mavis was away, the bride stepped forward on the arm of Henry Glass, the attorney with whom he'd corresponded. Rhett had jumped his schedule by a few weeks and hoped that wouldn't make a difference in the purchase of the deserted building across from the hotel. He'd caught a glimpse of the place when he'd stepped off the stage, and again when he'd agreed to escort Lavinia to the church, and now he couldn't wait to get back and take a tour. See if there was anything worth saving.

The beauty of the bride was undeniable.

Again, Mr. Little leaned over. "Don't let her fool ya. Belle's taken to ranching like she was born on a horse. She might look purty, but she

45

can shoot a fly off a post a hundred yards away."

People watched with rapt wonder. Weddings were a time of joy and hope. But Rhett didn't feel their excitement. All he could think about was atoning for Shawn's death. And maybe, once he'd done that, he'd discover whether he deserved a second chance at happiness.

CHAPTER SIX

~✦✦✦~

Before Lavinia had a chance to relax, the brief ceremony was over and she was marching back down the aisle on Trevor Hill's arm. In all the excitement, she'd forgotten about her eye, but as she glanced around she realized it felt a thousand times better. The church floors, walls, and windows had been buffed to a high sheen and never looked better.

Simplicity was what Belle and Blake had wanted after the lavish autumn housewarming the unofficial partners of the Five Sisters Ranch had thrown, during which Blake had proposed to Belle. Then, in late December, since the big snows had yet to fall, they'd had the idea to throw a Christmas party that would be rivaled by none. Henry had agreed, thinking their first Christmas back was something wonderful to celebrate. Blake and the ranch hands had gone in hunt of a Christmas tree befitting the festive mood. They'd set out to accomplish a daring feat, and they hadn't disappointed. Getting the monster into the house and firmly anchored took every ranch hand and still had been a struggle. The tree rose from the first-floor open living room almost to the second-story ceiling.

Lavinia sucked in a deep, cleansing breath at the memory. Life had been good here—not just with her sisters, but with the café and helping at the orphanage. Still, she found herself feeling invisible and a bit dissatisfied with her lot. Had she given up too much by leaving Philadelphia? She'd worked in a tailor's shop there, but just before coming to Eden, she'd secured a coveted apprenticeship with a well-known milliner—her true heart's desire. The opportunity was scheduled to begin in the summer, giving her time to stay in Eden until the conditions of their father's will had been met. But last week a letter had arrived, delayed months by the snowy mountain passes. Mr. Hansberry's plans had changed. She was summoned to return immediately if she was still interested in apprenticing with him. Heat stung the back of her eyes. She'd missed her chance and hadn't even known. And yet, how could she contemplate leaving Eden? If she were truthful with herself, that was exactly what she wanted.

Almost to the end of the aisle, Trevor glanced down and squeezed her hand. "We're all glad you made it, Lavinia," he whispered. "The day wouldn't have been the same without you."

The sight of his warm, endearing smile was accompanied by something else that made her blink and look away. The tall, handsome, broad-shouldered twenty-nine-year-old ranch hand, whom she considered a dear friend, had never made such calf eyes at her before. Perhaps Blake getting married had spurred these feelings—or maybe she was imagining things.

"Thank you, Trevor. I wouldn't have arrived in time if the new doctor hadn't shown up when I needed him." Her gaze sought out Rhett Laughlin in the back of the church. Finding him next to Mr. Little, their gazes met and held for one second before she skimmed across the crowd.

Again Trevor pressed her hand, nestled in the bend of his arm. "Then I'm glad," he whispered, his head inclined to hers. "How's your eye feel now?"

She gave a brief smile. "Much better, thank you."

The second they hit the entry, Lavinia pulled the sash from her head and relinquished the material into Karen's hand as she and Trevor passed by.

All around, people streamed out of the church and began tossing handfuls of rice—representing a rain of good fortune, the blessing of children, and a long and happy life—at the new couple, who stood laughing and smiling on the top step of the small church. Belle had sent away for the costly item last year, as soon as she and Blake had decided to marry. Lavinia extricated her arm from Trevor's and moved to find a safe spot to stand. She glanced over her shoulder, hoping to spot Dr. Laughlin. More than his handsome face, she'd been daydreaming about the man himself during the ceremony. His gentle hands and calming voice were seared into her thoughts.

"There's the doctor now," Trevor said, gesturing to Mr. Laughlin, head and shoulders above most of the rest. She'd forgotten Trevor was standing behind her. "Should we go say hello?"

"Surely not," she said.

Trevor tipped his head.

She hadn't meant to give such a strong reaction.

"I just want to thank him for getting you to the church on time."

Again the calf eyes. When on earth had this begun? She thought back, trying to remember if she'd given the man the wrong impression. He always shared a silly joke or two when he came into the café to eat or when she saw him at the ranch, but that was all—she'd thought.

She nodded at Elizabeth Smith and took two handfuls of rice, joining in the excitement that bubbled through the crowd. On the steps of the church, Blake swooped Belle into a dramatic embrace and kissed her long and passionately.

Cheers went up! They were Eden's darling couple.

Drawing back, the newly married couple gazed into each other's eyes for only a moment and then kissed again, this one not for show, but a promise of undying love for all eternity.

Shivers ran through Lavinia. Such love, such passion. A sight that was rarely seen, but a bond that was special and to be cherished. Belle had found her man and her future. Everything for them would be smooth sailing from now on. And Lavinia was happy for both.

With a tingle of apprehension, she glanced over her shoulder to find Rhett Laughlin looking at her. He pulled his gaze away immediately, but not before she saw something in his face.

That's ridiculous. I mustn't let my imagination sweep me away. I have plans, even if they've been disrupted for now. When the letter from Mr. Hansberry had arrived, she'd immediately sent a telegram explaining why she was responding so late, and that she couldn't leave Eden until the six-month stay had elapsed—their father's requirement to ensure that they made a commitment to the town before they'd be allowed to inherit the ranch. She felt her lips wobble. She hadn't heard back, and she probably never would. She'd need to figure out a new way to achieve her aspirations, and not forgo them altogether.

"They look pretty darned happy," Trevor whispered at her side. "I didn't think Belle would be the settlin' type the first time we met, but now I see different. I guess the right man will bring out the woman in—a—woman . . . ," he finished rather awkwardly. His face darkened as he looked down into her eyes.

Heavens.

She lifted one shoulder offhandedly. "We need to go inside and take the photograph now." She chanced one more quick glance over her shoulder, only to find Rhett Laughlin gone. That was all right. She'd have a chance to speak with him again at Mademoiselle de Sells. With a lightened step and a smile for Trevor, she hurried back inside the church and toward the altar.

CHAPTER SEVEN

~✦~

Beaming, Henry Glass ushered the wedding guests into Mademoiselle de Sells as if he were the father of the bride. And why not? He and John had been so much more than business associates. Henry had been at his side for years, and during his last month, practically every minute. He still had private papers and instructions John had given him concerning his children and the ranch that not even Blake knew about, nor any of John's daughters.

Being guardian over the sisters was a heavy responsibility, but over these past months, the burden had lightened. The girls had agreed to stay in Eden, at least for the time allotted in the will, and Belle and Blake had fallen in love. *They're man and wife!* Henry knew John would be overjoyed. *I wish you could have seen her, old friend. She looked so beautiful. And Blake, well, there's not much I can say except that he's never been happier. Rest assured, your plans played out just like you'd hoped. I only wish you were alive today to celebrate with us.*

Finished with the few group photographs at the

church, Henry had arrived at the restaurant ahead of the others to a cluster of excited faces ready to be treated to the sumptuous fare of Jean-Luc Boucher and his younger sister, Amorette. "Go on in while we wait for the guests of honor," he repeated over and over as the line passed him through the door. "Belle and Blake will arrive shortly. The courtyard is open today as well. There will be plenty of room for everyone. Enjoy."

A soft wind, warm for this time in March, lifted the hems of the ladies' dresses and ruffled the men's hair. Elizabeth Smith was already inside helping put out the food. Henry stifled an affectionate smile thinking of her. She'd come to town claiming that her son, Johnny, was really John Brinkman's illegitimate son. Though her claim had been a lie born out of desperation, he'd come to see her as an incredible woman—and a devoted mother. *How my life has changed since I've met Elizabeth.* At the moment, he was trying to be patient and give her time to settle into Eden before he sprang his feelings on her—feelings he hoped she reciprocated. He'd tell her he wanted to make her his wife and build her a home, a real home, and take her out of the boardinghouse where she now lived. That there was no one else on earth he wanted to spend his life with besides her and little Johnny.

As if his affection had conjured him, four-year-old Johnny appeared in the doorway and wiggled around several women to get outside.

"Johnny, hello." Henry smiled at the boy. Johnny's brown corduroy pants and neatly tucked-in white shirt were still surprisingly clean. A miniature black string tie rested below his chin and looked as cute as a button. *Such a good boy. I'd be lucky to call him my son.* "Is everything inside to your mother's liking?"

The youngster nodded.

"Is the food out on the table?"

"Sure is, but Jean-Luc—I mean, *Mr. Boucher,*" he quickly corrected, "said no one is to eat from the main table until the bride and groom arrive. My ma's hopping around like a grasshopper. Miss Amorette too." He let out a hearty laugh. "I'm supposed to get out from under their feet, so I came out to help you." His gaze flew around, his cheeks bright red with excitement. He was tall for his age and had his mother's striking blue eyes.

"Is that right?" Henry ruffled Johnny's sandy-blond hair. "That's good. I can use the help. Did you like the ceremony? Your mother told me today was the first wedding you've attended."

He nodded. "Yep. But I like now better because I can talk—out loud."

Henry chuckled, then nodded to Santiago Alvarado and his father, owners of the Spanish Trail Cantina, as they approached the door.

The strong resemblance between father and son had the attorney wondering what his own son would look like. If that were to ever happen, he'd be a much older father, since he was already forty-five. Still, he was in excellent shape for his years. He didn't have a foot in the grave just yet.

He glanced at Johnny. Would a child like an older pa? Nowadays, if you reached fifty-five, you were lucky. But Elizabeth had him feeling young, like a spirited colt. Had him thinking things he shouldn't. An embarrassing blush crept up his face. How he'd hate for anyone to be able to read his thoughts. He'd been in love once, with the daughter of his mother's best friend. Her painful rejection was the impetus that had marked his destiny. To outrun his pain, he'd applied for admission to Brown University in Rhode Island. Law school and Eden had followed.

Henry hoisted Johnny into his arms. "Look! Here come the bride and groom."

Johnny bounced with exhilaration, making Henry believe anything was possible. "And the rest of 'em too." The boy pulled his gaze back to Henry's face. "Soon we'll be eatin'!"

"That's right, son, soon we will." Patience, he reminded himself, was a virtue.

I can't rush a woman like Elizabeth. I'll know the right time, and when I ask her to marry me, she'll say yes.

CHAPTER EIGHT

~✦~

I ndecision warred inside Rhett. When his brother was alive, Shawn had actually mentioned Mademoiselle de Sells. The place had made a reputation with their succulent beef, savory sauces, and delicate pastries, so much so that word had traveled all the way to San Francisco. Amazing that an establishment that tiny was able to survive in such a place as Eden. But Mademoiselle de Sells had. The French restaurant would profit from the same boom of newcomers Rhett was counting on to get his place off the ground.

Today was the perfect opportunity to try them out. Not that his clientele would be the same as theirs, at least, not all the time, but he still had an obligation to be thoughtful about the new venture if he wanted the place he'd open in Shawn's memory to be a success. Their mother, rest her soul, had been a scullery maid, and from the moment Shawn was old enough to help in the kitchen, he had loved to cook. He'd badger her to let him try out recipes and then scribble the results of his experiments in a gravy-and-cream-spotted notebook, one that Rhett now kept close. He'd always been eager to eat whatever his little brother made, but Rhett never had the desire to create. That skill he'd have to acquire, and if he was going to compete in this town, it wouldn't hurt to see how a restaurant as successful as Mademoiselle de Sells pulled it off.

On the other hand, if he went to the restaurant now, Miss Brinkman—*Lavinia*—would corner him. That was a given. Then he'd be obliged to clear his conscience. He'd have to make good on his self-imposed promise and tell her he was not who she believed him to be. Was it worth the risk of causing a scene at her sister's wedding reception? He didn't think so. Best to steer clear of everyone for now and try the restaurant later.

With the decision made, and a faithful Dallas by his side, he turned from the alleyway and doubled back through the guests and made for the hotel. He walked briskly, confident in his choice. He had his trunk to collect from the boardwalk, and he needed to see about getting a room. By now, someone should be working, since the wedding was over. Maybe even someone who could rustle him up some grub—for Dallas too. Nothing fancy, just something hot and filling to dispel the aches in their bellies.

Now that he wasn't rushing to make the cere-mony in time, he took time to examine his new town. Poor Fred's Saloon was open and doing a fine business. The wedding hadn't hampered their day. There was a store advertising drugs and other tinctures that doubled as a telegraph office, a stage office, and a mercantile that also displayed a lawyer's shingle by the side steps leading to the upper floor. He stopped. Read the sign. "Henry Glass, Attorney at Law." Then he spun around.

Across from the good-size hotel sat the broken-down building he'd inquired about and would buy if everything went smoothly. Between the peeling paint and the sun-bleached letters, the sign read "Hungry Lizard Café."

With a name like that, no wonder the place went out of business.

"There's our dream, boy," he said aloud to Dallas. "Maybe the inside is better."

Excitement flushed inside as he took in the structure, followed by a dull pain he was used to experiencing whenever happiness tried to intervene on his guilt. Knowing construction better than cooking, he took in the bones of the dwelling with welcome anticipation of the job to come. Since he'd been old enough to hold a hammer, he'd followed after his father, hungry to learn everything he could about building. Boards crisscrossed the front door, barring entry. The front porch, with its drooping overhang, needed to be pulled off completely and replaced. Shutters dangled at odd angles, and window glass was broken out. But the place had a second story. A space he'd make into a home. The fit couldn't be better.

A lot of work.

Penance.

The rehabilitation would take a lot of energy and even more money. Looking at the Hungry Lizard now, Rhett wondered if he had enough of either, or if he'd lost his mind. Was such a challenge impossible? Would Shawn really want him to take this on?

"Hungry Lizard. Closed when I was five."

Rhett turned to a strapping young man striding his way.

Dallas watched his approach and then ducked his head when the kid reached down to pet him.

"About fifteen years ago?" Rhett asked, doing some fast mental calculations. "Why hasn't anyone opened the place back up since? Can't be all that bad."

The youth's amber-brown eyes snapped with humor. "Not fifteen. Nine." He thrust out his hand. "Cash Dawson. Sheriff's son. I'm fourteen years old."

This kid's fourteen? They grow 'em big in Eden.

"Rhett Laughlin. Just in from San Francisco. I'm looking to settle. Start a business."

Cash's eyebrows rose. "The café?"

"Maybe. I heard about a vacant building on the main street of Eden," he said, looking Cash in the eye. "Location is everything. Are there other eateries in town?"

"There's a few places over in the alley shops, but not set up as restaurants—more like open shells just waiting to be made into something. Of course, there's Mademoiselle de Sells, our most famous establishment, as well as the hotel café across the street." He glanced at the Hungry Lizard. "You're right about the location. Stage stops right here almost every day."

"I know. I just got off."

Cash chuckled.

The boy had strong arms and a powerful chest. He wasn't as tall as Rhett, but a few years would take care of that. His face and skin glowed with the exuberance of youth and the wonder of what was around the next corner, the next day, the next relationship. Looking into his face, his eyes, Rhett couldn't help but see Shawn. His brother had been all that and more. Until, at only twenty-two, he'd been cut off in his prime.

Rhett refused to allow his guilt to take over now, or his sorrow. They'd only keep him from moving forward.

"How come the place is still vacant? Is there something I don't know?"

"Ghosts."

"Ghosts?"

Cash shrugged. "Maybe not ghosts, but surely *a* ghost. Or the talk of one. That's why no one from around here has reopened the place in years. Ask anyone. They'll tell ya."

Ghosts didn't frighten Rhett. He'd been living with one for months. Thing was, he didn't ever want to be free of him.

My brother.

I'm sorry.

"You're not at the wedding?" Rhett said, surprised. *What young kid passes up a free meal? None I've ever known.* He took another look down the empty street. "Seems everyone's there except for the drunks in the saloon. The town feels empty. Why not you?"

Cash looked around too. His eyebrow played upward. He pulled a flask out of his pants pocket just far enough for Rhett to see. "I'm going back soon." He glanced over his shoulder. "Want a swig?"

Rhett's mouth watered, but he shook his head, a pain jabbing his heart. "No, thanks. Don't touch the stuff much anymore . . ."

"Suit yourself. You won't say anythin'? My pa doesn't stand for me drinkin'. Says I'm too young."

You are. Rhett shook his head. "Lips are sealed." He drew his fingers across his mouth. "I'm interested in seeing the inside of the café as soon as I can locate Henry Glass."

A group of riders passed in the street, a mite dusty and worn, but they didn't look like outlaws. And definitely not wedding goers. As a matter of fact, the way their eyes searched the near-deserted town made Rhett take notice. *What're they looking for?*

"He's at the reception. The mayor, Mr. Dodge, can help you too. Or my pa. What're ya putting in?"

"Restaurant."

The kid had the audacity to laugh. "Really? You don't strike me as the type, *you know,* that likes to spend time in a kitchen."

Astute. Didn't strike Rhett either. "Looks can be deceiving." *Or not.*

Cash withdrew the flask, unscrewed the cap, and took a drink, wiping his mouth with his sleeve when he was finished.

Rhett blinked and looked away. Not the road the kid should be traveling.

Cash winked. "I best get back to the reception before I'm missed. I don't want them to run out of food before I have a chance to fill my belly." He turned to leave but swiftly turned back. "If you need a hand fixing her up, I'm your man. I work at the livery, but I can usually get time off. Just as long as I get the stalls mucked out every day and do the other chores."

"Sorry. I don't need help." *I refuse to be responsible for anyone else. From now on, it's*

just little ol' me—and Dallas. Shawn paid for my
stupidity. I don't aim to forget that.

"Just so you know," Cash went on as if he
hadn't heard, "I have experience working with
tools. Just point me in the right direction and I
can handle any job."

The way he said it made Rhett think every
boy in these parts grew up with a hammer in
his hands. Not so in San Francisco. Most boys
with little education went down to the docks
when they were old enough and strong enough.
Sometimes opportunities turned up on ships as
deckhands or laborers. His ma would never let
him sail, but once she'd passed on, his pa had
given his blessing, and Rhett had shipped out
twice. Once as a deckhand to Italy on a cargo
passenger ship and once on a fishing boat to
Alaska. The fishing trip had cured his desire to
sail ever again. Fishing was cold, dangerous,
never-ending drudgery. Pitched overboard by a
stormy sea, a distracted sailor could disappear
forever. His little brother hadn't liked him being
gone for months at a time either. After that, Rhett
had put his wanderlust aside—until now.

Cash shrugged. "You might change your mind
when you see inside. If you do, you know where
to find me." He gave a wide smile. "And by the
way, I like your dog."

Rhett watched Cash stride away, a cocky tilt to
his shoulders. The kid took another quick swig

from his flask and was soon gone. That pa would know he'd been drinking the first time Cash opened his mouth. Rhett felt a smirk lighten his mood. He'd been young once, carefree and full of life, but those years felt like a lifetime ago.

The group of riders that had passed by before came back around and reined up in front of the saloon. The tallest made eye contact and Rhett gave an obligatory nod, not wanting any kind of trouble. He was done with trouble. He'd keep his nose clean and walk a straight line. That's all a man could do. The other two men dismounted, then lifted their stirrups and loosened their girths, as if they'd been on the trail awhile.

Intent on minding his own business, he turned away.

Across the street, at the hotel, he noted his trunk on the boardwalk. *Everything I have in the world.* He took one step in that direction—

And caught sight of Miss Lavinia Brinkman, in the lavender gown he'd so recently helped her settle into, marching his way. She was still too far away to see her expression, but he got the distinct impression she was angry. She was flanked by two of her sisters; a woman he'd never seen before; Henry Glass, the attorney; and a tall, serious fella who looked amazingly like Cash.

The sheriff.

Several locks of hair that had been up before now bounced loosely around Lavinia's face.

Even with the distance between them, he could hear the *tap tap tap* of her heels.

No way she could know the truth, could she? He hadn't yet told anyone. But there was no doubt under the sun she was coming for him.

CHAPTER NINE

D r. Laughlin!"
    The note of determination in Lavinia's voice made Dallas surge to his feet.

She and her group were still fifteen feet away. With an urge to put off the inevitable a little while longer, Rhett glanced wistfully at the hotel entry but made no attempt to move. He had to face the music sooner or later. And by the look of Lavinia's expression, the orchestra was just about to start.

The group stopped in front of him. Bright red flags colored Lavinia's cheeks. Her chest rose and fell, making the material of her dress swell out with each breath. He remembered how she'd dragged him up the hotel stairs. She was used to getting her way.

But she didn't appear to be angry. A warm curiosity shone from eyes he remembered all too well. Her sisters—Katie, he recalled, and Emma— sidled in on one side, the unknown woman on the other. The men stood behind as if keeping watch. A gust of wind caught the edges of Lavinia's hem, ruffling the garment and pushing the fabric against her slender legs. Another feature he was unlikely to forget.

"I thought you were coming to the reception, Dr. Laughlin? I've told just about everyone how you so gallantly jumped into service as soon as you stepped off the stagecoach. My eye is so much better. I can never thank you enough. But I'm disappointed that you seem inclined to turn down our offer . . ."

Oh boy.

She wasn't here to dress him down, but to bring him back to the party.

"Everyone is so thrilled to have you here at last. You see, we used to have an unscrupulous doctor. He was a liar, and, not only that, tried to scare me and my sisters out of town by doing horrible things. Even had Katie kidnapped." She closed her eyes momentarily at the bad memory. And then her gaze strayed to a sheer rock wall that jutted up from the road on the other side of the hotel.

He winced. *I should have told her after the wedding. Now the people of Eden will think I hoodwinked her.* What had happened to that lying doctor? Had they run him out of town? Was that about to be his fate?

He had to handle the situation carefully. With her standing before him wasn't the best time to think the possibilities through.

"I'd like to clear something up, Miss Brinkman, if you don't mind, before—"

She glanced around and smiled. "There'll be plenty of time for questions after I make introductions, Dr. Laughlin."

One of the fellows that had ridden into town leaned his forearms onto the saloon's railing, enjoying the show. Annoyed at being watched, Rhett frowned in his direction. "I think you'll want to hear what I have to say first." She went to say something else, but he stopped her with his palm. "Please. It's important."

Her smile vanished.

Annoyance etched the sheriff's face as well as the other fellow's.

"Very well," she said. "If you must."

"I must." Gathering his courage, he took one last look around the group and then opened his mouth. "Brace yourself for a shock. I'm not the doctor Eden was expecting. I have no idea what happened to him. I didn't see any signs of a medical person along my route here. Your guess is as good as mine."

Now shut up and give her a chance to respond.

"So you've picked Eden on your own? Well, a little competition can be healthy. We're growing, and reason says we may need two doctors."

She's a stubborn one. "I'm not *the* doctor, or even *a* doctor. I'm not a doctor at all."

She took a stumbling step back. Katie, the youngest Brinkman, steadied her sister with a hand to her back, and Emma scowled.

Lavinia cocked her head, her lips drawn into a frown. "W-what in the world are you saying, Dr. Laugh . . . ?"

There was little doubt she wished the ground to open up and swallow her whole. Her creamy complexion had gone white and now was turning a deep shade of red. He'd never met anyone before who so openly wore their feelings on their sleeve.

Henry Glass straightened. He'd held back before, perhaps waiting to be introduced, but now came forward, his face a stony mask of anger. "I think you'd better explain yourself."

"That's what I'm trying to do. I'm no doctor. Never said I was. In Miss Brinkman's moment of need, she mistook me for the doctor you were expecting. The one who I assume is scheduled to arrive today; at least, that's what I can make out from snippets of conversation I've heard."

Lavinia gasped.

Her sisters crowded closer. The older woman Rhett didn't know, but had seen at the wedding, withdrew a handkerchief from her pocket and wiped her forehead. "But you and Miss Brinkman were the only two people in her room, actually, in the whole hotel," she said, panic lacing her tone. "I, ah, well . . ."

"Alone at her bidding, ma'am. Please remember that. She dragged me into her room against my will. What was I supposed to do? Fight off this snippet of a girl who was walking around in her robe with her eyes clenched closed?"

Lavinia gasped again.

He slid a look at her, worried how she'd take the next thing he was about to say. With the look on the men's faces, he had no choice. Action was needed to avert a worse situation. "To tell you the truth, I was a tiny bit fearful she was touched in the head." Maybe that was going a little too far, but he *had* wondered at first about her sanity.

Lavinia jerked back as if she'd been slapped. Her hand flew to her throat, and tears sprang to her eyes. Her mouth opened and closed several times, reminding Rhett of the nets filled with fish they'd pulled from the ocean. He wondered if in Eden his offense merited jail.

But the sheriff didn't look in any way ready to arrest him. To the contrary, there was a humorous tilt to his lips, and his eyes twinkled.

"You, *sir,* are no gentleman!" Lavinia spat, her eyes snapping with anger. "You should have corrected the misunderstanding at once. But you didn't, and I think you actually enjoyed yourself."

Her assessment of him was the understatement of the year. "In defense of myself, I must remind you I never once claimed to be a doctor, and was reluctant to come into your room. If you recall, you tugged me up the stairs with a badger hold on my arm, while jabbering in my ear."

Fear flashed in her eyes. A red line began at the base of her throat and slowly worked its way up her face until even her forehead glowed crimson. *Is she remembering the same things I am? Slipping off her robe? Clutching my arm for balance as she stepped into her dress . . .*

"And then, even though I tried to refuse, when it was time to get dr—"

"—the hot oil!" she screeched, interrupting what he was about to say. "To get the hot oil for my eye. Yes, you kindly complied. I do need to remember that when I feel myself getting angry."

So she didn't want him to spill the beans about helping her with her clothes. That was fine with him. But the memories of her standing before him in nothing but her corset, pantaloons, and stockings brought heat to his face as he recalled how pretty she looked in her soft undergarments. That was a sight he wouldn't forget anytime soon.

The older woman looked aghast. "I fear this mix-up is all my fault. I was the one to see you get off the stagecoach and tell Lavinia the new doctor had arrived. I can't say how utterly sorry I am."

Without another word, Lavinia spun on her heel and bolted away. Her sisters and the other woman followed, leaving him and the two men standing in the street.

The taller of the two lifted a shoulder so, Rhett

was sure, he'd see the star pinned to his shirt. "I'm Sheriff Clint Dawson. If you're not the doctor, who exactly are you? And what is your business in Eden?" He gazed at Rhett through intelligent, narrowed eyes.

"Name's Rhetten Laughlin. I'm here about starting a business. A restaurant." He nodded to the old building and then looked at Henry. "In that building in particular."

The other man brightened. "Mr. Laughlin! I'm Henry Glass, the person who returned your telegram. I didn't put two and two together because you're early and I've been busy with the wedding."

Rhett reluctantly stuck out his hand and the men shook. This was not the way he'd pictured his new beginning.

Dawson followed suit.

"I see you made the trip from San Francisco without problem. Welcome to Eden."

"Thank you. But now I seem to have landed myself in more trouble than I can fix." He glanced down the street in the direction that Miss Lavinia Brinkman and her corset—*her cohorts*—had gone. "I never set out to fool Miss Brinkman. On the contrary. She single-handedly captured me in the vacant hotel lobby and dragged me up to her room. I can say honestly, nothing untoward happened besides that I lent her my assistance with her eye."

And helped her into her clothes. I hope she has the presence of mind not to say anything about that to anyone. If she keeps her mouth closed about the affair and so do I, no one will be the wiser.

Sheriff Dawson didn't look entirely convinced, but Mr. Glass smiled, giving Rhett hope that not all was lost.

"She'll get over the shock," he said, glancing at the sheriff. "Someday."

"I hope it's before she has the chance to turn the whole town against me. I know about the Brinkman sisters. I know how the town loves 'em."

Dawson stepped forward, his concerned expression reappearing. "Oh? How might that be, Mr. Laughlin?"

He'd gone and said too much. "Newspaper in San Francisco ran a series of articles. The *San Francisco Daily Call*, to be exact. Told how John Brinkman enticed his daughters back to town. Kept them here for six months. The inheritance. Wanted them to make the place their home."

The sheriff glanced at Henry and then back at him. "That's a lot of personal information. I wonder how many other men will find their way here in hope of landing a big fish. I don't recall any reporters sniffing around last year. I don't like this at all."

Henry scowled. "No, neither do I. The girls

won't be pleased. I wonder who put out the story in the first place. I'd certainly like to know."

"More than casual facts," Rhett went on. "Some of a delicate nature, embarrassing, actually, more than I would think printable, filled the pages." Rhett switched his weight to his opposite leg as Dallas sniffed around Dawson's boots. "Occurrences dating back years." He shook his head, still marveling at the detail the paper had gone into. "That's what made the articles so captivating—almost like a dime novel. People lined up on Sundays wanting to get the papers hot off the press. Unless all the details were fiction, they made for interesting reading. We had no way of knowing."

"We?"

Rhett felt a twinge of anger. He'd rather divulge information in his own time. He simply said, "My brother and myself."

The sheriff watched Rhett with a critical squint. "We better keep this information quiet until I have a chance to investigate. Did you bring these newspapers? Can I see them?"

He nodded. "I'll bring them by your office when I get unpacked."

"Thanks. You have an interest in the sisters?" Dawson asked.

Rhett quickly put up a hand. "No. Matrimony's not my intent at all. But if courting one of them was my aim, the fact wouldn't be your business to worry about, now would it, *Sheriff?*" Explaining his reasons for wanting to move to town galled him. As far as he knew, Colorado was a free country, or had been the last time he'd checked.

Sheriff Dawson just stared.

"Let me repeat. I have no interest in the Brinkmans. But I *am* interested in the men their situation will attract. Their inheritance will be tempting to a lot of fellas who aim to capitalize on their good fortune." He rubbed a palm over his mouth. "Nothing more. And speculation's not a crime. If Miss Brinkman is embarrassed over what happened, she has no one to blame except herself."

"Mr. Laughlin is what he claims to be," Henry Glass said to Dawson. "A new merchant for Eden. I'm sure he won't be the last to arrive, Clint, and we may as well prepare ourselves. Eden is growing. And maybe faster than we expected."

CHAPTER TEN

L avinia marched through the front door of Mademoiselle de Sells, tracked through the restaurant, ignoring astonished looks from the wedding guests, and continued out the back door, intending to keep going until she once again reached the hotel, where she could shut herself away. Where nobody would see her. Stare at her. Snicker behind their hands. In her blind rush to escape Mr. Laughlin and the embarrassing situation, she'd turned and marched back the way she'd come before realizing her best recourse was to seek solitude in her room.

Shame and mortification squeezed her lungs, making any rational thought impossible as she strode forward, her gaze glued to the cobblestones. Rhett Laughlin was *not* a doctor! He was some, some *man* whom she'd allowed to see her in her corset and stockings. No, not just that, she'd *begged* him for help dressing. The warmth of his skin beneath her fingers as she balanced on his arm was burned into her mind.

In a matter of minutes, the news would be everywhere! She'd told Belle and Mavis her intentions of finding the new doctor and returning with him to introduce him around, but that was only after she'd told half the merchants, their wives, and the town council. She'd felt a bit prideful, being the first to meet him and welcome him to town. When he hadn't showed, she'd joked he must have been too shy to come on his own.

Fiddlesticks!

Shy? Why, he was a predator, sneaking around to deflower any unaware young woman silly enough to fall for his tricks. How easily he could have taken advantage of her. Alone, in her room, in the deserted hotel, only her corset and bloomers between them.

Far off, the peaks of the mountains watched over the town as if nothing had happened, as if she hadn't just made such a fool of herself.

But Mr. Laughlin was a gentleman. If there is any blame to be leveled, it's at yourself.

"Lavinia, wait!"

She turned.

Emma was close on her heels and quickly halving the distance between them. She grasped Lavinia's arm and pulled her around. "What're you doing?"

"I can't stay in there another minute. I've told everyone what a wonderful man Dr. Laughlin is. Or was! How he came to my room. How gentle his hands are. How patient he is, what a splendid doctor Eden has acquired. That the children will love him. My gosh, I've all but put him up for sainthood—and now this! I'm so embarrassed, I want to die. I'll never be able to show my face again." She gulped in two deep breaths, and her eyes filled. "W-what am I g-going to do, Emma? I'm ruined."

"Just stop. You're making this into something much larger. You're not ruined and you're not a fool. You made a mistake, is all. Everyone does." Emma wiped away the fat tear that had slipped down Lavinia's cheek. "What happened isn't the end of the world. Like you said, nothing occurred between the two of you. But please, you have to come back inside, Lavinia. You can't run out on Belle and Blake's wedding reception."

Choking down her shame, Lavinia lifted a noncommittal shoulder. "They won't even notice I'm gone."

"What are you talking about? Of course they will. It's their special day. If they see you've left, they'll wonder why. And feel bad. Don't you see? You must come back and help celebrate. If the tables were turned, you wouldn't want Belle running off to hide. We all stand together. And we all stand behind you. You have to believe that."

No adequate words came to mind. Her mind twirled mercilessly, like an umbrella blown away by the wind.

Emma's right. I must go back to the party with my head held high. There's no other option. "I will for Belle."

Emma smiled. "And Blake."

"Endure the looks and the smiles. That can't be so hard," Lavinia whispered.

She'd been so stupid. She wished she could melt away. This would be a good time for her to get on a stage and head back to Philadelphia and beg Mr. Hansberry for that apprentice spot. No one here would miss her, and especially not bold Mr. Laughlin. She swallowed down her embarrassment.

"Lavinia?"

What was she supposed to do with her life now that her millinery dreams were most likely dashed? All her sisters had settled in, found their niche here in Eden. But she'd held on to the knowledge that change was just around the corner. That as soon as the papers were signed for the ranch, she'd be on her way back to Philadelphia for the summer apprenticeship. The waiting period for the ranch ran out in only twenty-one more days, and two days after that was her twentieth birthday. She'd planned to tell her sisters about the apprenticeship after the ink was dry on the contract. She'd had a secret, a wonderful, happy secret that had kept her going. And now . . .

She squared her shoulders. "You're absolutely

right, Emma. I don't know what I was thinking. I should stop worrying about myself so much and lift my chin." She had no other option. She couldn't hide away in the hotel or out at the ranch for the rest of her life.

As they returned to the restaurant, Lavinia forced a smile on her face and resolved to take the whole matter as a joke. *What else can I do?* At least Rhetten Laughlin wasn't at the wedding party. She'd get through this day just fine. She was a Brinkman. Little setbacks like this didn't bother them in the least.

CHAPTER ELEVEN

The next day, Lavinia drew the buggy to a stop in front of the Spanish-style stucco building of the Mother of Mercy Orphanage. The yard was spotlessly clean, as she knew it would be, considering Sister Cecilia's penchant for order. Aspens lined the long, winding driveway, and seven fruit trees dotted the front yard, their branches laden with small buds. The children would be out back playing in the fresh air at this time, Sunday service long past. Or perhaps in the barn with the cow and goats.

Peace.

She closed her eyes and raised her face to the sun, already feeling lighter than she had since before that wretched Rhett Laughlin had made her a laughingstock, before Mr. Hansberry's belated letter had dashed her dreams. It felt wonderful to be outside, away from her sisters, the ranch hands, and life. She blinked her left eye a few times, pleased not to feel any twinge of pain, though she did feel a twinge of guilt. Whether she wanted to admit it or not, the tall, handsome stranger had been her hero. For that, she was grateful.

Lavinia straightened her small lavender hat and then carefully descended to the ground. She gathered the box from behind the buggy seat and made her way to the front door, letting herself in. Aromas of warm bread, sugary syrup, and coffee hung on the air. She set the box on the long pine table that took up a good portion of the front room and crossed to the back door.

Hardly a moment passed before the alarm went up.

"Miss Lavinia!"

Jackie's high-pitched voice brought a surge of happiness. The eight-year-old with long, curly red tresses dropped the rake she was holding and dashed forward, a broad smile revealing her missing front tooth. It wasn't a baby tooth, which broke Lavinia's heart.

All heads popped up, swiveled around, or nodded in her direction. Children scurried forward, followed by her dear friend Sister Cecilia and a younger Sister Agatha. The younger nun had arrived at the orphanage last year shortly before the sisters had come to Eden.

In seconds, Lavinia was surrounded. Here she could breathe, and smile. It was as if nothing had happened.

"Children, children," Sister Cecilia called, clapping her hands. "Some of you have been in the garden. Be sure not to share your love of earth with our dear Lavinia and soil her pretty dress."

The nun's words were full of affection. In all the months Lavinia had been helping out at the orphanage, she'd never once heard the woman lose her temper, her tone always as soft as flower petals.

"Hello, hello." Lavinia laughed as the children snuggled near. Jackie wrapped her in a strong embrace, laying her head on Lavinia's chest. The others enfolded their arms around anything they could get ahold of. They had so much love to give.

The two nuns stood back, grinning from ear to ear. Their brown habits were tied at the waist by a leather cord and their rounded white collars were spotless. Their sleeves were wide at the wrist to make working easy. White veils covered their hair and flowed over their shoulders, ending at the backs of their knees. A white cross hanging on a thin leather cable around their necks was their only adornment. They were beautiful.

"I think they missed you, Lavinia," Sister Agatha said, a few wisps of chestnut hair showing at her forehead. Twenty-three, Mavis's age, and almost half the age of Sister Cecilia, the slight woman had professed her vows two years before. "This is a delightful surprise."

Where Sister Agatha was beautiful, spirited, and capricious, with the most gorgeous blue eyes Lavinia had ever seen, Sister Cecilia was handsome, steadfast, and wise. The older nun, slight in stature, wore round, wire-rimmed glasses and an endearing smile. Lavinia had no idea what color hair she had, because none was ever showing. The two were a perfect mix for the children in residence. Both were educators, in both material and spiritual matters, and took their jobs seriously, but they were also extremely fond of music and dance, incorporating singing and movement in most of the chores needed to keep everything running smoothly. The orphanage was a happy place.

"A surprise for me as well," Lavinia answered, tremendously glad she'd made the decision to bring the new bonnets and hats she'd made for the girls and boys out today. A dose of this was what she needed to get her thinking back on track. She'd lain awake all night going over and over yesterday's events. Thoughts of Philadelphia and her future. But worse, she'd finally fallen asleep hours after midnight and dreamed of Rhett Laughlin, with his piercing blue eyes and whiskey-deep voice. The memory was shadowy, but she thought they might have even kissed! She reached up and touched her lips, remembering how with the arrival of morning she'd been exhausted and confused. "Come inside," she said. "I've brought something for everyone."

Excited cries went up.

Sister Agatha held up a hand. "Before entering, remove your dirty shoes and wash your hands."

Shivering with excitement, the children dashed away, plopped down on the flagstones to untie their sturdy black boots and set them neatly, toes into the wall, next to the house. A line formed at the outside sink, and Miller, the oldest boy at twelve, thrust the pump handle up and down.

Sister Cecilia smiled and ushered her and Sister Agatha out of the brisk afternoon chill to the main room, where a small fire burned in the woodstove. They went to Lavinia's box of goodies.

First, Lavinia carefully extracted a cloth-covered plate. "Ada, the young woman who helps with the house, made these," she said, lifting the fabric to reveal several dozen molasses cookies. "If this visit wasn't so spontaneous, I'd have baked a cake as well."

"They look wonderful," Sister Cecilia said. "The children can have one now and more after supper for dessert. That was very kind of you."

Lavinia could never do enough for these little ones. She came often, to help with schooling, or gardening, and many times the meals. She never threw anything out at the restaurant, but instead brought leftovers here. Sometimes they took nature walks, or trips out to the ranch, or into town. The nuns were careful picking good homes, when homes were available. They'd told Lavinia that often orphans were looked at as free labor, and were taken in as farm or ranch help, not to be raised as a cherished son or daughter. Some of the children were what some people considered unadoptable, with a problem or disfigurement. Lavinia was dedicated to finding a way to help them all, more than just monetarily, if she could.

Freddie, a boy of six who had a clubfoot, came clumsily through the door first. He was one of her favorites. He held out his hands for inspection. When Sister Cecilia smiled and nodded, he shyly came a few inches nearer.

"Come closer, Freddie." Lavinia coaxed him with a smile. "Don't be shy. You can have the first cookie."

His face lit up. Knowing the rules, he went promptly to the bench and took his seat. Lavinia set a large cookie on the napkin in front of him.

"Cookies!" Others scrambled in and took their seats. Three girls and five boys, including twin brothers, five-year-olds of Italian descent, Alfio and Antonio, who'd ended up orphans when their parents took sick and died. They'd been sent up from an overcrowded orphanage in Santa Fe.

Once the children were eating, Lavinia withdrew the three bonnets she'd made in the prior weeks. A murmur of appreciation went around the table, but not a child spoke out of turn.

Lavinia held one up. "Well, what do you think?"

"So purty," little Brenda whispered, her fingers

taking tiny pieces of her cookie to her mouth. She was only four, and the youngest. The nuns had several families in correspondence that were considering adopting the child.

"I'm glad you think so, Brenda Blue Bird, because I made it just for you." Lavinia turned it back and forth so the children could see the white eyelet lace and decorative trimmings. Being gentle, she set the soft pink bonnet on Brenda's head and tied the bow beneath her chin, taking in the child's wary gaze. No one really knew the child's history, but her skittish behavior made them think it hadn't been easy. Lavinia kissed her forehead. Something about this mishmash of orphans reminded her of her and her sisters. The five little girls set adrift when their mother took them away from Eden, then died, leaving them to be raised by the thieving Crowdaires. "It will keep the sun off when the weather warms up. I hope you like it."

Brenda nodded and smiled.

"These are for you, Jackie and Judy. Matching yellow with blue bows, since you're very good friends."

The boys sat stone-faced, eating their cookies and sure they'd been left out. Lavinia almost laughed. "You haven't been forgotten, boys. I'd never do that."

She passed out five small sombreros she'd ordered from Emma's store over a month ago and then done her work making each one different. The twins' had brown velvet hatbands, which they were fingering at the moment. On Manuel's she'd put a silky red hatband and hung little red balls of material at the end of a string all around the brim, knowing they probably wouldn't last but a day. The children laughed when he put it on, but he seemed to like it. On Freddie's she'd molded the crown so it had a crease like the men's cowboy hats and sewed on a leather stampede string so he could hang it down his back. His eyes shined like gold and her heart squeezed. And for Miller, the oldest child, who'd been living here for many years, she'd fashioned a hatband from a rattlesnake skin she'd gotten from Trevor.

"There! Is everyone accounted for?"

The children cheered and thanked her profusely.

Sister Cecilia again clapped her hands. "All right, now let's not let this beautiful spring weather go to waste. Winter was long and you all need some sunshine. Out you go . . ." She gave Miller a direct look. "You're in charge until Sister Agatha and I come out. Go on, now . . ."

As soon as everyone was out the door, Sister Cecilia turned to her. "They will miss you when you go."

Straightening, Sister Agatha promptly went to the door. "I'm just on my way to see the goats.

We don't want them to feel left out of all the festivities."

Before Lavinia could stop her, Sister Agatha was gone. Mystified, she gazed at the nun by her side. "I'm not going anywhere." She'd not told a soul about Mr. Hansberry. And sharing her hopes now, after her chance was over, would be too hurtful. The sight of all those sombreros and bonnets had cheered her, and now the truth of her squashed dreams came rushing back.

Sister Cecilia went to the woodstove and fed the fire. "That was just my way of saying they appreciate all you do for them. Being they spend most of their days with us here at the orphanage, they enjoy an outsider, so to speak, taking an interest. They love you, Lavinia, never doubt that."

Here was her silver lining. Perhaps she wasn't meant to leave Eden. Her beloved family was here, and the orphans, they depended on her. Everything about Eden was perfect . . . except . . .

"Well," she said to the sister, "I guess there is something I'd like to share."

CHAPTER TWELVE

~✦~

I n the lobby of the hotel, Rhett waited nervously by the entrance to the café. Sunday and
Monday had come and gone and Lavinia hadn't
ventured into town that he'd seen. Surely he'd run
into her today, because early this morning she'd
driven herself to town in a buggy. He couldn't
help but notice, being right across the street with
nothing to do until he got some building supplies.
If he could avoid her, he would, but the drifting
aroma of hot coffee had lured him over. Trying to
appear inconspicuous, he gazed at the pendulum
clock on the far wall, wondering if he should just
seat himself.

Lavinia came through the kitchen door and
pulled up the moment she saw him, her expression one of surprise and distaste. Startled for only
a moment, she slowly approached.

He'd have chosen a more private place for their
first meeting since their discussion on the street,
where he could properly apologize. Tell her how
sorry he was that the mishap had happened in the
first place. But he'd have to make do with here
and now.

"Mr. Laughlin."

"Miss Brinkman."

Four boisterous fellas entered behind him, passed by, and took a seat at a center table amid sliding chairs and laughter. Lavinia watched and appeared as if she were about to start away when Rhett said, "I was wondering if I might get some breakfast." Yesterday he'd found a Mexican woman in the old part of town who sold beans and burritos, as well as other items. Today he needed something more substantial. He pushed his fingers through his hair, feeling much younger than his twenty-seven years. Would she turn him away?

Miss Brinkman glanced at the many empty tables. "Yes, of course. Choose any table you'd like."

He dipped his head. "Thank you."

She turned to face him. "Actually, I thought you might be gone by now. There was a stagecoach yesterday, if I'm not mistaken. I'm surprised you're still here."

As they spoke, she had to lift her chin to see into his face, the difference in their height substantial. "Are you planning to stay in Eden long?"

The sheriff or Henry hadn't told her his plans—they'd left the telling to him. "Actually, I'm making Eden my home."

He could tell she was struggling not to react to his news, but the pretty smile he'd been admiring a moment ago vanished and turned into a hard, flat line. He dreaded voicing the news that he knew he had to.

"I've bought the building across the way."

Her gaze flew to the front door. "The building across the road?" she repeated, blinking. "Why?"

That's a darned good question.

He nodded and gestured to the wall as if they both could see through it to the timeworn structure that represented his new life. After several hours checking the place over yesterday, and taking a good, hard look at what he might be able to accomplish with it, he'd signed papers with Henry, giving him half the owed amount. The attorney had legal authorization to lease or sell the building on behalf of its owner. Henry had actually warmed up to him, showed him around town, and introduced him to several of the other business owners as well as a handful of the locals.

The word about what had transpired between him and Lavinia had spread. People either thought the whole incident amusing and had a few good laughs at his and Lavinia's expense, or they appeared indignant, eyeing him as if he'd purposely set out to fool her for unscrupulous reasons.

She sputtered and pointed. "Are we talking about the same place?" She took two steps toward the door. "The Hungry Lizard Café?"

He nodded. More than a few heads had turned their way. People were listening.

"Yes, ma'am. The location is prime." With the difference in their ages, she was more miss than ma'am, but he didn't want to add to her ire. None of this could be easy for her.

"What are you putting in?" She jabbed a finger. "In the old place."

Here was the blow that would forever wedge them apart. When he'd taken up with this idea, he'd known a Brinkman daughter had inherited the hotel café, but he hadn't met Lavinia, or seen the depth of her eyes or how she bit her bottom lip when she was annoyed. He'd never known her heart-shaped face or noticed the tiny hourglass birthmark on the side of her neck. Those months ago, if you'd asked him if he cared that he'd be in competition with a Brinkman, he'd have smiled and said bring on the games. Now, standing in front of her dumbfounded face, he'd do anything to calm her annoyance at him. If taking a different place were possible, he'd do it. But this one was set up so nicely and came with a storage room full of chairs (in need of repair), several tables still usable, pots and pans, and some dishes. Enough to get him started. That was all he needed. Just a way and time to begin.

"With the stage office right next to you, I figure the town could use another eatery. I hear you get pretty packed with a full stage, and sometimes there's a wait." He lifted a shoulder. "They say competition is good for business."

A deep *V* formed between her brows. The coffeepot, which must be considerably heavy, sagged in her hands. Her eye, the one that had once been angry and red, seemed completely healed, and for that he was glad. A thick braid cascaded down her back and was tied with a dark blue ribbon that matched her dress. In her face, he saw vulnerability hidden by a cold exterior. Was she scared? His stomach fell and his appetite vanished. He didn't like to think it.

"An eatery? In direct competition with me." She swallowed and her nostrils flared slightly. He wouldn't be surprised if she were counting to ten.

"Yes, ma'am. I'd inquired about the building sometime before I arrived, and before we ever met. Corresponded with Henry Glass. So this has nothing to do with what transpired between us. I'm not trying to hurt you."

"*Nothing* has transpired between us," she spat back, and then glanced furtively around.

Sorry. Wrong choice of words.

A couple at the window table got up, the man leaving a few coins beside his plate.

"You're right," he replied, dipping his chin to the indignant-looking middle-aged woman who'd stopped to give Lavinia a hug.

"That was as tasty as ever, Lavinia dear. We'll

be in tomorrow, just like we are every day." That comment was leveled directly to his face, as if they would never set foot in the establishment of some woman wrecker.

A wobbly smile appeared. "Thank you, Mrs. Wilkerson. I'll be sure we bake fresh tomorrow, just for you."

Mr. Wilkerson waited for his wife outside the door, gazing across the street with interest. Women seemed much more loyal to their friend than did the men. Each and every one he'd voiced his plans to appeared eager for a new restaurant, somewhere different to sate his hunger.

With the couple gone, Rhett wondered if his eating in her café would cause Lavinia undue distress. Maybe he should go back to the Mexican woman over her fire. "I can go elsewhere, if you'd prefer. Henry introduced me to a nice woman who does tortillas and meat. She's not far at all. I've been taking my meals there but was in the mood for flapjacks. I need to fill this growing hole in my belly before I start lining up what I need to begin work on my own restaurant. Mr. Glass took care of the paperwork yesterday. I should have realized you'd not want to see me again."

Her expression darkened. "That's silly. We're going to have to get used to each other sooner or later."

Although he had no problem with her, her tone

said that was the last thing she wanted to do. She led the way to the table by the window the waitress had just cleared and wiped.

She looked around. "Where's your dog?"

Her tone had softened and the corners of her mouth had curled. "Waiting outside."

"He's well trained."

"He is." *When he wants to be.*

"Remind me before you leave and I'll find some scraps and bones for him."

"Thank you, that's kind." He tipped his head, remembering something he'd read in the newspaper articles—a tradition the girls had had growing up. "By the way, do you serve lamb on Tuesday evenings?"

Her brows drew down sharply as she looked deep into his eyes.

"I just, ah . . . really like lamb, and was hoping."

"We do, yes." She gave him another long look and then hurried away.

What a way to begin his new life. He'd had such plans on the trip out from San Francisco. Such hope. Anything to get past losing Shawn. The thoughts and plans formulated first on the train, and then on the rocking stagecoach ride to Eden had kept his mind off the sadness inside caused by leaving San Francisco, the salty air, and his pa. Those tragedies seemed a lifetime ago.

He hadn't been seated more than two minutes

when Cash Dawson came through the door. Spotting Rhett, he came over to the table.

"Mr. Laughlin," he said, respect in his voice. "I heard what happened with Miss—"

Before he had a chance to say Lavinia's name, Rhett gestured for him to sit and lower his voice. "I'd rather not rub salt in the wound, Cash."

The boy's face brightened in understanding. "'Nuff said. Just wanted to let you know I spoke with Maverick Daves—he's my boss at the livery. If you need me, he's agreed to let me off. As long as I don't fall behind with my responsibilities. I heard you signed papers with Henry yesterday, and wanted to speak with you before you had a chance to hire someone else. If you give me a chance, I won't let you down."

The boy, much younger than his looks, pushed a grain of salt around on the light blue tablecloth. Nerves pinched Rhett's stomach. For some reason, the kid wanted this job, but he was young, like Shawn. Actually, much younger.

"I'm doing this on my own, Cash, but I appreciate your offer."

His face fell.

"If I change my mind, you'll have the job. If you're dependable."

A wide grin appeared. "I am!"

Miss Brinkman walked up. "Cash. Did you want something to eat?"

"No, thank you, ma'am. Just looking for Mr.

Laughlin, being he's a new business owner in Eden."

She blinked. "Oh, all right."

Her gaze slid to him as if to say, *and now it starts*. He wished he could put her fears to rest, but he couldn't. He had no idea what tomorrow would bring, any more than she did.

CHAPTER THIRTEEN

Rhett jerked to a stop just before the heavy oak bridge leading to the lumber mill. His breath hissed through his teeth. He eyed Aspen Creek, the rushing tributary that was more river than creek that kept him from the timber office nestled amid the trees on the opposite bank. A large rock in the center of the waterway divided the current and created a mist. Dallas trotted over the bridge without concern.

Rhett felt as if a gun were pointed in his face. His breathing doubled and sweat broke out over his body. His mouth dried to sand and his feet felt anchored to the spot. The sound of the river grew in his mind. *Your fault. Your fault.*

His heart twisted. Shawn had stepped in for Rhett so he wouldn't be fired for missing his shift. The day was typical, foggy and cold. A young boy had chased a ball into the docking area, where crates were piled too high. A strong gust of wind toppled the highest. Saving the child, his brother had taken a blow to his head and was knocked into the icy-cold water. Dallas plunged in to save him without success. Two agonizing days passed before they'd found Shawn's body.

Feeling eyes on him, Rhett drew his attention from the swirling current to find Mrs. Gonzales, the Mexican woman he'd bought food from, watching from down the road. He nodded and looked away—but still didn't attempt to cross.

The three days since his talk with Lavinia in the café had been busy. Avoiding her was easy—with his measuring and researching, he didn't have time to search her out even if he'd wanted. When he needed something to eat, or a cup of hot coffee, he walked over to Mrs. Gonzales's fire. Today, the March sun was lukewarm, but much warmer than a San Francisco spring.

If he didn't move soon, someone would notice. Closing his eyes, he concentrated on the scents of the freshly milled lumber. They tickled his nose, brought a sense of relief as well as an outpouring of homesickness. He swallowed, gave a brief smile to Mrs. Gonzales, and then strode across the bridge—and away from his ghosts. On the other side, he let out the breath lodged in his lungs.

At the moment, the saws were quiet and the rush of the river was all he heard. A buggy parked close to the office, the horse unharnessed and tethered in the shade of a tree, told him the woman he was looking for must be inside. He approached the office and pulled open the door.

Katie Brinkman looked up from the front desk. Surprise crossed her face. She stood and glanced over her shoulder to the door to another room. "May I help you?" she asked.

Her tone was icy.

"I'm Rhetten Laughlin. I need to order some lumber. As well as roofing material. A number of things."

She slowly came forward. "Yes, I know who you are. I was with Lavinia when you admitted your true identity."

The man who hoodwinked my sister. She didn't have to say the words for him to know what she was thinking.

A middle-aged man poked his head out of the other office, taking stock.

"I've got this, Howard," Miss Brinkman said, giving the fellow a smile. "No need for you to stop what you're doing."

Katie looked up at Rhett through her lashes, her intense gaze making him uncomfortable. She could effortlessly stop his restoration progress. He needed lumber.

"I'm surprised you'd show your face at my mill, Mr. Laughlin. After the trick you played on my sister. I'd think you'd be too ashamed to come around."

"I have no other option but to show my face if I'm to get my restaurant up and running. I'm sure you can understand that." *I needn't waste my breath explaining. She's heard the story by now. Either she believes me or not.*

"Yes, I heard about that. And right across from my sister's place. Feels like you have a vendetta against her. Is that true?"

"Not at all, Miss Brinkman. My intentions only concern my business."

"Yes, well, I'm not sure if I believe that or not, but I'll have to take you at your word. But be warned, the truth has a way of coming out. If your intentions are to hurt Lavinia in some way, more than you already have, just know you will have the rest of us to contend with." She drilled him with what he thought must be her most imposing stare. She reminded him of a puppy after you've taken away his bone. "And me mostly, Mr. Laughlin. Lavinia and I, being the two youngest, are exceptionally close. We look out for each other." She arched a brow. "This is a gentle warning."

"Yes, my father says the same—about the truth coming out, that is. And I'll keep your words in mind—what you've said about the two of you looking out for each other. That's a good thing."

She took a form from a slot in her desk and licked the tip of the pencil she already held in her hand. "What do you need?"

"Twelve two-by-four-by-twelve Douglas fir, ten one-by-twelve-by-twelve smooth pine, six one-by-four-by-twelve door-and-window trim—

whatever you have will be fine—and a couple bundles of new shingles. When the rain starts, I hear the roof is plenty leaky."

"When would you like them?"

"Yesterday."

Her brows dipped, but she didn't smile.

"Uhh, at your convenience," he quickly amended.

She scribbled his requests on the paper.

He swallowed, his nerves getting the best of him. "I'd also like to start an account. I'm sure these won't be the only supplies I'll need. And paying at the end of the month would be more convenient."

She gave a quick glance to the back room where the other man was working. "Howard usually handles the accounts and bookkeeping." At the moment she looked much like Lavinia as she tried to decide what she should do. If he was indeed good for the money.

"How can I trust you'll pay promptly what you owe?"

He'd known he'd have to bare his soul sooner or later, but doing so to a snippet of a girl was galling.

"I have savings I deposited in the bank. I'm a man of my word. I'll pay my debts on time, Miss Brinkman. Check with Henry Glass if you want more information about me or my affairs." He'd said more than he'd wanted to about himself already and was almost ready to walk out the door without the lumber. "If you'd rather I do business in Dove Creek, I can do that. I don't want to make you uncomfortable."

Her expression darkened.

"That won't be necessary, Mr. Laughlin. If you've dealt with Henry, who is our close friend, I trust you."

She actually smiled. Or maybe, as a rule, she smiled at all her customers. His wounded pride eased a tiny bit.

But as he finished the transaction and walked outside, he loosed a long sigh. He felt worn-out, and he'd only taken care of one chore on his long list of duties.

CHAPTER FOURTEEN

E mma sorted through the heavy wooden crate the stagecoach had just delivered. Mr. Buns had kindly pried off the lid before he left for his noon break. Having a man around did come in handy, and now that the two were better acquainted, they'd become friends. Originally from the East, he'd confided in her that he was forty-two years old. He hadn't said what brought him to Eden, but as the months passed, she was sure he would open up further.

Corsets, pantaloons, several factory-made dresses, and shirtwaists overflowed from the crate, as she pulled garments out one by one. The Toggery's inventory was growing nicely, but now, seeing the brimming crate, perhaps she'd been a little too zealous with her monthly order. But she *enjoyed* pretty garments. She liked folding them, touching them, and mostly helping women who'd depended on their own talents for years try on something store made. Their faces lit up like a Christmas candle. She was doing a good deed for the women of Eden. Until she'd arrived, they hadn't known what they'd been missing.

After taking possession of the Toggery last fall, Emma had immediately knocked out a sidewall and enlarged the building by fifty percent. The new space was a dedicated women's department, with clothing of all kinds. Some items factory made, some tailored by her dear friend Elizabeth Smith, others on consignment made by a local seamstress who had a knack for beauty. Her sister Lavinia had contributed three attractively crafted hats, one bonnet and two small tulip-shaped felt. One blue and one green. Her store wasn't on par with those in Philadelphia by any stretch of the imagination, but she was getting there, slowly but not so surely.

Emma sighed and pushed away a nub of anxiety in her belly. The signing of the contract that bequeathed the Five Sisters Ranch fifty percent to the Brinkman girls and fifty percent to Blake Harding was swiftly approaching. If any of the girls decided to back out or leave Eden before that, they'd each receive a fifteen-thousand-dollar payout. With that amount of money, she could open a shop in Paris or live in New York in style. She glanced around at the vacant room.

Is Eden the best fit?

Things'll pick up. We've just come out of winter. I must give the women a chance to get to town before I begin to worry. Many don't even know I'm here. Leaning on her elbow, she blew some stray hairs out of her face. *Anything of value takes time . . .*

But how much time? In the months since she'd taken over, the Toggery's expenditures had surpassed the monies coming in. First with the renovations and then her ordering new items every single month. Her business wasn't moving in the correct direction.

She lifted a soft pink corset and turned the garment over in her hands. *What would Father think? This was his store prior to my inheriting. Back then, surely the place was always in the black.*

Concerning accounts, and ordering, she received enough censuring expressions from Mr. Buns to know what he thought—but for the most part, he kept his comments to himself. Action was needed to get more females into Eden before all was lost. She'd not pour good money after bad. The store would survive on its own or not at all. She'd made that promise to herself the first week she'd had to rein herself in with the order.

The bells above the door chimed. Expecting Mr. Buns, Emma placed the corset back into the crate and swished around the counter, coming face-to-face with Rhett Laughlin, the fake doctor who had assisted Lavinia in her moment of need.

She pulled up short. "Oh!" Her cheeks tingled with warmth. *Mr. Laughlin and Lavinia were alone in her room. The only two in the whole empty hotel.* Was there something her sister wasn't telling? She acted much too embarrassed if the man had only assisted with her eye.

She and Lavinia were two of the three middle sisters. Two peas in a pod, they liked to say quietly, for only their ears. Preferring to do each other's hair rather than their own. They held hands in a thunderstorm, their heads together whispering comfort. And when feelings were hurt, who rushed to apologize first was a toss-up. They thought alike over almost everything. They weren't the older, more responsible sisters like Mavis and Belle, philosophizing and theorizing about everything under the sun, Emma thought with a half smile, her heart warming. And they weren't the needy-but-lovable baby like Katie, flighty at times and sometimes immature. She and Lavinia were their own little set, and Emma liked it that way.

She straightened her shoulders, trying to look taller. "May I help you, Mr. Laughlin?"

She actually flinched when her voice wobbled, but hoped he hadn't noticed. He was tall and muscular. Unlike the day he'd arrived, his face was free of whiskers and tanned—*sun-kissed,* she thought. The messy hair she remembered from the day of Belle's wedding had been trimmed and perhaps even combed.

He glanced around the quiet store. "I'm in need of some garments."

A customer! Even one that had shamed her sister. For that thought, she asked the heavens for forgiveness. Would she be considered a turncoat if she were kind to him? And sold him some trousers?

"What can I show you?" she said, keeping her tone all business and her expression stern. Perhaps she could sell him some things but not develop a friendship. She'd not want to hurt Lavinia.

She wove her way into the men's section, smiling over her shoulder to be sure he followed. An assortment of different types of men's work clothing as well as some dressier items were staked on displays or hung on racks. "I'm sorry, my clerk, Mr. Buns, is not here at the moment. But I can assist you with whatever you might need."

Mr. Laughlin's face turned a ruddy hue. He didn't seem like the type who would be introverted around women. But perhaps he was not what she and her sisters expected. Perhaps they'd pegged him in the wrong hole.

"Would you rather come back when Mr. Buns returns? He's worked here for years and has much more experience than I do." To break the awkwardness, she lifted a linen hankie from a stack on a middle-of-the-room display and let the sensation in her fingers ground her runaway nerves. "He usually only takes half an hour for lunch. I expect him back any moment."

He did his own nervous fingering of a folded cotton shirt.

"No, ma'am. I have things to accomplish when I'm finished here that take manual labor. Best I pick something now before I get sweaty so I can check this chore off my list."

She didn't know how she felt about being called a chore. "All right. Tell me what you're looking for and I'll see what I can do."

"I need some town clothes to wear when my new restaurant opens. I hope that will happen quickly, but there is considerable work to be done, and some details that will take time." His gaze strayed back down to the shirts folded beneath his fingertips on the display shelf.

She felt her eyes brighten. "The old vacant building across from the hotel? Yes, I've heard."

"I thought you might have."

"To be truthful, Mr. Laughlin, I believe what you're doing is a great service for Eden. Not only cleaning up an eyesore, but adding commerce. I agree with your opinion that more women will follow men who'll come to Eden in hopes of winning the hand of a Brinkman. Please forgive me if I sound supercilious, that is not my intent. I just hope you're right, for my business's sake." She laughed softly. "I'd like to entice more women here, and faster."

He chuckled. "Interesting. A Brinkman after my own heart."

She jerked her gaze away.

"I only meant that we're thinking along the same lines," he quickly amended. "And that I must not be as crazy as my hopes might sound. I'm not going to sit and wait for opportunity, but foster growth and profit along." He smiled. "We should sit and have a talk someday soon. If we worked together, the outcome would be more abundant and swifter. Don't you think?"

Heat infused her face. This conversation was completely inappropriate. She needed to change the subject. "What were you thinking, in terms of clothing?"

His smile disappeared. "A white shirt and new pants. I need a set and another for whomever I hire. I haven't yet found anyone."

"Oh? How are you going about looking?" she asked, tipping her head so she could guess what size he wore. Surely larger than large. They'd had a few men who'd fit that description.

"I haven't even begun. Does Eden have a newspaper?"

"Less a paper and more a notice sheet. Comes out once a month around the first, or second, or third. If you can wait that long, I'm sure the proprietor will be happy to run a notice for you—at a cost, of course."

"Of course. But I'll need someone sooner than that, I hope." He glanced around and his gaze landed on her bulletin board by the door. He raised his brows.

"You're welcome to post a note there, if you'd like. I don't have as much foot traffic as I'd hope, but I'll also put out the word. See who we can find. Are you looking for a man or a woman?"

"Preferably, a man. But if I can't find one, I'm not against a woman."

Emma was beginning to feel sympathetic toward Mr. Laughlin's plight. Everyone who'd heard the accounting of what had happened on Belle and Blake's wedding day had jumped to defend Lavinia's honor, when in all reality, Mr. Laughlin had been a victim too, so to speak. He'd only tried to help. At least, that was all she'd been told. If there was more to the story, she hadn't been privy. *But there is that feeling that Lavinia isn't telling me everything . . .*

She left the folded work shirts and went to some finer-quality garments hanging on the wall rack. The problem was, she didn't know if there were any large enough to fit Mr. Laughlin. "I think this fine fabric blend of cotton and linen is lovely. It's durable, looks nice, and will wash and wear well. The only thing is"—she reached for the largest one she had—"I don't think this will fit you."

He took the shirt and held it to himself, a doubtful tilt to his forehead. "I don't think so either."

"That's the largest we have." *But I do have a*

sister who worked for a tailor for years. As long as I don't let on who Lavinia is altering for, she's always willing to help.

"We'll let out the seams and lengthen the arms. We'll doubly reinforce the seams so the garment will last. But all that will take a little time." *If I can get the alterations accomplished at all.* Elizabeth sewed new garments for the shop; she didn't usually do alterations, but she might if Lavinia said no. He carefully inspected the shirt.

"Do you like the texture?"

He shrugged. "I'm not knowledgeable on fabric and what's nice and what isn't. If you say this will be durable, that's all I need to know. I'll take your word. I'm most interested in getting something that fits."

"Well, this will when I get through with it, but I'll need to take some measurements . . ."

She glanced around at the still-empty store. She'd hoped Mr. Buns would have returned by now. He was overdue by five minutes. She normally wouldn't care, but . . .

Mr. Laughlin appeared as uncomfortable as she felt.

"Have you always been in the restaurant business, Mr. Laughlin?" she asked to fill the void. "You certainly don't look the type. My sister mentioned your case of knives. Frightened her to death, thinking they were for surgery. Now we know the truth."

114

He chuckled low. "I shouldn't have scared her like that, but she did ask me what I had inside. I bought them in San Francisco when I made the decision to come to Eden and open a restaurant. And no, I've never been in the restaurant business before. This is a first for me."

The bells chimed again and a rush of warm air flowed into the shop as Elizabeth Smith came whooshing into the room. Since Elizabeth had come to town with her son, Johnny, in hand, she'd fit right in. Especially with Henry. Emma wouldn't be surprised if they had an announcement sometime soon.

Elizabeth pulled up short, much the same way Emma had, when she spotted Mr. Laughlin.

"Elizabeth." Emma stepped to the side as if Mr. Laughlin couldn't be seen behind her. "Look who's here purchasing clothing. Mr. Laughlin. Have the two of you met?"

Elizabeth's face turned three shades of scarlet, and Emma almost laughed. For some strange reason, she was feeling generous toward this tall, quiet man. He *had* helped Lavinia's eye, after all, just under false pretenses. She didn't feel the need to make him more of an outcast than he already was.

"No. We haven't. But Henry has told me all about your plans, Mr. Laughlin. Having a new eatery in Eden will be a blessing. I, for one, am looking forward to more choice."

Emma held out a hand. "Mr. Laughlin, Mrs. Smith."

Mr. Laughlin politely nodded, and then smiled. Emma was surprised at how handsome he was becoming in her eyes as they got better acquainted. She admired his clear, blue eyes and the way he'd been a bit skittish around her, and soft-spoken. His attractive good looks reminded her greatly of two special brothers back in Philadelphia. Memories of the wool shop surfaced. She'd loved helping women choose what wool they needed, straightening the shelves, and doing anything else that needed doing. But mostly, she'd loved the proprietress, the brothers' mother, like her own mother. Tamping back her melancholy, she smiled.

"And here are our Levi's and slacks for men." She moved around the display. "What did you have in mind?"

"Dark trousers, please. I think that best with a white shirt and apron."

A lopsided grin appeared and transformed his face. Emma blinked and glanced away. Mr. Laughlin was *quite* attractive when he wanted to be.

He shifted his weight. "Unless you have a better idea. I'm not much for imagination and am open to suggestion. If either of you ladies has a better notion, don't be shy."

"No, that sounds perfect to me." Emma pulled

her cloth measuring tape from her pocket and handed the implement to a flustered-looking Elizabeth. "Let's get these measurements done. Do you have time, Elizabeth? You're so much better at this with all your experience." She stopped, her brows lifting. "But did you need something specific, or are you in to visit? I didn't ask."

"I just stopped by to tell you I saw Belle earlier this morning, and she said she was coming in later today. She wanted me to pass that along so you wouldn't go out."

"Where else would I be? Only at Lavinia's restaurant," she said, sliding her gaze over to Mr. Laughlin, who was intently examining a pair of pants. "Do you have time for Mrs. Smith to take a few measurements?" she said.

He stretched out his arms. "The sooner I get these chores finished, the better."

With deft experience, Elizabeth called out numbers and Emma jotted them on a sheet of paper. She was relieved Elizabeth was the one who had to run the tape over the expanse of his wide shoulders, over and under his arms, around his middle, from the nape of his neck down to his . . .

She jerked her thoughts back on track. In a matter of minutes, Elizabeth was finished.

Mr. Laughlin looked relieved.

"I'll have three shirts altered to these specifications, Mr. Laughlin," Emma said, "so there'll be backup in case you find you need another one anytime soon." She touched Elizabeth's arm, knowing her friend could hardly say no to her coming question. "Can you take care of these for me?"

Elizabeth smiled. "I'd be happy to."

Emma released a deep breath. "Wonderful."

"Thank you," Mr. Laughlin said. "And whoever I hire, I'll send in for matching garments." He paused for a moment. His gaze traced to Elizabeth and then back to Emma. "And I'd be pleased if you called me Rhett. If that's proper by now. I feel we've become friends. We have the same ambitions."

Emma didn't have to look at Elizabeth to feel her questioning stare. Emma wasn't choosing Rhett's side over her sister's, but that's the way her actions would look.

"Thank you, Mr., ah, Rhett. And you may call me Emma, if you choose. We're both business owners in Eden. It's only right. If I find someone I think is suitable as an employee for you, I'll send him or her down to your place."

And hope I'm not in hot water with my sister.

CHAPTER FIFTEEN

*D*amn. Clint Dawson opened the third install-ment of the Brinkman sisters' saga in the tattered *San Francisco Daily Call*, uneasy under the watchful eye of Rhetten Laughlin, who was observing with one shoulder against the wall. Clint wasn't a deft reader. He hated feeling weak about anything—especially in front of the new-comer who had captured Cash's interest. The man was practically all Cash talked about from the moment his son got home from the livery in the afternoon to the time he left in the morning to go to work. Him or the man's dog, who now lounged on the small rug in front of the door, sprawled on his side. Laughlin had lived in San Francisco, and from what Cash had found out, he hadn't been a restaurateur his whole life but wasn't talking much about his past. Laughlin's secrecy made him all that much more fascinating to Cash. Nicole, Clint's much younger half sister, was almost as sick of hearing about the man as he was, if her expressions around the house meant anything at all.

I'm jealous!

Clint glanced up when Rhett straightened and looked out the window.

Finally finished reading, Clint closed the paper and wiped a palm across his moist brow. Feeling at a disadvantage, he stood. "Shocking. The amount of personal information in these pieces is beyond the pale. As far as I know—Henry too—there wasn't anyone around after the girls arrived who could have ferreted out all this information. To tell you the truth, I'm mystified." He glanced down at the paper and the name of the reporter.

Harlow Lennington.

"Do you know the reporter?" he asked.

"No."

"You mentioned that these articles were popular, well read."

"Extremely," Laughlin said. "Everyone likes a good rags-to-riches story. It's almost as if the sisters have followers. When I'd go for a meal, I'd overhear conversations. Women wanted to know more, what they wore, how they spoke, what they thought. Men had only one desire, and that was to marry one—didn't matter which. The Brinkmans are a huge hit in San Francisco."

Clint pushed back in his chair. "I don't get the personal information about their guardians. How someone could have known about them. How they treated the girls as servants as soon as they were old enough to be of use. Even some personal conversations. Doesn't make any sense. Unless some of what's written is fiction." He struggled to get a breath of air, thinking how Mavis would be affected. For two months she'd been working a few hours a week for him in his office. Keeping the filing straight, writing reports, and all the other chores he didn't like to do. He'd be a liar if he said he wasn't smitten, always counting the hours until she'd show up. They'd talk, laugh, and maybe a bit more, if you could call long, heartfelt gazes anything. He didn't want to see her, or any of the sisters, be hurt by these articles. He'd hoped the articles would enlighten him as to why Mavis always wore gloves, whether it was propriety or something else—but, sadly, the writings hadn't said.

"Could be this"—he looked again at the byline under the headline—"Harlow Lennington is lying. Embellishing the truth to sell the articles. Fabricating something that he knew would titillate."

Belle's birthday letter, and what John told her about her being nursed by an Indian woman . . . Who would have so much infor-mation? Henry, Blake, the girls themselves—no one he could see gaining anything from exposing their private lives. Their former guardians, the Crowdaires, were out there somewhere, but they wouldn't know the details of the girls' lives in Eden. *So who's up to such mischief?*

When Laughlin chuckled, Clint didn't know

what the man thought was funny. None of this boded well. The girls would have to be told—but not just yet. He imagined Mavis would be furious. Right when everything was going so well for them. Belle's wedding, Emma and the rest settling in to Eden as if they'd never left eighteen years ago. The contract to inherit the ranch ready to be signed in fifteen days. He didn't like this turn of events one bit.

"So you can see why I decided to come. I'm not interested in landing a *Brinkman,* just making a living from the others who are. Have you seen an increase in the town's numbers?"

Clint hated to admit it, but they had. They'd been happy about Eden growing. That was before they had all the facts. "Yes." He stood, strode to the window, and looked out. Two cowboys he'd never seen before rode down the street looking around with interest. Those weren't the first. Almost every day he was being told about a new-comer and going to introduce himself. Available housing around town was at an all-time low, and Katie had seen an increase in orders at her lumber mill. Now he understood why. Surely John hadn't anticipated this when he'd worked so hard to make the ranch a success, all so his daughters would have something to be proud of when they finally returned to Eden.

"Can I keep these for a few days?" He looked over his shoulder at Laughlin.

"Sure."

Outside, Blake and Belle rode up to the office hitching rail. *The newlyweds make their first appearance in Eden since becoming man and wife.* They dismounted and, through the window, Belle nodded and smiled as she tied Strider's reins. Blake was at her side.

Clint folded the papers and covered them with some old paperwork. He stepped outside, followed by Laughlin.

"You made the ride to town," Clint said, feeling a bit embarrassed. The sight of Belle's shy glance took him back years, to the time before Cash, when he and his own young wife had only been married a few days. Clint's face heated at the memory, and he had to smile wide to keep Blake from guessing at his thoughts.

"We did." Blake patted his chest and glanced around proudly as if he'd never seen the town before. "Time we get out, see what trouble the town's got itself into without our guidance." He laughed and sneaked a look at his new wife.

Belle was uncharacteristically quiet.

Little do you know. "Not much," Clint said, not ready to burst any bubbles. "You remember Mr. Laughlin?"

Blake thrust out his hand. "Sure we do. Even though we never got a chance to meet on our wedding day."

They shook a bit violently.

"Mr. Laughlin," Belle said, holding back approval.

Clint was sure she'd heard everything from her sisters. A simple introduction was not going to win over her support. As asinine as that sounded, Clint was glad.

"I'm pleased to make your acquaintance, Mr. and Mrs. Harding. Congratulations on your marriage. I'd like to extend an invitation to my place as soon as I open for a free meal."

"That's generous," Blake responded. "We'd be happy to take you up on that. When do you expect to be finished?"

Laughlin let out a deep sigh. "The place needs more work than I originally thought. Just bought some lumber from your sister. She said she'd have the order to me later today. After I begin the work"—Laughlin glanced at him and smiled—"shouldn't take more than a week."

All Cash talked about was his hope Laughlin would hire him.

"Roof needs patching as well," Laughlin went on.

I'll rue the day Cash is grown if he ever wants to move away. Can't stop a young man, though. He'll have his own dreams that won't include me.

"I'm pushing out one wall a bit."

"Thinking big," Blake said. "I like that."

The building was directly across from his

sheriff's office. There was room to go toward the Old Spanish Trail that ran out front. And on the opposite side toward the mercantile. The man had options. That was a good piece of property.

Belle snagged the newcomer's gaze. "You're expecting a lot of customers, Mr. Laughlin."

Laughlin glanced at Clint, his expression saying a million things. "I am. I think Eden is a diamond in the rough. I'm banking on the fact."

She tipped her head. "Positive thinking. That's good for a new business owner."

Clint liked the fact that Belle wasn't warming. He lifted one shoulder, feeling the weight of the large chip residing there. He should try to remember that Laughlin hadn't written those articles himself. He'd actually done them a favor by alerting them to their existence. Now Clint could be watchful for unscrupulous characters hanging around the sisters.

"I ordered some clothing from your other sister at the Toggery an hour ago, and am on my way to the forge and livery to speak with Mrs. Applebee about getting the stove in better working order. I'd hate to have to buy a new one with all these other expenses I wasn't counting on." He turned to Clint. "Who's her man? Maverick Daves, I think? How good is he with metal?"

Her man?

"He can fix it, I'm sure," Blake responded. "He's handy. Some men would buck at having a woman to answer to for a livery and forge. He seems to have risen to the challenge."

Belle blinked up at her husband. "Challenge? You make us sound incompetent, Blake. My sisters are doing a fine job." She slanted her gaze at Laughlin. "Take Lavinia, for instance. She's up at four most mornings, dressed and on her way to town. They don't come more dedicated than that. Don't you think? The hotel café is busier than ever these days. She's even looking to hire another girl."

Blake laughed and slung his arm over Belle's shoulders. "I only meant in the instances where a man is the usual proprietor. Restaurant work is for wo—" He jerked his gaze away and then said, "Workers who are industrious, man or woman. But I've never seen a female in a forge, or a lumber mill, for that matter."

"Or tannery?" Belle laid her hand on Blake's chest and smiled prettily. "I guess us women should stay home and raise babies."

"Now you're being plain silly. You and your sisters have backbones of steel, and I don't think there is a thing any one of you couldn't accomplish once you set your minds to the task. I retract my narrow-minded comment, boys. Don't listen to a thing I just said." He smiled and looked between the men. "I sometimes forget I've married into a family of five women."

Belle nodded, satisfied, and Blake added,

"Heed my words, Laughlin. You won't win in a competition. I guarantee it."

"I don't doubt it," he said. "And it's Rhett. I hope you all will consider me a friend."

Blake smiled, but the veiled suspicion in Belle's eyes wasn't going to go away anytime soon.

Good, thought Clint. They didn't know everything about Laughlin. Harlow Lennington wouldn't be the only person he'd look into. For all they knew, Laughlin could be in cahoots with Lennington, or anyone. Clint's job was to be suspicious of everyone, especially someone who would be such a presence in Eden.

"You too, Sheriff, please call me Rhett."

There was an edge to his voice, as if he'd been able to read Clint's thoughts. If he had, he'd know he'd better watch his steps. Clint wouldn't put up with anyone who might hurt Mavis in any way.

CHAPTER SIXTEEN

꧁ꕤ꧂

I just love your quaint little restaurant,
Lavinia," Lara Marsh gushed as she moved
around the café kitchen, looking into every nook
and cranny. "You're an accomplished business-
woman, now! That's amazing. I'm proud of
you."

Lara had gone to the same school as Lavinia
and her sisters. Their acquaintance began when
the sisters' guardians, the Crowdaires, moved
to a nicer neighborhood. Lara was Belle's age,
but was close friends with all the sisters. She
was considered a sixth sister among them all,
and at times, could argue as such. They hadn't
had a true goodbye when the sisters left Philadelphia, because everyone had believed they'd be
returning in a week, so the reunion had been a
delight.

"Thank you, Lara. Sometimes, I'm still amazed
myself. Each morning I wake up and wonder
what the day will bring." *Like a new café opening
across the street.* She gave a small laugh to
disrupt her runaway thoughts.

"You sound as if you don't mean that."

"I do. Not every day a woman is a proprietor at nineteen."

"Almost twenty," Lara replied, wagging a finger. "Your birthday is swiftly approaching. I'm so happy I'll still be here to help celebrate."

The rectangular kitchen, separated from the dining room by a swinging door, was not much larger than their old bedroom in Philadelphia. Everything one might need was crammed into the small space. The two long counters were a blessing. Working space was one thing they had a lot of. Her stove was reliable and never gave any trouble since the thing had been replaced some five years ago. Karen had many humorous and not-so-humorous stories about the previous appliance, and Lavinia hoped she never experienced any such calamities. A deep sink and water pump under the window took up the end of the kitchen, and trash bins set close to the back door made an easy job of lugging out the waste. There was an additional, much smaller stove on the other side of the room that they lit in the cold winter months to help keep the place warm. Three windows along the back wall gave plenty of light. A mirror for checking one's appearance was tucked away on the far wall where floor-to-ceiling shelves kept the aprons, tablecloths, and napkins organized after they'd been pressed. Lavinia yearned to feel it was *home*.

"My dining room is small and somewhat

rustic, nothing like the eateries we're used to in Philadelphia, but, day by day, the place has grown on me. Knowing my father once walked these floors, and touched the same china, linen, and utensils, gives me much comfort." She lifted a small china creamer, feeling his warmth. It bolstered her happiness. "He and Karen were close friends, from what she tells me. She has many anecdotes about him to share, and she does often."

Lara turned to face her, one of the café's flowered teacups in her hands. Tall and willowy, anything she wore looked stylish. She had an easy smile and dark brown eyes that matched her hair. She was soft-spoken, smart as a whip, and funny. Best of all, she was a staunch supporter of the sisters, and if ever there was a disagreement at school, she'd rush to their defense. "That is so nice, Vin," she replied, using the nickname she'd given Lavinia, saying the four syllables of *Lavinia* were cumbersome on her tongue.

Lavinia hadn't minded at the time, and actually felt special at being singled out. Lara had that special thing, that allure, that natural magnetism that attracted people like honey did bees. Her appeal wasn't about being beautiful, although Lavinia thought she was, but more the special look in her eyes. All she had to do was glance your way and the room lit up. The fact that Lara was closer in age to Mavis and Belle meant

Lavinia had secretly pined for her attention. Now she had their friend all to herself for the afternoon. The attention felt delightful.

Lavinia, who had been in the café since early morning, felt a bit bedraggled, especially compared with Lara, who was clean and shiny with not a hair out of place. "How was your ride in from the ranch? Did you see anything unusual?"

Lara's eyes lit with pleasure, and a smile bloomed on her face. "The scenery is just breathtaking, Vin. How could anyone ever tire of seeing those mountains? Or the rushing river, the animals, just the wide-open sky free of soot is amazing. Trevor and KT purposely kept me laughing, I think. The ride was extremely enjoyable. I can see how you've fallen headfirst into Eden, never to come up again. I'd never want to return to Philadelphia either, if I were you."

Lavinia blinked and looked away. *She's right. But I can't forget about my dream of making hats. That's been my desire my entire life. I feel steadfast to the vision. I can't be wishy-washy.* "And the buckboard wasn't too rough?"

"Not at all. The bumpier the better. I can ride a smooth buggy any old day of the week, but a ranch wagon?"

Her brows lifted with delight.

"And Moses came into town as well, correct? Friday is when they usually do their heavy supply run."

Lara put her hands on the counter and glanced out the back window. "He did. He rode his horse most of the way beside the wagon." She turned and leaned back. "Just think, a year ago you all were wondering what you would do with your lives. Mavis was a newlywed, and Katie was talking about becoming a teacher." She wagged her head. "Look at you now. Heiresses, all of you. When I heard the news, I couldn't have been happier."

The love in Lara's eyes was so real, Lavinia had to cross the room and take her into her arms. "Having you in Eden for the wedding meant so much to Belle and the rest of us. Thank you for coming."

She pulled back with a laugh, so typical for Lara when a situation became emotional. She didn't seem to know how to handle sentiment, unlike the Brinkmans. "Mother and Father were delighted to get me out from under their feet for a few weeks. They're amazed at the turn of events as well."

Karen pushed through the door, her face shiny from exertion. She glanced around and smiled. "Is lunch made for Mavis and the men at the livery?"

"Yes. I'm putting on the finishing touches right now." Lavinia wrapped the three large sandwiches she'd made in clean napkins and set them into the basket with three slices of pie and a small crock of coffee. On days Mavis spent at the barn, getting dirty, she'd request a meal delivered for her, Maverick, and Cash. "I'll take the basket over in a few minutes. I'm surprised Mavis is spending so much time at the livery, but I'm glad. The air is fresh and clean, and she works outside. Seeing her glow with health after being shut away in her accounting job for so many months is nice. The change in scenery has helped her get past the loss of Darvid."

"Is there anything I can do to help?" Lara asked. She plucked an apron from the hook on the wall and slipped the garment over her head. Reaching back, she tied a bow and, with a folded dishcloth, lifted the heavy coffeepot from the stove.

Scandalized, Lavinia rushed forward. "No. You're a guest. Karen and I have been taking care of this for months. And for some time, she did the job on her own, with just one cook."

Lara tottered under the weight. Her arms were soft and silky, not used to any kind of work. "Where's your cook now?" she asked.

"He's only here during the busiest times." Karen lifted the lid of the kettle on the stove, picked up the wooden spoon off the dish on the counter, and gave the stew a gentle stir. "The lunch rush is over, and it'll be some time before many diners arrive for supper."

Determined to fill the coffee cups, Lara turned

back. "Humor me. I aim to learn as much as I can about living in the West. This morning I went out to the barn with Belle, and she taught me to saddle a horse. Imagine that. Me, flopping on the saddle blanket and pulling the under thing tight." Her smile was bright.

"That's called a cinch."

"Yes, well. Not that I'd be able to accomplish the chore on my own anytime soon, but hopefully by the time I leave. I think my two younger brothers will be well impressed upon my return." She winked her long, dark lashes and was about to go through the swinging door with the coffeepot in her hands, but paused. "Vin, I just had the most fantastic idea!" She placed the pot on the wooden floor and clapped her hands. "Why don't you turn the Five Sisters into a travel destination? A resort. A place to visit for fresh air and healthy constitutions."

Lavinia humored her with a laugh. "What on earth are you suggesting?" She glanced at Karen, who looked as shocked as Lavinia felt.

"You remember hearing about White Sulphur Springs in West Virginia? Rich people go there for a reprieve from the heat and coal-filled air of the cities. Well, on my trip out here, I actually heard someone speaking about visiting a cattle ranch to ride horses and camp out. They're willing to pay to have a Western experience. One fellow told another that a cattle ranch in North

Dakota had opened their doors to Easterners. Their ranch hands take guests on hunting and fishing trips, or just plain horseback riding in the mountains. Supposedly they have a steady stream of Easterners willing to pay a couple of dollars a day just to drink coffee brewed over a campfire, sleep under the stars, and see some authentic Indian artifacts. Think about that, Vin! That's a lot of money." She glanced at Karen. "Can you envision what I'm suggesting?"

Karen mumbled something noncommittal.

Lara's smile stretched from ear to ear. She was always at her best when organizing something outlandish. She was the only girl in her family, with three brothers, one older and two younger. She'd told Lavinia often that she longed for female companionship within her family. Her mother, as delightful as she was, was totally dedicated to Lara's father and the two did every-thing together, almost as if the children didn't exist. Lara had been raised by a string of nannies. If the Brinkmans could provide a sense of family for her, Lavinia was more than happy to oblige.

"After my trip here," Lara went on as if the coffeepot on the floor was a natural thing, "with the buckboards, calves, and horses, not to even mention the *handsome ranch hands*—I've been contemplating booking my own visit to that North Dakota ranch." She tapped her temple. "I wish I could remember the name. Anyway, when I do, I'll sleep under the stars while a fine-looking cowboy strums his guitar and sings some sad song about his long-lost love. Last night as I stood on my bedroom balcony, I heard a song just like that coming from your bunkhouse. The velvety voice put gooseflesh on my arms." She waved her hand to the back window that had a view of the distant San Juan Mountains. "That's gold ready to be mined, Vin. You're *already* in the Rockies! And your old homestead would be perfect. It's vacant now that you have the new house. With a little work, think how quaint the place would be! Wouldn't that be a nice tribute to your mother and father? That's where your family started." Her face glowed with excitement.

Lavinia was sure she was completely serious. Lara wanted to bring outsiders into their home for money. That sounded so strange. "I think the ranch hands just might have something to say about escorting citified people around by the nose." She shook her head. "We'd have a mutiny on our hands. They'd all quit if they had to entertain such a notion."

Lara flashed her saucy smile. "I don't know about that. Every time I'm at the barn or corral, I find myself surrounded by not one but several attractive, *single* men competing to do my bidding, show me around, or make sure I'm having a nice visit. I think they were born to the position."

Lavinia blinked as she felt her face warm. Was Lara right? Could the Five Sisters become a resort, so to speak? *What a fascinating idea.*

Karen, who'd been quietly listening, snapped her open mouth closed. "John Brinkman, what have you done?" she whispered, before turning back to the counter to put the dirty dishes she held into the sink. "This town will never be the same."

Lara laughed. "It's not all that bad, Karen. You'll see. The wheels are turning in your mind, Vin. You can't hide that from me." She lifted the heavy coffeepot back into her hands. "The income might someday overshadow the big dollars you're bringing in with the cattle. But don't wait too long. Right now, you'll be one of the first to open your doors to the public." With a flouncing of her skirt, Lara was gone.

Karen blinked. "My! That girl has a runaway imagination."

Lavinia turned to Karen and felt a smile growing on her face. "One thing about Lara, she *is* determined, but she also flames out quickly. You can see why, with the way she exudes energy. When she gets tired, I'll make sure she rests in my room upstairs, so she's not too worn-out."

"Not too worn-out to present her great notion . . ."

"Actually, I think she's onto something. On

the trip out from Philadelphia, we spoke about the difference a woman's touch could bring to a ranch—not that we knew then we'd inherit one, we were just passing the time. But a woman does have attributes to contribute in the West, to make the place better. Ideas. Dreams."

Lavinia let those thoughts linger in her mind. Maybe her millinery ambitions weren't all she had to offer. Maybe she did have a future here . . .

CHAPTER SEVENTEEN

~❧❧~

Rhett didn't know why he felt so nervous about speaking with Mrs. Applebee, except that she was the oldest Brinkman and he'd received more than a few censorious glances from her since he'd been in town.

I shouldn't have a guilty conscience. I didn't touch Mrs. Applebee's sister in any inappropriate way. I was a perfect gentleman—well, maybe not perfect, but a gentleman indeed.

Right. He could tell himself that until he was blue in the face, but that didn't change the fact that he'd stood next to nineteen-year-old Lavinia in her undergarments and enjoyed every moment. His thoughts hadn't been completely innocent, but what man's would? He shouldn't be so hard on himself.

And Lavinia was a beauty. And sweet too. Henry Glass surely sung her praises. And Rhett had experienced that firsthand in the café—as embarrassed as she'd been over the incident, she hadn't thrown him out of her establishment or refused to serve him. She'd also gone out of her way to make sure Dallas had some fresh bones. She didn't have to do that.

"Dallas," he called to Shawn's dog, who trotted ahead on the road. As well behaved as Dallas was, if the dog caught sight of some small animal, he'd bolt.

Without looking back, Dallas stopped in his tracks and waited for him to catch up. Once Rhett was alongside, he continued as if a command hadn't been given. Sometimes it felt like Dallas had read his mind. They passed a quiet butcher shop and then the gun shop. He'd ventured to Colorado without a weapon, but had been thinking of purchasing one. Some men wore a gun on their hip every day, like Sheriff Dawson. Others had a Winchester in their wagon. He was new. He'd best take heed.

"Bonjour, Monsieur."

He turned to find a young woman wearing a quaint farmer's dress and white apron. A triangular, blue-paisley kerchief covered some of her blond curls, and a small cape covered her shoulders. She wore a wide smile and her pretty eyes were filled with curiosity.

Dallas stopped by his side as they waited for her to catch up. "Hello."

"You are Mr. Laughlin. I've heard much about you."

He stuck out his hand and they shook. "You're correct. But you have me at a disadvantage. I don't know who you are."

Her brows rose. "Can you not guess by my accent? I'm Amorette Boucher. My brother and I own the establishment just down this street." She pointed to the narrow, curvy lanes that made up the area of small, prebuilt shops.

"Ahh, Mademoiselle de Sells. I've heard much about your place. Actually, word spread all the way to San Francisco."

She gave a small shake of her head. "I am not surprised. Jean-Luc is tremendously talented. Nobody can create sauces like his."

"I didn't hear you behind me. Your step is very light." He glanced at the wicker basket, the handle nestled in the crook of her arm. A blue napkin covered the contents.

She gave a small laugh and her cheeks tinged pink. "I came from the butcher's as you passed." She slightly lifted the basket. "Getting ready for supper. We have a small group coming in tonight." She smiled down at Dallas, who gazed intently at the basket of meat. She laughed when he licked his chops. "Au revoir. I must be on my way before Jean-Luc comes looking. Come to our restaurant sometime soon. You will enjoy."

He nodded as he watched her turn the corner and hurry down the cobblestone lane.

Rubbing his palms together, he approached the tall ponderosa pines, narrowleaf cottonwoods, and a few aspens that sprinkled the area around the large livery barn and cluster of outbuildings. The place had a good feel, cool, refreshing. The aroma of stock animals lingered on the breeze.

The tall barn doors were open. He saw Cash out in the back paddock approaching a horse with a halter in hand. Several wagons parked along the side of the fence displayed red-and-white "For Sale" signs. He entered and looked around. Heard laughter. Proceeded down the aisle of stalls to the back. There was an ample shed roof for when the weather turned hot, but for now, Mrs. Applebee, Lavinia Brinkman, and another woman he'd yet to meet sat on three-legged stools in the sunshine next to a cottonwood tree, laughing with a man he suspected must be Maverick Daves, the smithy. Lavinia and the other young woman wore capes over their shoulders, but Mrs. Applebee wore a much-too-large man's coat. An open basket sat on a small makeshift table. They were eating and drinking out of china cups.

Cash, now on his way in from the field leading a bay horse, called out, having seen him first. "Mr. Laughlin!"

The others jerked around.

Lavinia's smile disappeared.

Still nursing her bruised feelings.

Everyone stood, looking more than a little uncomfortable.

"Cash," Rhett replied. Nerves scuttled up and down his spine. He stopped. "I don't want to

142

interrupt your afternoon meal. I'll come back when you're not busy."

Maverick Daves, his sleeves rolled to his elbows, and mightily smudged as most smithies often looked, set his cup on the table and waved him over.

"Don't be ridiculous," Mr. Daves called. "You have a question about somethin'?"

Dallas bounded up to the group, sniffing and wagging his tail at the women, who smiled and petted his back.

"Dallas, here." Coming forward, Rhett tried to keep his gaze far from Lavinia. She wore a gray-blue dress that reminded him of the overcast skies of San Francisco. Her gaze gleamed, probably with animosity. The other young woman smiled like she had a secret. Edginess pushed at his arms and legs. He wished he could turn around and leave without making a scene.

Don't be inane, man. You'll just state your business and be on your way.

Dallas ignored him, so he answered the smith. "Yes, I do, Mr. Daves. I need you to look at my cookstove. Dallas!" he called again to the dog, who had taken a shine to Lavinia.

The dog trotted over and sat at his heels, his tongue lolling out.

"You must be Mr. Laughlin," the unknown woman said.

He nodded.

"This is Miss Lara Marsh," Mrs. Applebee provided. "She's a friend from Back East. She came for the wedding."

"My pleasure."

"And you already know my sister."

"I do."

They all stood there in the uncomfortable silence.

"I've never seen a dog like that before," Lara said. "What kind is he?"

"A mongrel." He reached down to scratch behind Dallas's ear now that he was behaving like a gentleman. To tell them more, Rhett would have to go into detail about his brother, and how Shawn had rescued a young Dallas from cruel hands. The dog had been loyal to Shawn without question, somehow knowing Rhett's brother had saved his life.

"So, the stove," he said, looking at Maverick and then Mavis. She was half owner, and must have a say in what business they took on. He'd probably get further with Daves then he would her. "The flue doesn't seem to draw properly. I've yet to be able to get the fire hot enough to cook anything." Not that he knew much about that at all, except that his eggs never seemed to cook completely through.

Maverick's smile looked genuine. "I can take a look anytime you want. How about I swing by in an hour or so? Will you be there?"

Rhett actually laughed. "That's the only place you'll find me. I appreciate you taking the time. Thank you."

Maverick closed the ten feet and shook hands. His raised brow seemed to say, *stick with it. Things are already getting better. Walk softly.*

Rhett turned, and Miss Marsh called his name.

"Lavinia and I are heading back to the restaurant. May we walk with you?"

Lavinia gaped at her friend and the color in her face deepened. She looked like she wanted to object but couldn't without sounding like a cranky cow. Others, it seemed, had begun to soften toward him. Surely Miss Brinkman had noticed the change in atmosphere the last couple of days. Even her sister Emma had been accommodating. Should he mention that?

"I'd enjoy that, getting to know you both. I had a nice conversation with Miss Katie and also Miss Emma." His exaggerated smile felt ghoulish to him, but the others didn't seem to notice.

Lara lifted the already repacked basket and stepped forward. He took it from her hands when she was within reach. Lavinia held back under the tree, as if still uncertain.

"Well, come on, Vin. Let's not keep Mr. Laughlin waiting," Lara said. "He has work to do, by the appearance of his place."

Mrs. Applebee gave her younger sister a slight

145

nudge. "I'll see you tonight, if not sooner."

Lavinia nodded and hurried forward, taking the position on the far side of her friend and away from him.

For something to do, Rhett glanced down into the basket, the contents obscured by a hastily placed red-checkered cloth. "You had a picnic," he said, desiring to break the silence. "That's a nice way to pass the afternoon."

A scruffy, gray-striped cat slowly tiptoed through the grass in their direction, mewing. Obviously the animal hadn't noticed Dallas, who was watching with great interest. Before Dallas could lunge forward, Rhett reached down and touched the top of Dallas's head to break his concentration. "Dallas," he said low. "Stay." The dog's muscles bunched to chase.

Mavis hurried over and lifted the feline into her arms, giving Dallas a stern eye.

"We did have a picnic," Lara replied as they stepped quickly away to circumvent any problem, keeping an eye on Mavis. "The weather is lovely. May we go this way?" She smiled up at him, as pretty as a Brinkman, but different. She pointed through the back pasture of the livery over to the Old Spanish Trail, a route that would take several minutes longer to reach the hotel than the more direct course. "I've yet to explore the southern part of town, and I find myself captivated by everything Eden. The oldest buildings are over there. I don't want to leave one stone unturned by the time I have to return home."

The basket on his arm swung with every stride as they walked. "I don't mind if Miss Lavinia doesn't. She's the one who probably has tasks waiting for her." He glanced around Lara to Lavinia. "Are you pressed for time, Miss Brinkman?"

To his surprise, her pretty eyebrows arched and she actually smiled, an expression he remembered well from her hotel room and then again at the wedding. He longed to get back onto firmer footing where she was concerned. Life would be so much simpler. And a measure of his guilt would ease. If he wanted to be a viable part of the community, he'd have to win back her favor. Even if the doing took him months. They'd be working across the street from each other. They didn't have time for senseless games.

"A little. I do need to get ready for supper," she said.

She glanced up, and it seemed something in her eyes felt the way he did. Maybe he'd been forgiven.

"Biscuits to make, a couple of chickens to put into the oven, those kinds of things."

Lara shivered, making them all laugh.

"I guess a few extra minutes won't put me too far behind." Lavinia slid a censuring look to her friend, who only smiled.

"In that case, we'll go the long way." He opened the gate to the back pasture and they crossed the field as the handful of horses watched. On the other side, he assisted the women through another gate, lifting the lowest board high over some mud. There was an expanse of open ground that led to the back of the Spanish Trail Cantina, where a wagon sat and a few horses were tied in the shade of the building. He'd been into the cantina a couple of times and met Santiago Alvarado and Miguel, his father.

"Look at this old adobe building," Lara said as she gaped around at the place. "It's a saloon? Right? Shall we go inside? I'd like to see a real Western bar. I've noticed Poor Fred's, down from the hotel, but didn't dare look inside." She raised her brows at him. "Alone."

Rhett glanced at Lavinia, wondering what she thought of the unusual idea. He was sure she'd say, *Absolutely not. Ladies don't visit saloons,* but something in her expectant expression made his lips twitch. *She's game. I'd never have expected that response.* But then, that wasn't quite true. Maybe of her here and now—in Eden. But he knew a few things about Miss Lavinia's past that she didn't know he knew, and some of them were a bit astonishing. He wondered what other aspects of herself she liked to keep hidden.

CHAPTER EIGHTEEN

~❧❧~

L avinia recalled the invitation that the handsome Mexican Santiago Alvarado had issued all those months ago when they'd first met him in front of the hotel. His eyes had seemed to devour her younger sister in a way an unfamiliar man's should not. But somehow, coming from him, the caress hadn't been offensive. The man wouldn't have invited them to his establishment if doing so would put John's daughters in danger, would he? His exact words had been an invitation to stop by for tea, of all things. The months had flown by and Lavinia realized not one of them had taken him up on his offer. That was not only rude, but mean as well. Today, she could make a start on alleviating that wrong.

"I say, why not?" Mr. Laughlin's astonished smile created a small flutter inside. Lara could be adventuresome, so why couldn't she?

Two paints and a sorrel gelding stood at the hitching rail, along with one mule draped with a colorful blanket. The walls of the pink adobe building were worn from years of rain, sun, and snow, but the stairs and the porch that ran the length of the building were spotlessly clean, as were the few chairs and one small table. On their approach, they'd passed a long water trough on the side of the structure half-full of murky water.

"You sure?" Rhett asked.

His half smile directed at her sent a little zip of excitement up Lavinia's spine. Being in his company without going over and over what had transpired between them was refreshing.

She glanced at Lara. "I wouldn't want to put our guest in any danger. Her parents are expecting her to return to them at some time—and in one piece. Do you think going inside is safe?" There, that hadn't been so difficult, speaking directly to him as if they had no history at all. He nodded slowly, regarding her, as if he were thinking the same thing.

"This time of day should be fine."

"In that case, I'd like to." She gave the building another moment of scrutiny. "Mr. Santiago Alvarado invited all of us for tea, but that was some time ago. I wonder if he'll remember."

Rhett gave a slight shrug. "There's only one way to find out. Stay," he said to his dog as the three of them climbed the porch and he opened the door.

A rush of cool, musty air cascaded outside. Two men of Mexican descent stood hunched over the bar, one with a tumbler of dark liquid in his hand, the other an empty glass. Another sat slouched in a chair in the corner, his boots propped on the edge of the next table, his hat covering his face.

The bartender's eyes widened when he saw them on each side of Rhett. He glanced quickly at the stairs. "Senor Santiago! Come quickly."

The men at the bar looked around at the bartender's frightened tone, but the sleeper never budged.

Santiago appeared at the top of the stairs, his signature grin on his face. His lean, powerful build would be attractive to any woman.

His arms thrust forward. "Welcome, ladies!" he called, moving down the steps at a fast pace.

He kissed the back of Lavinia's hand, his warm lips a strange sensation. He quickly did the same with Lara. The men shook hands.

"I wondered if my invitation had been forgotten." With a sweep of his arm, he ushered them toward the back of the room. "Come into our kitchen, where you will be more comfortable away from curious eyes. These men have never seen such beauty. Let me take your mantles."

Lavinia thought of the day he'd helped rescue Katie from the Chinese peddler, and another time he'd been so protective after Belle found a rattlesnake in her wardrobe. She'd seen him other times too, at their ranch parties, and recently at the wedding, but their talk had always been superficial. She liked his face and the inviting challenge in his eyes.

The inside adobe walls appeared as smooth as satin and looked cool and inviting. Splashes of color, illuminated in the light of many lanterns, made the shadowy room appealing. The two other saloons in town, Poor Fred's and the Hole in the Floor, couldn't possibly hold a candle to this wonderful old structure that must have a thousand exciting stories to tell. She'd never been inside either of the others, or had a desire to do so, but in her heart she knew neither one could possess a smidgen of the history and charm of this ancient building.

Santiago laughed as he watched both her and Lara take in their surroundings with amazement. He slapped Rhett on the back, a wide grin splitting his face. "I owe you a favor, amigo. You bring a spot of spring to my establishment."

They all ambled through a doorway in the back of the saloon into a wide-open kitchen. Aromas of spices, sweet and savory, met her as she took in the tidy room.

Santiago's father glanced up in surprise from his place at the table. An assortment of pastries were arranged on a platter before him, as was a delicate teacup she thought much too small for his hands. His surprise was chased away by a smile. He stood. "Why, Senorita Brinkman, this is a lovely surprise." He nodded to Lara and Rhett.

"Please forgive our dropping in on you unannounced, Mr. Alvarado," Lavinia said. Warmth rose to her cheeks. She realized too late that this was tantamount to someone dropping in on them at the new house out at the ranch without a word of warning. The Spanish Trail Cantina was more than a business; it was Santiago's home, as well as his father's. She'd heard from Blake about Santiago's older brother, Demetrio, being incarcerated in Sugar House Penitentiary. The name of the penitentiary sent shivers down her spine. She couldn't imagine how she'd feel if one of her sisters was locked away in such a ghastly place. Shame filled her for having thought this visit a lark. Her father would never have been so thoughtless. "Your place has always held such charm and allure; we stepped inside to see the interior. We hadn't expected to be invited into your home." She glanced at Santiago, who watched her closely. Behind his eyes seemed to be some kind of secret, or test?

"Nonsense, Miss Brinkman!" the older Alvarado said. "You are *always* welcome in my casa." He glanced at Santiago. "Our casa. Drop in any time. Your father, God rest his soul, did often, and each time, we considered his presence an honor. We will consider the same of you and your guests." His gaze flicked from her to Rhett and Lara. Miguel was a handsome older man, not as tall as Santiago, but he certainly would have been as attractive in his younger years. The lines that fanned from his eyes and across his forehead did nothing to detract from his appeal. His dark hair was sprinkled with silver in a striking way.

"Thank you, Mr. Alvarado. Let me introduce my dear girlfriend from Philadelphia, Lara Marsh. She made the journey to Eden for the wedding and is staying on for some time. And this is Mr. Laughlin, our newest citizen, who is opening up a restaurant across from the hotel." The words held much less sting for her each time she said them.

Lara gave a small curtsy and smiled, spreading her ample charm around the room, and Rhett dipped his chin in acknowledgment.

"We are acquainted," Santiago said with a smile. "Rhett enjoys Mrs. Gonzales's cooking as much as we do."

So the cantina owners and Rhett knew each other already. Rhett hadn't let on a few moments ago. Instead he'd acted as if he was just as keen on seeing the inside of the establishment as they were, when he probably knew the saloon as well as the back of his hand. *Shame on him.* Did he make a habit of fudging the truth?

Santiago gestured to the large, round table. "Please. And speaking of Mrs. Gonzales, she has just delivered an assortment of cakes. You must join us. There are plenty."

How kind. Lavinia smiled. "We'd love to, but only for a moment."

Santiago pulled out a chair for Lara, and Rhett did the same for her. How strange to be falling into such an easygoing routine with him. The man who had thrown her world upside down not that long ago. This day seemed impossible.

He carefully pushed in her chair. "Comfortable?"

"Yes, thank you."

Mr. Alvarado sat as well. Santiago brought more plates to the table. He pointed to the platter of delectable-looking treats, and the pinkish ones, shaped like seashells, first.

"This is concha, a sweet roll covered in a cookielike crust. If you like vanilla, I highly recommend you try one."

He pointed to the largest of the selections, a puffed dough baked to a golden color. A snowy-white cream oozed from the middle seams, making her mouth water. They looked delicious.

"*Pan de muerto*, also known as bread of the dead."

Lara looked over at her with wide eyes.

Mr. Alvarado smiled. "The sweet cream inside the light pastry is some of my favorite, and Mrs. Gonzales, in her kindness, indulges me. Usually the cross-marked pastries are saved for *Día de los Muertos*, or Day of the Dead, a tradition of central and southern Mexico. Mrs. Gonzales's family migrated many, many years ago from southern Mexico, but she still holds many tradi-

155

tions close to her heart. This is a general explanation, of course, but might help you understand the markings. Do not be afraid. They are only flour and sugar, some vanilla as well."

"They look delicious, Mr. Alvarado, but so large. I think I'll choose one of these smaller offerings," Lara said, carefully reaching for an oval-shaped goodie coated in pecans.

"That is *ratón*. Quite good as well."

Santiago chuckled as he poured four cups of tea from an already hot teakettle as if he were used to doing the chore every day. Returning the kettle to the stove, he sat at the open spot and took a pastry for himself. "Translation, mouse."

Lara had just taken her first bite but stopped chewing. She covered her mouth with her fingers, blinking several times in quick succession, and then reached for her cup of tea.

The men laughed.

"I can assure you, there is no part of a rodent cooked into your pastry, Miss Marsh." Santiago's eyes twinkled. "You are safe."

Steps sounded on the back-door stairs, and a moment later Katie stepped inside, seemingly comfortable with entering on her own. She pulled up in shock when she saw Lavinia and the group at the table.

Santiago stood.

"Katie!" Lavinia gasped. *What on earth are you doing coming in the back door?*

Without missing a beat, Santiago, unbothered by whatever situation was unfolding before their eyes, went to Katie's side, taking a parcel out of her hands. "Katie." Her name rolled off his tongue like a sweet caress.

Color scorched her sister's cheeks, and she kept her gaze far away from Lavinia's or Santiago's.

It was evident her arrival was no surprise to the senior Alvarado either, as his smile was warm and endearing. What had been going on all these months that Katie had been riding out to the lumber mill in her buggy? She'd become so proficient with her horse and conveyance that she often drove herself. No one thought a thing of her doing so as they settled into their new lives. Lavinia had assumed that she went straight to the mill and came straight back to the hotel, for the sisters often stayed in town or the ranch, but not here to the cantina.

Katie has fooled us all. And so has Santiago! Anger at the swain, proudly puffing out his chest, burned inside. *If he's compromised my little sister, I'll kill him!* Lavinia didn't care how much her father had thought of the Alvarados. If Santiago had hurt Katie in any way, she'd take him apart limb by limb.

Mr. Alvarado had stood, and Rhett as well.

"You are just in time for tea with your sister and friend," Santiago said softly.

His dark gaze assessed Katie from head to toe.

Did he think she might run off now that they'd been discovered? Surely Santiago, older than Katie, and five times as worldly, had known their relationship would someday come to light. He didn't look all that displeased that the secret was out. Was Friday an agreed-upon meeting time? Or did Katie come every day, God forbid? Surely not. If yes, someone would have noticed at some point and reported to Blake or one of her other sisters.

So many questions and no answers at all. Perhaps the satisfied grin stretching Santiago's handsome face was answer enough.

CHAPTER NINETEEN

~❦~

With most of the day spent at the livery, Mavis had just enough time to stop in at Clint's office and finish a quarterly report that needed to be posted this week. Clint was capable of finishing the report, but he much preferred her to do it, because of her handwriting skills and the fact he just wasn't a man who liked to work with pen and ink. In all honesty, she was happy to help when she could. The work here was peanuts compared with all the book work she'd been responsible for in the accounting department back in Philadelphia. A heartfelt moment slowed her feet for only a moment when she thought of Darvid, now gone almost seven months, and their first meeting at Thornton House. That time felt like an eternity ago. And once she and her sisters signed the contract for the ranch, she'd be tied to Eden for the rest of her life. Was that really in her best interest?

Opening the door, disappointment filled her at the empty room.

"That's fine." She slipped the well-worn coat she'd confiscated from her father's bedroom closet off her shoulders and hung it on a hook by the door. She cherished the garment as if it were made from the finest silk. The room was chilly, but she didn't want to take the time to start a fire. "The job will be done more quickly if Clint's not here to chat with every few minutes." *But that's what I enjoy the most. His little anecdotes make me laugh.* She went straight to his desk and tried to get comfortable in his walnut chair, the shiny, smooth seat much too large for her frame.

She lit the desktop lantern, then tugged the right-hand drawer open, withdrew the form she'd begun the other day, and then patted around for the pen. *Clint. He'll go to all measures not to have to write, even misplacing his writing implements.* She glanced across the desktop. Then opened the narrow center drawer. There were plenty of pencils, but she preferred to work with ink.

She knew the left-hand drawer was stuffed full with old wanted posters, outdated correspondence, and other things she should somehow make sense of and file away on another day. Had he put the ink there? There were only so many places it could be.

The drawer stuck on her first attempt, and then screeched, giving way. She reached down, around, pulled the lamp closer with her right hand, all the while searching with her left.

There! Something.

Ink! Wet in the bottom of a drawer? Who would

put ink where it was sure to spill and make a mess?

Mavis's breath hissed through her teeth when she looked at the black-stained fingertips of her glove. Ruined. Feeling disgruntled, she flopped back in the chair. The lamp illuminated the edge of a newspaper under a few things on the corner of the desk.

Excitement raced through her. Back in Philadelphia she'd read the daily paper religiously, keeping up on news of the city and other places. Oh, how she missed that. Last month, she'd subscribed to the paper back home, but the first issue had yet to arrive. Starved for news, she pulled the paper out, surprised to find two more beneath, and that they came from San Francisco. She'd heard of the bustling coastal town, of course, everybody had. The city was booming. With a mixture of old and new. Rich and poor. Dreams and devastation.

Being a good reader, Mavis devoured the news hungrily and flipped the page. Her fingers splayed and the paper dropped to the desktop.

BRINKMAN SISTERS OF COLORADO— A BOOM OF THEIR OWN

Mavis blinked, not believing what was before her eyes. An article about her and her sisters took up most of the inside second page. Everything from when they'd learned of their father's death, to the trip on the train, escorted by Lesley, Belle's beau at the time. Her gaze jerked farther down— here were described events in their childhood, where they'd worked, everything! As bile rose up in her throat, she ripped open the other two papers. Here was news about Thornton House and Darvid! What in the world? The articles had been written by a *Harlow Lennington* and went into great detail about everything from their feelings of abandonment to what clothes they'd chosen to bring to Colorado.

Mavis gasped and smashed the last rag closed. *How? Who?*

Her heart slammed painfully in her chest, and before she knew what was happening, scalding tears gushed out of her eyes. She buried her face in her hands and wept.

Clint was just returning to his office when a strange sound made him pull up. He glanced around. A buggy passed on the street behind him. At his side, Cash looked at him in question. Clint held up his hand, and his son clamped his mouth closed. They exchanged a disconcerted look and Clint preceded him through the door.

Mavis, sitting at his desk, must not have heard his approach. The size of his chair made her look like a small child. Her face was buried in her elbow, but the fingers of one of her gloves were stained in black.

Clint turned to Cash. "Son, go order our supper. Hunger's gnawing my belly. I'll join you shortly."

Cash nodded and strode out the door.

Hearing him, Mavis stood and whisked up one of the newspapers Laughlin had brought by. "What's the meaning of keeping this hidden from us, Clint? I thought you were our friend. And where did it come from? I can't imagine."

He held out a calming hand as he slowly stepped forward, seeing the anger flash in her eyes. She reminded him of the young Mavis he'd known so briefly before their mama took them away from Eden. One day she'd been outside on the ranch, watching the men brand cattle. Clint, only a youth himself, had helped out when he could at John Brinkman's small ranch.

Thing was, in addition to the branding, they had at least a dozen bull calves that needed castrating. He'd thought Mavis too young to watch such an event, but she wanted to stay. Her pa had sided with Clint and sent her into the house. The whole way up that path, she'd sent him daggers over her shoulder. Looking at her now, he almost chuckled, but didn't.

"Easy, Mavis. Just settle down." He hated to see her so upset but was a bit relieved the truth was out. They'd have to deal with those articles sooner or later. He'd only hoped to wait until he'd uncovered something about where the writer's information had come from.

"Settle down?" she asked in a strangled voice. "How can I do that?" She opened the page and scanned the beginning of the article. "This person, this *Harlow Lennington,* has exposed our personal life for the whole world to read. Where did these papers come from?"

"Mr. Laughlin. That's how he'd heard of Eden in the first place."

"And that's why he believes more men are moving to Eden?" she asked, her hand moving to her throat. "Because our private history has been spelled out?"

"And your inheritance."

"Is that legal?"

He shrugged. "That's a question for Henry."

"Does he know?"

Clint nodded. "Since the wedding, but Laughlin, with all he's been doing, only just had time to dig them out of his belongings. Henry read them before me."

"Who else? Who else knows every detail of our lives?"

"That's all."

"That's all here in Eden, you mean?" Mavis's face clouded over. "And Mr. Laughlin believes after the men come, the women will follow. How callous. Treating us like an enticement."

She was overwrought. Tears brimming in her blue eyes were about to spill over. Mavis, always the strong sister, the wise sister, sounded like a hurt pup. Again, her ink-stained fingers came into view. There was at least one piece of personal information that hadn't made it into the papers. Why she loved those gloves so much was a mystery.

"Laughlin's not responsible, Mavis. He didn't write the articles. He just read 'em. And was good enough to tell Henry and me about 'em. You should be thankful. The person to be angry with is the one who's betrayed all your confidences. Who is Harlow Lennington? Do you have any idea?"

Her lips wobbled. "I've never heard his name before today."

"I didn't expect you would. Henry is digging up what information he can."

Seemed her anger had finally been replaced with hurt. Then her eyes narrowed. She took a step back.

"Wait one minute here," he said, dropping his voice as he followed her with a stride forward. "I see that look in your eyes. Get that notion out of your head this instant. I may have known a few things about your family, but not that Emma had a crush on both of her employer's sons. That Belle couldn't stand the woman she thought would someday be her mother-in-law.

That Lavinia skipped more than a few days of school pretending to be ill. That to get her teaching credentials, Katie had to take her teaching test twice. Or that you and your husband had a favorite restaurant that once made you wash dishes when you ran short of what you owed."

Mavis gasped so loudly, Clint knew he'd gone too far.

Her eyes flashed with outrage. "Have you memorized everything?"

"There is so much, how could I?"

Her face fell.

"I'd like to get to the bottom of who's responsible. John would be furious his girls have been unknowingly exposed like this. And I'm sure your sisters will be as unsettled as you are."

Her anger faded away and her lips wobbled, bringing a surge of compassion.

"When did you plan to break the news?" she asked, turning away to pace the length of his office. She stopped at the front windows and gazed out, watching a group of miners walk by. She turned back to him, her fingers tented below her chin, a stance that almost looked like prayer.

But his eyes kept returning to her gloves, badly stained on the fingers of her left hand. In a moment of insight, he remembered the bottle of ink he'd spilled in the bottom of his drawer. Embarrassment for the mess in his desk burned in his chest. He could never be what she deserved.

And maybe he'd never even had a chance. For the past few months, she'd been spending plenty of time with Maverick Daves. Maverick was his good friend, but he wasn't fit to wipe her boots either. Neither one of them was good enough.

"Sorry I ruined your gloves," he said quietly, feeling like an oaf. "I'll pay for a new pair."

She swept her hands behind her back. "No need."

Why did her face, her eyes move him in such a way? Suddenly pulled by a power larger than himself, he went to her side and gently reached around her back. She leaned away, staring into his eyes, her expression unreadable.

"Let me see the damage," he whispered. When he tried to bring her arm around, she resisted but didn't break her gaze. His face close to hers, her breath came fast. She let him take her arm, but it wasn't until he'd started to peel off the stained glove that she seemed to regain her senses.

"Let me have this before you ruin your dress." A chuckle slipped between his lips. "My salary can't afford a new gown too."

Her eyes widened. "No, Clint. Let me go." She shook her head frantically and yanked her arm away—

Leaving the stained glove in his grip.

"What's wrong, you silly girl? It's just a—"

She gave a strangled gasp and whipped her hand behind her back—but not before he saw her missing little finger. Her face contorted—with pain? No, he realized. Embarrassment.

Remorse filled his stomach like a hot slug of whiskey. It didn't matter that he didn't think a missing finger was a big deal—he'd seen far worse injuries during the war. What mattered was that he'd carelessly exposed something deeply private to her, more private than any of the stories in those papers. He felt like retching. "Mavis?"

She backed slowly away, her gaze riveted on the floor.

"I'm sorry. I didn't know. A missing finger doesn't mean—"

He was digging himself in deeper. He could tell his words were like glass on ice, hitting hard and then shooting off into the unknown. There was nothing he could say to make this better. Why had he been so stupid? Why hadn't one of her sisters warned him? She was the most beautiful woman in the world and he'd never, ever wanted to hurt her.

She'd already started for the door.

He silently urged her to turn around, to meet his eyes. *Can she feel how sorry I am?*

With a jerky nod, she continued toward the door, and then looked back.

"May I take them?" Her gaze was trained on the newspaper. "I'd like to read them more carefully. And I'll have to show my sisters."

He'd told Laughlin he'd not lose the papers. "I'll bring them when I come by the house tonight—with Henry."

With a final nod, Mavis disappeared out the door, and a deep anguish whooshed from his lungs. He hoped, in time, she'd trust him with the story of what had happened to her finger. He hoped she wasn't gone for good.

CHAPTER TWENTY

‿✕‿

Lara's hand slid down the smooth banister as she and Lavinia descended from the upper floor of the ranch house side by side. "I wonder what your family meeting is about, Lavinia? Blake wouldn't say a word. And I tried my hardest to pry the secret out of him over supper." She winked in her ever-familiar way.

"I'm sure I don't know," Lavinia answered. *These days, it could be anything.* "Something to do with the ranch or the cattle, I'm sure. Maybe water is running low like it did last year—but we limped our way through. There're so many conditions that can go wrong with so many animals. I'm sure we'll talk about business, because if not, he would've invited you to join in. You know we consider you one of the family. I'm sure he just didn't want to bore you to tears." She laughed, touching the delicate cap perched on the side of her head. But her heart hadn't been in the making of it, not like before, not like when they'd been living in Philadelphia.

"You're right," Lara said. With her free hand, she gestured to the room below. "I just love what you and your sisters have done. Someday, I hope to be able to persuade Mother and Father to travel to Colorado for a visit. Perhaps my parents can be your first paying guests."

"Guests?"

"Didn't you listen to a word I said at the restaurant?" She grasped Lavinia's arm and pulled her to a halt at the bottom of the stairs. "I truly think you'll miss an opportunity of enormous proportions if you dismiss the idea. Promise me you'll at least bring it up to your sisters."

Lavinia had to admit that Lara might be on to something—she hadn't stopped thinking about the idea since Lara broached it. It was just that everyone had had their hands full ever since arriving in Eden. And there was still the silver mine to open and begin work on. That opportunity sat dark and quiet. Henry had encouraged them to begin thinking in that direction, and she supposed they should. Another source of income that didn't depend on weather, water, or disease would be a good thing.

"Yes. I'll bring it up if the suggestion means that much to you."

"Tonight?"

"I don't know about that. First I have to hear what Mavis is about. At supper, her face was stony and she avoided my glance. I have the sneaking suspicion that she's been crying. When I pressed her, she'd say nothing."

A line formed between Lara's eyes. "I'd think you'd be concerned about Katie. What in the world are you going to do about her? She swore us to silence before we left the cantina, but I'm not all that convinced that's the correct course of action. Doesn't she realize how her reputation will be ruined if word of her clandestine meetings with Mr. Alvarado gets out, especially in a small town like Eden? And now Mr. Laughlin knows as well. What do you think about him? Will he keep the knowledge to himself?"

Mr. Laughlin. After learning about Katie, Lavinia's troubles with him didn't seem quite so bad. Katie was partaking in a risky business that could completely change the course of her life. Had Mavis, with her red eyes, learned Katie's secret too? Was that what this family meeting was about?

"Vin? What're you thinking? I've never seen you so quiet."

Lavinia laid a comforting hand on Lara's arm. "Don't worry, Lara. You're here on holiday, not to shoulder all our problems. I'm sure whatever Mavis has to discuss can't be all that important. The livery may have some unknown expense that she wants our opinion on, or maybe this has something to do with Katie. If the mood feels right, I'll bring up your suggestion."

They embraced.

"That would be wonderful. If you decide to

take my advice, I'll feel like a *real* Brinkman."

"You are a real Brinkman!"

"Go to your meeting while I walk down to the bunkhouse and see which handsome cowboy I can sweet-talk into escorting me on a moonlight walk. I'd not like to go off the trail and get lost."

Lavinia couldn't stop a wide smile. "You're incorrigible."

"And that's why you love me."

CHAPTER TWENTY-ONE

E ntering the library, Lavinia gave her normal sigh of approval as she looked around the room. A large wool tapestry depicting a prairie filled with cattle, woven by a famous artist from Santa Fe, hung above the fireplace. A large leather sofa and two polished cotton chairs and ottomans sat in a semicircle around a coffee table made from large rocks. A small baby grand piano took up the far corner. A desk along the wall with more hand-carved chairs, and a large bookcase on the opposite wall, balanced the room. All their father's books from the old house filled the shelves, along with others the sisters had added. Blake usually had a story or anecdote to share when he'd pull out a volume, regaling them with tales about their father. His personality. His likes and dislikes. Those stories were better than any novel. Because of that, Lavinia thought this room her favorite. A packet of their father's favorite tobacco and his preferred pipe was kept in a special box on the shelf, scenting the air. Floor-to-ceiling drapes, made from red-printed French cotton they'd ordered from Denver, accented the large windows that looked down on the ranch.

Closing the door behind her with a quiet click, she turned, then drew back. She'd expected Mavis and her sisters, who were all there, but an edgy-looking Clint and Henry, who she hadn't expected, stood when she entered. Blake already waited at the window. He wasn't thinking about a dwindling water supply or sick cattle. Something else was on his mind.

I've been totally wrong about tonight. This is serious. Is it Katie? An issue with the inheritance?

She glanced around, trying to figure out the quandary before she was told.

The door opened again, and Ada entered with a tray filled with cups, a coffeepot, and cream and sugar. She arranged everything on the table. "The coffee you requested," she said pleasantly, glancing at Mavis. "Enough to go around."

Lavinia smiled at the housekeeper on her way out.

"What's this about?" Lavinia asked, finding it strange that the men were so silent. She couldn't think of one subject about the ranch that they hadn't yet discussed to death. The men, she had been amazed to discover, *liked* to talk. But only if the subject matter was to their liking. They could go on for hours about beef prices, cattle or horse breeding, or the Rocking J Ranch, the competing outfit that always seemed to cause the Five Sisters difficulties.

Mavis patted the spot on the couch beside her. "Come get comfortable, Lavinia. Have a cup of coffee."

Lavinia narrowed her eyes. Had Mavis heard news about the Crowdaires, their duplicitous guardians who had absconded? Was that what had her upset? Lavinia couldn't think of any other reason why Mavis would look the way she did. Blake, Clint, and Henry weren't giving anything away.

The sooner she sat, the sooner they could get on with it. She joined Mavis and Belle on the cool leather sofa. Emma and Katie were in the two Queen Anne chairs bedside the fireplace.

"This is all quite mysterious," she remarked. "Clint, how was your visit to Durango last week? I haven't had a chance to ask you with all the wedding preparations and then the wedding."

Clint tipped his head in a nod. She'd never seen him so stiff. His gaze darted to Mavis for one instant, but she ignored him completely.

"Short. Uneventful. Just the way I like 'em," he said, his deep voice constrained. "Durango's growing. I don't recognize some of the streets since my last visit. The silver boom has the place hummin'. My hat's off to the law and mayor for keeping the place so civil. Can't say that they have much crime."

He cleared his throat and then stood to pour himself a cup of coffee. Henry seemed lost in thought. Finally, Blake walked from the window and stood by the piano that had been delivered last month. The shining crown of the room. "There's been some news," he began, glancing for a moment at Belle.

She blossomed as she usually did when their eyes met.

Katie sprang to her feet. "You're expecting! I knew it! Mother and Father would have been so happy." She waited with a bright face for Belle's reply.

"Really, Katie, think about it. Blake and I aren't expecting—*yet,*" Belle replied, a blush tinting her cheeks. "We *just* got married." She turned and looked at Mavis. "You need to have a talk with her about . . . well. Before something happens."

Katie sank down to her spot, and Lavinia sent her younger sister a supportive smile. Belle was right. She'd promised Katie she and Lara would keep her secret, but only for so long. If she and Santiago wanted to court, they needed to do it openly—and properly.

Blake cleared his throat. "We'd best not dither any longer. Mr. Laughlin has brought some disturbing news to Eden."

CHAPTER TWENTY-TWO

B lake's tone was all business. Lavinia jerked straight, her attention snapped back to the issue at hand. Had he just said Mr. Laughlin? Hadn't she just been daydreaming about him? Did Rhett's "disturbing news" have something to do with him helping her dress in the hotel? She flushed.

Katie, though, had gone white, no doubt convinced Rhett had decided to say something about her and Mr. Alvarado. "What is it?" she asked.

Mavis, surprisingly not worrying the cotton-filled little finger of her glove, kept her eyes on her lap. She glanced up. "A newspaper in San Francisco has run a series of articles. There are three," she said. "They're about Eden, Father's passing, and how his beloved daughters have returned home. Our earlier lives are mentioned as well."

News? Articles? Stunned, Lavinia glanced around. *Is that so bad? Why is everyone acting so strange? There must be more to this story than that . . .*

"I've had a peek at them. There is a level

of private information about all of us that is shocking." She cast her gaze to the window, where nightfall was not far off. In the ranch yard, the bunkhouse windows glowed cozily.

"What?" Emma's eyes darted around the room. "What kind of private information? You're being too vague."

With her handkerchief, Mavis blotted her forehead. "That you, Emma, had feelings for *both* of your employer's sons at the wool shop. Tim *and* Cooper. At the same time. That to you, choosing between the two of them would be impossible, like picking cake over icing. That they are the handsomest men in the world, and kind."

Emma gasped. All color drained from her face, and she turned away. "No! I'm so ashamed. I pray Mrs. Gamble never hears of this. She's a private person. She'd never forgive me."

"What else?" Katie blurted. "What about me?"

"You'll get to read them yourselves," Blake said, and then gave his youngest sister-in-law a consoling gaze. "Mr. Laughlin told Clint and Henry about their existence the day of the wedding."

"Finding information on the author, Harlow Lennington, is proving difficult," Henry said. "But I've really only just begun. Just like everything else, this will take some time."

"Apparently, these articles were tremendously popular," Blake said to Henry. "We'd like to know if any other newspapers have picked up the stories. The author would know that, or the publisher in San Francisco."

"You've known since the wedding? I want to read them!" Lavinia stood and held out her hand. A sickening awareness seeped through her as she thought of all the possibilities that could be written about her. "Who would do such a thing?" Her stomach tightened into a knot. "And who would know so much about us to begin with? My heart is shattered at the betrayal."

"We don't know," Henry said. "That's the problem." His gaze tracked over to the library doors, and she wondered why. Henry, for all intents and purposes, had stepped in as their father figure after the death of John Brinkman. His steadiness, his integrity, his concern, made him all things good. The sisters loved him dearly.

"Could it be Mr. Laughlin himself?" Lavinia hoped it wasn't true. She thought of his eyes, and the endearing smile she'd seen a time or two. The way his gaze seemed to reach deep into her heart. A flutter in her tummy made her hands clench. They might have gotten off to a rocky start, but the warmth that infused her cheeks whenever she thought of him wouldn't let her believe he was that much of a scoundrel. *Remember how he misled you about being a doctor, and again at the Spanish Trail Cantina? He acted as if he'd never been inside before,* a little voice said.

Mavis shook her head. "There was a recounting of the Crowdaires as well. Quite detailed. I don't know how we'll ever live everything down." She glanced at Belle. "You smoking at the Bomann's party." She turned to Lavinia. "You swimming naked in the lake."

"No one was there!" Lavinia protested, blushing to think that Rhett, Henry, Clint, and Blake all knew she'd acted so brazenly. She'd been a good swimmer since she was a girl. They'd swum often, for Lara's parents owned a cottage by a lake. "It was bloody hot, and I knew the last person had left the building because I stood watch until they did. I can't believe this has happened."

"But a groundskeeper returned," Emma mumbled. "Velma and Vernon were upset."

"That's so mean," Katie wailed. "Is it illegal, Henry, to write about someone without their permission?"

"Only if the things they claim aren't true. That would be libel. If what the articles claim *is* true, it's considered news. Since your father was wealthy, and known by many, it's thought of as a good-fortune story, something people can't resist. Now, if any of the things that have been printed are lies, we'll have a solid case for defamation, and we'll bring a lawsuit like none the newspaper and journalist have ever seen. But only you girls can tell us what is true and what is false. Only you can be the judges. You'll have to read and let me know."

He drew the newspapers from his satchel and held them out. "These belong to Mr. Laughlin. Clint had permission to bring them out."

How horrifying. To have so many strangers know all the private little details about one's life. Lavinia wondered what else was included about her.

CHAPTER TWENTY-THREE

E xerting many lungfuls of energy as if fighting an invisible opponent, Rhett ascended the rise behind Eden in the light of the full moon, feeling his heart thump against his chest. The sensation grounded him, pushed him onward, upward. Golden light extended over the meadow he'd just crossed and into the more forested area. Puffs of chilly evening air wrapped around his thoughts as he pushed himself to the top of the slope. He'd felt a need to get away from the town, the people.

Dallas roamed ahead and was a speck in the distance, almost impossible to see. Was the dog looking for ghosts from the past, as he was? With no heart to call him back just yet, Rhett let him run. He'd been obedient, for the most part. Giving Dallas some freedom was the least he could do after taking his master from him.

Rhett stopped and closed his eyes. Sucking in deep breaths, he imagined the sound of the wind in the tall trees was the sound of the ocean, the roll of the waves, their crash against the rocks.

That brought a swift punch to his gut. A vision of Shawn running on the docks, being hit by the falling crates, then plunging into the sea almost made him gulp in a mouthful of air.

Rhett hadn't seen it, but the recounting was horrific enough that he'd never forget.

Gasping for breath, he hunched over, his hands resting on his knees. As if moved by a force from within, he straightened and let out a tormented howl of anguish, crying up to the moon. It went on and on until suddenly Dallas was at his side, circling, whining, his dark eyes assessing, troubled, scared.

I'm sorry. I'm sorry. It should have been me, it should have been me. I'd readily switch places if I could. I'm sorry. I'm sorry . . .

Turning a full circle, the night suddenly felt too big. The mountains, and trees, the few stars visible over the light of the full moon. Rhett crumpled to the earth, scents of grass and dirt filling his senses. He wrapped himself into a ball and wept until he had no more tears, Dallas's comforting warmth at his side.

As boys, he and Shawn had grown up on the cold shores of San Francisco and surrounding towns, with the sand between their toes and the cries of gulls in their ears. The fog and chilly temperature were second nature to them. Memories of his kid brother tagging along behind him to explore damp, dark ocean caves when the tide was out. Shawn had been cautious, always wanting to leave quickly and climb back to safety before they'd be trapped. But not Rhett. Oh no, he liked to push life to the limit. He'd laugh at Shawn's wide eyes and tell him to toughen up.

More guilt, more tears, more crushing despair.

Then as young men, extended days on the docks had inspired Rhett, as long as there was plenty of hot coffee and food to go around. He'd liked the ribald talk of his companions, the stories that came in on the ships from different parts of the world, the physical aspect of the work, the sharp bite of whiskey. And the money was decent enough. Rhett worked hard and saved his money, content with continuing there for the rest of his life. But not Shawn; he'd always known he wanted to give up the life as soon as he was able and open a restaurant, be a chef.

Rhett missed his father too. A simple man. A laborer, humble and kind. After Shawn's death, he'd tried to comfort Rhett, but the truth was always there, lurking in his eyes. He blamed Rhett. And who wouldn't? When Rhett shared his plan to leave California for Colorado, pain had crossed his father's face, but relief too. Seeing Rhett was a constant reminder of Shawn, and his absence in their lives. As much as his father tried to refute the truth, Rhett's leaving was best for all considered, so he'd given his oldest son, his *only* son, his blessing.

Taking a deep breath of mountain air into his lungs, Rhett finally sat up and wiped his eyes, tasting the saltiness of his tears on his tongue.

Dallas, only inches away, climbed to his feet and stared at him as if expecting some kind of declaration.

"Thanks, boy," Rhett finally said and pushed to his feet. He strode through the trees. Kept pushing farther until he emerged into a smaller, hidden meadow. Tall, golden grass swayed softly in the moonlight. An owl startled off a high branch, swooped away across the moon, and then sailed back toward town, bringing thoughts of Lavinia and her sisters.

And now the Brinkman sisters had something more to be sorry over, since he was the one who'd brought them news of the articles written about them in San Francisco. Clint had stopped by to let him know they were meeting to discuss them tonight. Would not knowing have been better? He wouldn't like his life on display for all the world to see, and he was sure the women would feel even more so. But this way, they could be on the lookout for unscrupulous opportunists. Still, Lavinia's face did haunt his memories. He hated to cause her any more grief. Seemed that was all he was good for.

Crossing the meadow by moonlight, he came upon a place where the grass had been trampled. Deer? A small herd could easily make such a disturbance in a short amount of time.

He glanced about. No, not deer. Men. At least

a few. He found ashes from an old campfire that had been covered over with soil and grass. Whoever had camped here wanted to cover their trail. Why? Hunting was legal. What was going on that wasn't?

Glad to feel curiosity overtake his guilt, he tracked over to the nearest stand of trees and discovered where they'd staked their horses. He kicked a pile of manure, finding it dry but not bone-dry. Dallas trotted back and forth, sniffing and whining.

Rhett searched the area for more clues, finding nothing substantial. The camp was cold. The inhabitants had been gone for a good three to four days. He'd inform Clint tomorrow, and also stay alert. Hiding from a known sheriff was easy, but concealing troubling activity from someone they weren't aware of was something entirely different. And Rhett had a great spot on Main Street from which to do just that. He'd keep his ears and eyes open and see what he could find out.

CHAPTER TWENTY-FOUR

T he men excused themselves, closing the doors to the study with a soft click. Lavinia slowly advanced toward the desk against the wall where the papers were laid out, wondering if she was ready for what was in store. "Is this much different than the obituary Henry sent to the major papers?" she softly asked. "Father was well-known, or should I say parts of his story were. His wealth. His ownership of thousands of acres. The fact that he had estranged daughters. Or at least known to some." Now at the desk she glanced down, flanked by Emma, Katie, and Belle. Mavis had taken the desk chair. Her usually pretty blue eyes were troubled.

"It *is* different," Mavis said. "And once you begin reading, you'll see what I mean. Having one's dirty laundry, as well as their clean, and ragged, hung out for the world to inspect, is unnerving."

Katie squeezed in and turned the lantern a little brighter, then bent over the papers. "But these are the only copies in town. It's not like everyone here knows our deepest, darkest secrets, is it?" She straightened. "Oh!"

Her face looked like she'd just bitten into a sour lemon. She blinked several times and then resumed her reading.

Emma gave a small gasp. "Mavis, I didn't know you lost a Thornton House bank deposit bag filled with hundreds of dollars. You never said a thing."

Mavis pulled back. "Why would I? I was reprimanded and almost lost my job. I didn't want to worry all of you. I was embarrassed."

"Did your employer ever recover the funds?" Lavinia asked. Such a serious accusation could ruin a person's reputation.

Mavis nodded. "Yes, thankfully." She brought her hands up and folded them on the desk as she continued reading. "It was in my bottom desk drawer. The only thing I can figure was that Darvid had played a very juvenile prank. But that was the day he'd taken sick and went home before he could tell me." Her lips wobbled. "It was the start of the illness that led to his death. I'm sure I would have been fired if the money hadn't been recovered."

"But who could have known about that?" Belle asked.

Belle had been conspicuously quiet as she scanned the sheets. She'd turned the page first, reading the back side of the print by holding it

189

up while the rest of the sisters read the front.

"Well, Darvid for one. Perhaps Fred, the man who sat to my left, may have seen him do it, or was in on the not-so-funny prank from the start. My boss surely knew. Maybe he told his wife."

No, none of them feel right. Something else entirely is going on. "Those are unlikely suspects," Lavinia said. She pointed to the story. "Those people you mentioned might know about you at work, but would they also know that to pass, Katie had to take her teaching test twice? Or that before moving here, I was totally frightened of cattle and thought of them the same way I would an alligator?"

Katie actually smiled. "You've said that so many times, Lavinia, everyone's heard you. What about"—she pointed to the paper—"that married man, Mr. Brakchester, who took a shine to you, and who made a pest of himself at the tailor shop? Remember? Your boss finally had to demand he leave you alone?"

Lavinia felt her cheeks heat up. She'd thought Mr. Brakchester so nice, so considerate, always offering to walk with her and carry her belongings. She'd accepted his invitations to pie and coffee three times before she'd learned he was a married man—*with a family.* "How is a girl to know if a man doesn't wear a wedding ring? Reprehensible, to say the least."

Emma nodded. "Exactly!"

Troubled, Lavinia paced to the study window and looked out. The men would have to ride back in the dark. By now, Lara would be back in her room, reading or getting ready to retire.

She turned from the window. "There has to be a common denominator. I'd almost say one of us—but I know that's not possible. Or Velma Crowdaire. Maybe she and Vernon have run out of money. Could she have sold the information from overseas? That wouldn't explain how this writer knows the things that have happened here in Eden, though, like Belle's birthday letter, unless Velma has a spy. To me, that's the most likely explanation. Or could they've returned?"

"Although that's not likely, it's not impossible," Mavis said. "I just spoke with Henry at length yesterday about the Crowdaires. Communication overseas takes time. His contact working the case hasn't yet sent a report."

Silence filled the room, so Lavinia continued. "It has to be someone who knows us all so well that—"

She snapped her mouth closed.

Her sisters stared.

Suddenly, she didn't like the direction her thoughts had traveled. It couldn't be true, *wouldn't* be true. There had to be someone else.

Belle came over and put a steadying arm over her shoulder. "What, Lavinia? Who do you suspect?"

She shook her head. "No one. Nothing." She'd say twice as many prayers tonight asking for God's forgiveness just thinking such a thought. "I have no idea . . ."

"Don't be silly," Mavis added. "We're all trying to figure this out together. Five heads are better than one. Who do you think has been snitching on us? Someone who knows us as well as we know ourselves, maybe even better."

Still standing in the center of the room, Lavinia gripped her trembling hands together in front of her skirt. Her sisters surrounded her. None of them could ever keep a secret from the others for long.

"Who?" they said in unison.

"The only person who would know all these facts about each and every one of us, and would have the ability to do something about it, and as much as I can't believe it's true, would be . . ."

Lavinia swallowed, not believing what she was about to say.

"Lara."

Her sisters gasped. Accusing Lara was like accusing one of them. Horror and doubt were etched in each and every face.

"I know. The thought is too horrible to even consider," Lavinia rushed on. "I have no idea why she came into my head except for the fact I remember telling her about Mr. Brakchester. And that's not all. I've written to her almost every month. But just because she knew those things doesn't mean she's the one who passed them on to a paper."

"I wrote to her too," Emma whispered. "Mavis, did you share with her about the deposit?"

Mavis nodded.

"And me, of course," Belle said. "We've been close for years. It wasn't that long after my birthday that I shared the story about Father taking me to the Indians as a newborn."

"Noooo . . ." Katie whispered. "Such a claim can't be true. It just can't."

Her gaze pulled away, and Lavinia could nearly see Katie's thoughts. She believed the accusations as well, despite her declaration of loyalty.

"We all wrote to her," Emma said. "She was there the year I gained so much weight I had to buy a new corset. I can't believe that fun little fact is listed here." She nibbled her lips. "I wish the author would have included too that soon after, I started walking each morning before work and fixed the problem. As much as I hate to believe it, I think you're right, Lavinia. Who else could have known so much about us?"

Emma's eyes filled with tears. "Our dear friend has betrayed our confidences."

CHAPTER TWENTY-FIVE

F lanked by her solemn-faced sisters, Lavinia raised her hand to knock on Lara's bedroom door. None of them wanted to believe Lara was responsible, Lavinia least of all. But since she'd been the one to voice the thought, she'd insisted on shouldering the task of going to Lara and asking her if their fears were true. Dread that she was making a horrible mistake pushed painfully on her heart. Anything would be better than this.

The door opened, and a bright smile appeared on Lara's face.

"Lavinia, girls, come in! I had a beautiful walk with Garrett. He's really quite the lyricist, did you know? Poetic rhyme rolls off his tongue with ease. Now, the subject matter may be cattle, cactus, and roundups, but still." She gave a small laugh. "He said Henry and Clint are here. Were they at your . . ." Her brows drew down, and her smile disappeared. "What's happened? You all look like you've lost your best friend." She held the door wide and Lavinia stepped inside, followed by the rest. "Tonight's meeting must have been a disaster. You all look quite morbid.

Please, Lavinia." She glanced around at them again. "Tell me what's troubling you. I'll do all I can to help."

With the large bed positioned by the window for a nice view of the distant mountains, there was plenty of room to get comfortable. Lavinia, too nervous to sit, rehearsed in her head how she'd broach the heartbreaking subject. Mavis and Belle leaned against the bed; Emma took a seat at the desk chair; Katie took the reading chair. Poor Lara, not knowing what was about to descend on her, just watched them through worried eyes.

"What?" she said more insistently. "Don't keep me in suspense. I fear something horrible has happened and you want to spare me the details. Take my word on this, not knowing is much worse than the things I'm thinking."

Lavinia stretched out a shaky hand, her thoughts growing darker. Were the articles the reason Lara had chosen to stay in Eden after the wedding? To learn more about their lives here to sell to the newspapers? How could someone they loved as a sister have betrayed them so horribly?

Lara, her brow crunched in consternation, came forward and took Lavinia's outstretched hand. To Lavinia's surprise, the warm connection she'd always felt between them was still there. Maybe Lara had a good reason for doing what she'd done.

"I'm sorry," Lavinia said. "We don't mean to scare. It's just that it's been brought to our attention that a newspaper in San Francisco has run some articles about our family."

Lara's palms flipped up and her smile was back. "Isn't that to be expected when such a man as your father passes on, making heiresses out of you all? The story is fascinating. I'd think you'd enjoy some of the notoriety. I'd also think that kind of noteworthiness would be good for the Brinkman-Harding name and business."

Lara straightened, just a little, as if she only now felt the tension in the air. Would she deny her actions? Would she actually lie?

"Something else is the matter. I'm sorry, but as close as we are, I'm not a mind reader. You'll have to spell things out for me. That is, if you want my help."

Mavis mercifully picked up where Lavinia could not. "The articles, a series of three, actually, ran three weeks in a row. Mr. Laughlin brought them with him and showed Henry and Clint, who in turn brought them to our attention. They're the reason he decided to make Eden his home."

Lara was nodding along. "Exactly what I was saying. I think they'd be good for Eden."

She was an extraordinary actress for the blank look of ignorance on her face. Had she received a large amount of compensation for her knowledge? Did she betray them for money?

"And?" She shook her head and laughed. "I just don't know what to think of your odd behavior. Stop this and spit out the problem."

"The articles contained untold amounts of personal information about all of us," Mavis went on. "Not just how Father left us the ranch, silver mine, and businesses, or his letters, and such. It told how I almost got fired when I lost a deposit from Thornton House, how Katie almost failed getting her teaching certificate—"

"How *in love* I was with both my employer's sons!" Emma added, her face still a bright pink over the embarrassing fact.

"All exceedingly personal accounts," Lavinia went on, having had a small reprieve. She tried to read Lara's thoughts, but their friend was holding her reaction close to her chest. "And that's only a small sampling. There is more—*much* more . . ."

"That's horrible!" Lara's face was rigid in shock as she glanced around the room. "I can't imagine how you're all taking this so calmly. I'd be sick. I'd take to my bed. I'd, I'd . . ."

Belle nodded. "Exactly. How I accidentally spilled the inkwell on the teacher's desk and then lied so I wouldn't be punished. That's something I'm embarrassed about, even though I finally confessed and took the penalty."

"I can see why you all look like someone has died." Lara released her clenched fingers and rubbed her forehead, thinking. "What else was written? Can I see the papers themselves?" She paced a trail back and forth across the room. Finally she stopped.

Glanced around.

All color drained from her face. Hurt flashed across her eyes. For several long seconds, Lavinia thought she might burst into tears. That didn't happen.

"You think I've done this?" She slowly punctuated each word. "Went behind your back to spill all your precious confidences?" Her mouth snapped closed, and her eyes gripped tight for one moment. "How very kind of you. Your silence now gives you away. That's exactly what this is about."

"We've all shared our closest secrets with you, Lara, for as long as we can remember," Lavinia said. Perhaps she'd gotten jealous when they went off and left her. And then, mad when she learned they were all very wealthy. Lavinia could point out how easy it would have been for her to write to the paper in San Francisco, to any paper, for that fact, but it would be best for Lara to simply confess and ask for forgiveness. They all loved her like a sister. Everyone was guilty of some transgressions in their life—the sisters certainly were. They'd all forgive her, and things could go back to normal.

"How could you suspect me after all our years

of friendship? My heart is shattered. Has your new station changed you all so much?"

Lavinia stepped back, astounded. "Our hearts have been shattered as well, Lara, to have been so badly betrayed. Your older brother, Calvin, left two years ago and now resides somewhere in the West. Is he in San Francisco?" Lavinia didn't recognize the hardness in her own voice.

"I, I . . ."

With all the seats taken, and most likely not wanting to sit on the bed so close to them all, Lara went to the fireplace and lowered herself down on the hearth. Her face, the one Lavinia knew so well and *still* loved, was set in an expression Lavinia had never seen before, never once over all the years. Lara's gaze was riveted on the floor, probably trying to figure out how they'd put two and two together. Didn't she think they'd suspect her? Who else had every tiny bit of background on them, even about the Crowdaires' treatment, how their guardians had made them wear aprons and serve them in the parlor like little maids? Would she and her sisters ever live down that humiliation, especially now that it was public? She didn't think so.

"Do you have anything to say?" Mavis whispered, her tone soft, conciliatory.

Everyone, Lavinia was sure, would be willing to put this behind them the moment Lara admitted her transgression and asked for forgiveness.

That's all they wanted. But it didn't look like Lara was thinking along those lines. And at the moment, the opposite appeared true.

"I didn't sell your confidences to any newspaper." Lara glanced away but couldn't stop her tears. They spilled over and coursed down her cheeks.

That was almost Lavinia's downfall. She glanced at Mavis, then Katie, Belle, and Emma. What should they do?

Standing, Lara marched to the bed, hunkered down, and pulled her travel satchel from beneath. She brushed away her tears with the back of her hand. "I'll pack tonight. If the men are still here, I'll ride back to Eden with them. That is," she said stiffly, "if they can stand being in the company of a snitch."

"They're on horseback," Lavinia said, when she really wanted to beg her not to go. Not yet. Things had gotten murkier instead of clearer. They needed to bring this to a resolution. Talk it out. The arguments her family went through usually ended in tears, more talking, and then hugs and forgiveness. Lavinia would not sleep tonight, and neither would her sisters if things were left unresolved.

And neither would Lara. She'd drawn blood on her lower lip by her munching with vengeance.

"You don't have to go tonight . . . *or ever.* That's not what we want," she found herself

200

saying. She tried to take Lara's hands, but her friend snapped back defensively, the first time in her life she'd ever done so. "We don't want you to leave, Lara. Just tell us why."

"Not go?" Fury filled her voice. "You just want me to admit to something I didn't do and apologize as well. You want me to say I did it so you can forgive me and we can all get back to being best friends. Well, that's *not* going to happen. So sorry if I disappoint you, *again!*" She opened a drawer on the tallboy and began stuffing her clothes into her case, not caring in the least that she was rumpling them all.

A knock sounded on the door.

"Belle?" Blake asked through the door. He and the others had listened to the sisters air their suspicions before coming upstairs. "Is everything all right?"

Lara whipped around, facing them all. Her eyes narrowed as she glanced between them. "The men know? All of them? Blake, Clint, Henry? Couldn't you have asked me first before whipping me and hanging me out to dry?"

Lavinia sought Mavis, then Belle.

"I don't keep any secrets from Blake," Belle answered.

Blake knocked again, this time with a little more force.

"We're fine," Belle called back, then did what Lavinia felt like doing. She drew a handkerchief

201

from her skirt pocket and dabbed at the corner of her eye.

This had not gone the way they'd all thought. Something horrible had happened. Something that could never be fixed. Lavinia felt as if they'd crossed a burning bridge that was crumbling into the river. Going back was impossible.

"All right," he said. "I'll go back downstairs."

They remained like blocks of ice, unsure how to proceed. Lara, on the other hand, couldn't pack her bag fast enough. Her pretty face was twisted in a horrible expression that Lavinia thought she'd never forget. After enough time had passed that all of them were sure Blake was good and gone, she marched to the door and opened it wide. "Thank you so much for the enlightening talk. I don't want to take up any more of your precious time. If you don't mind, I'd like to finish my packing, and in the morning, if it's all right with you, perhaps one of the ranch hands might drive me into town. I'll stay in the hotel until I get a ticket home. Thank you for your hospitality. You've been exceedingly kind."

Lavinia wanted to pull Lara into her arms in the worst way. She'd had tirades before, but they were always directed at someone else. Unfortunately, there was nothing Lavinia could do now to save the situation. There was no fixing this.

CHAPTER TWENTY-SIX

In a silence born of worry, Clint rode alongside Henry in the moonlight, the light bright enough that they could see the way twenty feet ahead. Tonight had been troubling. The sisters had been devastated to learn their good friend had betrayed them.

He thought he felt Alibi falter. Nothing big, just a slight step off. Maybe his horse had picked up a stone.

Clint reined to a halt.

Henry pulled up himself. Looked over.

"Alibi's off." Clint dismounted and ran his hand down the sixteen-hand sorrel's right leg, lifting it in the darkness. They weren't that far from town, maybe a mile or so, with several hills to pass. He rubbed his fingers over his gelding's hoof, probing the frog. Finding nothing, he set it back to the earth.

"Anything?"

Henry's voice sounded old. For the first time ever, his age was showing. The sisters had been in Eden not yet six months, and poor Henry was the worse for wear. Clint wondered if John had realized what bringing five citified girls to Eden would do to his friend.

To all of us. He slipped a quick look at his friend, nine years older than himself, which made Clint thirteen years older than Mavis. He shook his head. She needed a younger man than himself. "Nothin' I can see now. I'll walk him back. You go on ahead, if you want."

They started forward, Clint leading Alibi and Henry again riding by his side.

"I'm in no hurry," Henry said. "I'm enjoying this evening air. My rooms above the mercantile can sometimes feel like a prison cell."

Hmmm. Was Henry getting ready to pop the question to Elizabeth Smith? The two had been keeping close company for the last few months. They sat together in church. Spent Saturday nights in the hotel café, he and she and little Johnny, eating supper and finishing up with pie. Perhaps Elizabeth was getting impatient, still living in the boardinghouse. Once they married, they'd have to get a new home, a proper home, maybe one of the small ones where Clint lived, along the river.

"I know how you feel." Clint glanced up at the few stars that could be seen in the night sky. "Sometimes I yearn for the trail. Every night a different horizon."

"You've been in Eden a long time. You were here when I came."

"True enough. Since I was sixteen, only leaving to fight in the war."

Those were years he didn't dwell on often. Once Cash's mother came along, the nightmares had softened. Remembering, Clint smiled. Ella had waltzed into his life, a tall, strapping girl with a smile as wide as her hips and hands. They'd stood eye to eye—he should say smile to smile. He couldn't ever remember that girl not smiling. His heart stumbled and he looked at the north horizon. Well, he could actually. Once. The day she'd learned she was dying.

Far off in the mountains, coyotes took up their song.

Thank God he'd had Cash to get him through those months and years. He and his son were a good team. Cash looked a lot like his ma in his smile and expressions. That was one way he'd been able to hold on to her memory for so long.

"You're pretty quiet over there," Henry murmured. "I hope me mentioning the war didn't dredge up bad memories for you. I know it does for a lot of fellas."

"No. Actually I was thinking about Ella. I haven't done that in a while. Seems less and less these days."

"Any reason why?"

Henry had that tone. He never asked a question he didn't already have the answer to—or at least think he had the answer to. Clint had seen him

205

standing in his office window plenty, watching the town. He couldn't have missed the many times Mavis dropped by the sheriff's office. Perhaps with what happened today, those times were over, he thought with a pinch of sadness.

"No, not really. Just life getting lived. You know Nicole lives with Cash and me. As easy as my son is, never getting into any trouble, Nicole keeps me guessing. I worry about her gallivanting all over town by herself. She thinks she's invincible, and I don't want to see her hurt."

Henry nodded, swaying with his horse's stride. "I hear ya. How old is she now? Nineteen?"

"No! That's the problem. She's sixteen going on twenty-five. Give me five sons over one headstrong, well-developed, sassy-mouthed half sister. I swear. She'd drive me to my grave if I let her."

"What about Mavis? She has all those sisters and years of experience. I've seen her visit your office. Can't you ask her to help?"

Sly as a fox but you don't fool me. That was Henry's lawyering voice, used when he was fishing for information. He was worse than a gossipy old lady.

"Sure I can. And I have. But Nicole is a day-to-day battle. She just needs to settle down . . ."

"And find the right man?"

"Hell no! She's only—"

Henry laughed into the darkness, the sound

squelching the owl that had taken up with the coyotes.

Clint snapped his mouth closed. His friend had baited him with ease.

"You like the control, Clint. I worry about the man who ever tries to win her heart."

With a shrug, Clint moved on. He wondered if Henry knew the truth behind Mavis's habitual wearing of gloves. What a stupid ass he'd been. He'd never forget her horrified expression as the glove dangled from his hand. Or the way disgrace and hurt had replaced the horror. What did one little finger mean out here in the West? *Nothing!*

"You still with me?" Henry asked. They only had one more sloping hill and they'd be back in Eden.

"Yeah, I'm here," he responded.

"Where's Nicole tonight?"

"I assume she's home with Cash—at least, that's where she's supposed to be. For the last week, she's been helping ol' man Little set up the new tannery and get the place running properly. Once that job is over, she'll have more time on her hands, and that means trouble." He huffed out a disgruntled sigh. His sister really was turning him into an old man.

Clint lifted his gaze, and what he saw made him pull to a halt. "A campfire. I wonder what that's about. You hear of anyone, or any strangers, out on the land?" The light twinkled, barely a prick of light, way off, and high in the mountains. He'd thought he was the only one to ever ride out that way.

"Sure haven't. I wonder if this has anything to do with Laughlin's idea about the Brinkmans drawing men to town."

"If that's the case, why camp? And by the size of the fire, I'd think they don't want to be spotted." He reached over and ran a hand along his gelding's neck. "If not for Alibi's possible lameness, I'd check it out right now. I got nothing better to do."

"You want to take my horse? I don't mind walking. We're almost to town."

"Tomorrow will be soon enough. I'll get a horse from Maverick." *And maybe have a chance to smooth things over with Mavis in the process.* If she came into Eden tomorrow. With the way the sisters looked when they'd left, Clint wasn't all that sure any of them would show up. And he couldn't blame them in the least.

CHAPTER TWENTY-SEVEN

R hett rolled out of his bedroll laid out in the middle of what would someday be the dining room of his restaurant and went to the dark window. A high mountain chill was in the air. Sunrise had yet to appear over their mountains. His mountains? That was a strange thought. Would this place ever feel like home?

From his blanket not far away, Dallas raised his head questioningly, but didn't get up.

Smiling to himself, Rhett pulled an undershirt over his naked chest, added his boots, and headed to the back door. The squeak of the outhouse door made him cringe. He'd oil all the hinges today, take care of that offending sound sooner than later.

The crisp morning air chilled him to the bone as he glanced around. Eden was quiet. Just before sunup was one of his favorite times of day. The time when he and Shawn would discuss their day's plan over a cup of hot coffee and an egg sandwich. They'd slug down several mugs of thick brew, letting the strong coffee slam their minds awake. Worn-out from the emotions that

209

he'd expended last night, the guilt that usually held Rhett prisoner wasn't anywhere to be felt, and that was a blessing.

He rubbed a hand over his face and turned a half circle.

Dallas, finally deciding to get up, came out the back door, padded to the outhouse, and lifted his leg, bringing a smile to Rhett's lips. *Smart dog.*

A buggy appeared far off in the road that led to the Five Sisters Ranch. He stepped away from the outhouse and moved toward his back door. Lavinia usually arrived early, but he'd be surprised if five thirty had passed. As the conveyance got closer, he recognized her, sitting straight in the passenger's seat, while Moses held the lines. Usually, she drove herself.

The buggy stopped at the hotel. He heard the murmur of conversation but couldn't hear their words. She went to the front door and let herself in with a key. The buggy turned around and headed back to the ranch.

Why so early? Saturdays weren't that busy. Since his food shelf was barer than a bear's lair, he decided he'd head over to the café sometime around six, when they unlocked the door and turned the sign. He'd give Lavinia a little time to get things going. He hadn't eaten there for three days, and he was hungry. Until his lumber arrived, he was at a standstill.

He scraped his palm along the side of his jaw

again, deciding to take the early opportunity to go to the bathhouse for a wash and shave. He was overdue, and he'd not like to offend Miss Brinkman, or any of her customers, when he ventured in.

A little of his sadness eased. One day at a time. Take the good with the bad. He'd heat the water himself if the proprietor of the bathhouse was still asleep upstairs.

"Come on, Dallas." Dallas appeared at his side as he started off.

Rhett found he was looking forward to a long soak in a hot tub followed by a hearty breakfast at the café. Someday soon, others would be thinking the same thing about his place. At least he hoped so.

Almost there, he turned and absorbed one last glimpse of the mountains, the emerging sun making the wispy clouds blush. He thought of the campsite he'd found in the hills. Maybe he should buy a horse so he could get out of town when he needed to feel some space around him. The thought of another expense he didn't need wasn't smart, though, not while he was working to get his place off the ground. He picked up his stride, stepped up on the porch, and pulled open the door to a silent room. He'd have to have a good, hot fire going before anything else.

Just like everything in life, nothing of value came easy. A favorite saying of his pa's. What did his father think of his oldest son now? Rhett shoved the question out of his mind. There was nothing to be done for the past. But he could plan for the future. As soon as the lumber arrived, he'd attack the building. Finish it straight away, and then get it stocked. The thought of actually cooking a meal for a roomful of patrons made his mouth dry up. There too he needed some practice.

How difficult could it be to bake some bread and fry a chicken?

CHAPTER TWENTY-EIGHT

❧❦

At the café window table, Lavinia, a damp cloth in her hands, polished a small vase. Later, she'd collect what wildflowers she could find above the town when she went out on her midmorning break. Karen had told her that by summer, the plateau above the hotel would be covered in rock roses, daisies, and others whose names she didn't know.

She lifted the small cut-glass vase, something she'd bought for all the tables the first week she'd taken over the restaurant. She buffed away dust and smudges caused by sticky fingers. The vases were sweet, and not inexpensive, but she'd felt extravagant back then, only recently beginning to realize the windfall of funds their father had left them. As a matter of fact, she remembered with a smile, all her sisters had made a special purchase at that time.

Mavis had wanted a pretty, and unexpected and impractical, stained glass window of a bird in flight. Maverick had carefully installed the colorful piece of art in the loft of the livery, giving the large barn a touch of beauty. The sight greeted incoming customers.

Belle had ordered a handmade cutting saddle from a leather master in Wyoming. The one she rode now was much too large, because the finished product had yet to be delivered. As well, she had rebuilt the old tannery, more for Mr. Little than herself.

Emma, in her quest to upgrade the Toggery and bring some elegance to Eden, had had the place remodeled, building an extension and remodeling the dressing room, where Elizabeth could take measurements with ease. The men who entered the shop expecting to find the same masculine fare came out with a shock on their faces, followed by a smile.

Progress was coming to Eden. She, like her sisters, had decided to celebrate and purchased fifteen small cut-glass vases that gave her much pleasure each and every day. Whenever flowers were available, she'd gladly hike the trail, enjoying the walk. She'd be sad when all the blossoms were finished for the year.

Their baby sister, Katie, having acquired the lumber mill, hadn't known what to buy. There were only so many ways to sort and store wood and boards, so instead of changing anything at the mill, she'd focused her attention on the swinging footbridge that crossed the river just west of her establishment. She'd beautified the area on the mill side and had a small plaque made that sat at the top of a short, round pole. It read "Dedicated to John Brinkman from His Five Daughters. Thank You for Loving Us from Afar." A white iron bench under a tall tree finished the area.

So much change already for the small town.

Finished, Lavinia set the vase on the table. Her eyes still ached from the tears she'd shed last night when she should've been sleeping. Such a tragedy. *Lara,* her heart whispered. What was to become of their friendship? Frustrated with her lack of sleep, Lavinia had rolled out of bed at three, gone downstairs and made some tea and toast, and waited for morning to arrive. She'd been tempted to go to Lara's room, try again to talk things out. Instead, she'd dressed early and ventured in the darkness to the bunkhouse and asked if anyone could please hitch the buggy for her.

All the men were adamant that she couldn't drive to town alone in the darkness. Now, Karen had arrived and was in the kitchen with their cook.

Across the street, Mr. Laughlin came around his building and stood at his front door taking in the street. He looked different. His crisp-looking shirt was neatly tucked in. He'd shaved and she'd guess he'd bathed as well. In the morning breeze, his shiny hair gently whispered across his brow.

When he turned and looked at the hotel, she quickly stepped back from the window. *This is silly. I love to look out on the town. Am I going to change my whole routine just because of one man?*

Yes.

"He looks mighty nice today."

Startled, she turned. Karen stood behind her with a playful smile, as well as a hotel guest waiting by the entry stand who hadn't been there a moment ago.

"Oh, I'm sorry," she said. She plastered on a smile and glided over to the hostess stand. "Take any table that you'd like. I'll be right back with coffee."

The unknown man nodded and went into the dining room.

"Woolgathering?" Karen asked. "Or day-dreaming?" She gave an affectionate laugh. "They are different, you know."

"You're a tease." Lavinia started for the kitchen with Karen on her heels. "I was polishing the vases, as I do every day." To change the subject, she glanced back at the kitchen door that had closed them off from the dining room. "Who was that man? When did he arrive?"

"You'll not believe me even if I tell you."

Karen hadn't had her quota of spoken words yet this morning, and Lavinia knew there was no way to hush her up until she had. She played along. "You're correct. I can't guess. Why don't you tell me since you're dying to, by the look on your face."

"Jeremy Gannon. Eden's new doctor. He arrived yesterday, late. I was just locking up when he appeared. Seemed he had a medical emergency that delayed him seven days. Now he's here and eager to get to work."

What? After her fiasco with Mr. Laughlin, she'd forgotten all about the new doctor. But she shouldn't have. They'd been limping along without one since last year. His arrival was good news indeed.

"Well, that *is* a surprise. But why did he stay in the hotel last night? His office and the living quarters above it have been ready for ages. Maybe he's rich and planning to rent a house in town."

"He said he's going to use the apartment above his office, but first he wants to clean and spruce the place up a little, paint maybe. Things like that."

"What! The town council already did that. The place looks perfect."

Karen laughed heartily. "He'll be the judge of that, as you will find out for yourself soon enough. Now, you better get that coffee out there before he comes looking. And get prepared for a busy day. After you and your sisters headed out to the ranch last night, an extra stagecoach came in. It's been a long time since we've had a chartered stage. Besides the doctor upstairs, five rooms were taken. I've already passed on the news to the cook, and that's why he's moving like lightning."

Lavinia glanced over, only now noticing the man hadn't said one word to her this morning. "You should have sent a message out to the ranch. Are we ready?"

"For breakfast—yes. But today will be a whirlwind. We may think about hiring on."

Lavinia felt her brows rise. "I could probably get Nicole for the day. Should I?"

Karen's face lit up. "That's a grand idea. I don't know why I didn't think of her already. Before the hordes descend from upstairs, I'll write a note and run across the street and leave it in the sheriff's office. Clint will get her here if she's available."

A brisk knocking sounded on the kitchen door.

Karen's eyes went wide. "Too late!"

The new doctor pushed the door open. He was tall and rangy, and looked to be in his early thirties. Thick, dark blond hair, nicely combed (so unlike Rhett's the first time they met!), though on the long side. A serious tilt to his eyebrows made Lavinia take note. He wasn't a man who was used to being kept waiting.

"May I get a cup of coffee myself?" he said sharply. "Would that be improper of me to ask?"

Irritated at his rudeness, Lavinia grasped the coffeepot and advanced, making the doctor step back. "I'm sorry to keep you waiting, *Doctor*," she replied. "I'll fill your cup straightaway."

A surprising thought made Lavinia smile. If this doctor had shown up a week ago, she might never have made it to Belle's wedding. She was glad her hero had been Rhett.

CHAPTER TWENTY-NINE

~❧~

Feeling like a new man with a new purpose, and leaving Dallas on the hotel porch, Rhett eagerly stepped across the threshold, his hunger a pressing need. Inside, Lavinia marched from the kitchen with a stranger on her heels. Seeing a new face was good news. One he should be applauding. His plans for Eden were going to play out exactly as Shawn had thought.

The man took a seat at a corner table, and Lavinia turned his cup over. Rhett seated himself at the window table that had a perfect view of his own place. In his mind's eye, the broken-down Hungry Lizard took shape.

"Karen tells me you're the new doctor," he overheard Lavinia say. "Welcome to Eden."

She sounded strained and not her normal, happy self. He wondered why.

"Thank you," the man replied stiffly. "I'm sorry for my delay. It couldn't be helped."

The man took his napkin off the table and set the blue cloth in his lap. Rhett did the same.

Finished pouring, Lavinia said, "You're here now, and that's what's important—I guess . . ."

He felt a small smile tug his lips, and he looked down at the table, already familiar with Lavinia's tone. She wasn't pleased . . .

"What do you think of your office and living quarters?" Lavinia asked. "You've been there, I presume."

"Yes." He gulped down almost his whole cup of coffee before going on. "I have a few adjustments I'll make to the office and examination room in the next few days. Bring it up to standard."

Lavinia's rigid back looked almost painful as she refilled his cup. Rhett wiped his hand over his mouth to hide his amusement.

"The town council took a good many days doing that already, Doctor," she said. "What in particular do you find lacking?"

"There is no reflection on the town," he replied gruffly. "I like things just so. And taking the time to get things right doesn't bother me in the least. Now, may I order my breakfast?"

Rhett turned to the window, noting a few people about. The door to the hotel opened, and more strangers came inside. A small family clambered down the stairs, and the children rushed to a booth along the wall. Lavinia looked over her shoulder at him, a small smile changing her expression.

The new doctor gave her his order, and she came hastily to Rhett's table, turned his cup without asking, and filled it with coffee. She looked vexed.

"Good morning," he said. "I see your doctor has finally arrived. You might have him take a look at your eye, to be sure nothing was left behind. Do you ever have any more pain?"

She flushed. Was she thinking of her scanty state of dress as he'd aided her into her gown? Her lying on her bed waiting for his help? If she wasn't, he surely was. Especially the soft swell of her breasts at the top of her corset. Her skin had looked as soft as a baby bunny's fur, and tempted his touch. He took a deep breath.

"No, no pain," she replied in a low voice. "But thank you for asking. What would you like to eat?"

More patrons had arrived and were filling the tables.

"A tall stack of flapjacks, three eggs, and an extra side of potatoes and toast?" He glanced around. Seemed most of the hotel's guests had decided to descend at once. "That is, if you think you won't run short of supplies. My gosh, Lavinia, I've never seen such a crowd in here. Will you be able to handle it?"

"I assure you, we can." She glanced to the other tables. "I'll be with you all right away. Who would like coffee?"

All the adults, and several youths, nodded and raised their hands.

Inhaling, she smiled. He gave her credit for not crumbling under pressure. If the tables were turned, he didn't know if he'd handle the situation with such poise, but it was a skill he'd have to learn.

It wouldn't be long now until he made Shawn's dream a reality. *I need to get my place up and running. Perhaps this will turn out better than I hoped. But only if I learn the things I need to, like how to cook!* He watched Lavinia disappear into the kitchen with the coffeepot. Would she be willing to lend a hand to her competition? He'd take a chance and ask.

After all, hadn't he helped her in her time of need?

CHAPTER THIRTY

At the end of the morning rush, Lavinia noticed the ranch buckboard roll to a stop in front of the hotel. A stone-faced Lara sat beside Trevor. Her gaze was trained forward, as if to avoid catching anyone's eye.

A deep, dark hurt pushed up in Lavinia. No matter the reasons Lara had had, she was still their dearest and oldest friend. How would Lavinia feel if that were Katie or Emma out there, nursing a broken heart?

Trevor set the wagon brake, stepped down, and then assisted Lara to the ground. The breeze kicked up dust and skittered leaves around her feet. She clutched the shawl around her shoulders, a garment the sisters had given her for her birthday. The two said a few words, he nodded and smiled, and she nodded back. Reaching into the back of the buckboard, Trevor lifted out her travel case, set it down, and then lifted out a small trunk. Stacking the two, he again picked them up and they started for the hotel. Unable to stop her emotions, Lavinia spun, feeling her eyes fill, and bumped into Karen.

"What's the rush?" Karen asked, catching Lavinia by the arms and steadying her before she fell.

"I, well . . ."

Trevor and Lara entered.

Karen's face lit up, but when she saw their expressions and the trunk Trevor held, she cut a questioning glance to Lavinia.

A quiet tension filled the room.

Lara looked about for the clerk. Finally she said, "Karen, can you please check me in?"

Karen took a startled step back. "Uh, yes, right away," she said, going to the far side of the entry where a narrow counter took up half the wall. She hurried behind, took a ledger from beneath the counter, and opened to the page marked with a burgundy ribbon, the fabric faded with age. "Just sign in and I'll get the key." Turning, she went to the wall where a board held only three keys from their twenty-five rooms. The hotel was almost filled to maximum capacity, and because of it, they'd already had the best morning of business Lavinia could remember since coming to Eden.

Feeling Trevor's gaze, Lavinia looked up to find him watching. His gaze was neither condemning nor sympathetic, but she could see the questions in his eyes.

Unable to stay in the room another second, Lavinia reached around and untied her apron, lifting the garment over her head. She balled the fabric in her fist and turned. "I'm going out for a few minutes. I'll be back in plenty of time to prepare for lunch." She went to the hooks where she'd hung her straw hat.

"Take your time, sweetie," Karen called. "Cook and I have this handled. And Nicole is supposed to be here in a few minutes. Take all the time you need."

Lavinia darted across the front porch, keeping her attention trained at her feet. Why did she feel so guilty? She hadn't done anything wrong. Lara had. Lavinia's heels clicked along the boardwalk purposefully. She circled around the building and made for the trail that would take her up to the plateau. There, in the meadow, she'd be able to make sense of her feelings. And breathe easier.

Climbing at a good clip, her face heated. She usually took her time, went slowly, didn't work up a sweat. Enjoyed the views and nice, clean air. Not today. Today she had demons to chase away.

Reaching the top, she stopped. Ahead of her, Rhett, deep in thought, was staring at a pile of three rocks. The little tower was perched on a large flat slab of granite maybe an inch or two out of the grass. Close enough to the edge of the cliff that the view overlooked the town. Rhett, intent on his task, sat in the grass and hadn't seen her arrive.

Shocked, she drew back. The path was not well

traveled, and she credited the trail to deer or other wild animals, not people. But his presence made sense. Did she think she was the only one who wondered what was up over the next rise?

Dallas climbed to his feet.

Rhett looked up.

Their gazes locked.

He sat straighter and his gaze darted to his unbelievably balanced stack of three irregularly shaped rocks, almost as if he were embarrassed to be caught in the act. A crimson hue climbed his face.

"You've caught me," he said, a crooked grin pulling his lips.

As if released by his words, Dallas bounded to her side, wagging his tail and sniffing at her shoes.

Feeling sentimental after seeing the despair in Lara's eyes, Lavinia squatted and put her arms around Dallas, his head turning this way and that as he tried to lick her. She dug her fingers deep into his fur, and then kissed the top of his head, his acceptance alleviating a portion of her sadness. Finally, she stood and came closer to Rhett. "I guess I did catch you. What is that thing?"

"I call it the watcher."

"The watcher? How strange."

"Watching over the town. See how the top rock almost looks like a man's head tilted toward the north?"

Now that she was closer, the stack seemed even more unbelievable. The stones defied gravity. "You've done the impossible." Wariness made her take a tiny step back. "Why?"

Rhett let out a hearty laugh, and his eyes crinkled in the corners. She'd pleased him with her question. That actually brought her a spurt of happiness.

"It's not anything evil," he said, taking in his creation. "Not a curse, spell, or superstition. More than anything else, an exercise in patience and balance. Each rock has a point of balance, and if there are three points of contact I can use to stabilize it on top of another rock, I'm in business. Come closer and I'll show you how."

She glanced back the way she'd come, realizing they were all alone—*again*. She really didn't know Mr. Laughlin—*Rhett*—all that well. They'd come to a truce the last few days, but other than that, he was a mystery. Henry, being the consummate professional that he was, had avoided her questions about the town's new man with ease each time she'd asked about him or asked why Henry hadn't told her about the impending competition across the street with the coming restaurant. He'd politely informed her that telling her about the competition wasn't his place, and that the Brinkmans didn't have exclusivity over the town. All business was good for Eden—and she should welcome the challenge. Then he'd flashed her a pleased smile and gone about his business.

Relaxed back in the sprouts of green, Rhett looked incredibly handsome. His hair was moist at the temples from sitting in the sun, and his eyes, so close to the azure sky, were amazingly blue. As if drawn by an invisible cord, her feet moved forward as he patted the ground beside him.

"Don't be frightened. Only thing is, to rock stack, you have to get on the ground and study the surfaces you're working with. I'll understand if you'd rather not get your skirt mussed on this nice, soft grass."

What can it hurt? Still a bit unsure, she folded her knees and lowered herself to the earth.

Dallas sat by her shoulder as if interested in what the humans were discussing.

"That's better." He tipped his head. "I like your hat."

She warmed. "Thank you. I decorated it myself."

His eyebrows rose in appreciation. "How did your doctor like his first breakfast in your café?" he asked.

He was in a playful mood today. "He's not *my* doctor."

"Well, yes, I meant Eden's doctor. The one you've been waiting for."

She wanted to bite her tongue for speaking before thinking. "Of course you meant that. I was just saying . . ."

Again the hearty laugh that reminded her of the large seals at the Philadelphia zoo. They'd clamber up a rock and bark away, sounding like a man laughing. Like Rhett. Who, at the moment, looked quite pleased with himself. Growing up with the Crowdaires, she wasn't used to such easygoing banter. Vernon had rarely smiled, let alone laughed.

She looked at the strange rock tower. Rhett Laughlin was a surprise. "Are you going to show me how?"

"If you'd like. It's a nice way to soak up some sun."

"What's that?" she asked, looking at a fourth rock sitting by the tower. "He already has a head."

He lifted the rock, testing the weight in his hand and turning the object over several times. He held it up for her inspection, smiling when she shrugged. Then he slowly leaned forward and carefully set the stone on the top of the tower, not pulling his fingers away. He stared so long, she almost thought he was asleep with his eyes open. "A watcher has to have his hat . . ."

"Yes, I suppose so." She tipped her head. "How come you're not working on your place, Mr. Laughlin? I thought you were in a rush to open."

His hand trembled and the whole thing almost fell.

"Sorry!"

He smiled. "I did all I could until I have more lumber. I'm waiting on another delivery from your sister. She said this afternoon would be the soonest. So . . ." He took a deep breath and glanced about. His eyes sparkled in the sunshine, and she remembered seeing him this morning freshly bathed from the bathhouse.

"So you climb the hills? That's a different pastime for someone like you."

"Someone like me?" He tipped his head.

"Someone who is no longer a boy. More mature." Embarrassed, she looked away.

Another bark of amused laugher.

She glanced over, a bubble of irritation sticking in her craw. Dallas, now lying down, crept forward and laid his head in her lap.

"He likes you."

His words sounded wistful.

"I'm twenty-seven, Miss Brinkman, not fifty. I'm no boy, but I'm hardly old. And I could ask the same of you. What're you doing out here on a workday, playing hooky when you should be cooking and waiting tables? When I was in, the tables were filling quickly."

"I'm gathering flowers for my vases. I usually get out here sooner, pick and return, but the people wouldn't stop coming down the stairs. We ran completely out of bacon. Karen had to make a mad dash to the butcher shop and beg that they open up early for us."

"That's good news."

"I guess your calculations are coming true. People are flocking to Eden because of us." She couldn't keep the hurt from her voice. How she wished she could turn back the hands of time.

He instantly looked up from the rocks and studied her face.

Uncomfortable, she glanced away.

"Something wrong, Miss Brinkman?"

"Lavinia, please."

"And I'm Rhett."

"I think you know what's wrong. We were made aware of the articles last night. It's a horrible feeling to have one's whole life on display."

He nodded. "I see. I'm sorry to be the bearer of bad news. It seems I'm not very good for the Brinkmans. Keep in mind, though, everyone has a skeleton or two in their closets."

His smile faded and a shuttered look dropped down over his eyes, making her wonder just what his skeletons were.

"You shouldn't lose too much sleep. Most of your family's secrets, or whatever you choose to call them, were sweet. Merely entertaining, not condemning, or against the law." He swallowed and looked away. "Nothing between life and death."

Even though she'd like to ask what he'd meant when he said *most,* she didn't. A faraway look in his expression had stolen her voice. Rhett, as happy-go-lucky as he liked to act, had his own heartaches, and they seemed to be much larger than hers were at the moment. Compassion stirred within. It might take time for the two of them to trust each other, but maybe one day he'd feel comfortable telling her his story.

For now, though, she stood and brushed off the front of her skirt. Reaching up, she adjusted her hat. "Good day, Rhett. I'll leave you to your stacking, then."

CHAPTER THIRTY-ONE

Annoyance and uncertainty hummed within Rhett as he watched Lavinia walk away as if she hadn't just thrown his thoughts into a pickle barrel and rolled them down a hill. He stood, brushed off the back of his pants. He needed to get back to work. The restaurant wouldn't finish itself. He thought of Cash and how much faster the job would be completed if he'd accepted the boy's help.

That might be so, but he wasn't going to crumple to the temptation. Each time he saw Cash walking down the street leading a horse or driving a wagon, Rhett saw Shawn. And all he'd lost. Shawn would never get a chance to fall in love, have a family, or open his restaurant. Rhett never wanted to be responsible for anyone again, especially someone who reminded him of Shawn. The sight was just too painful.

On the far side of the clearing, Lavinia stopped at a patch of small flowers and began picking. He remembered the cold campfire he'd discovered yesterday. He should have said something, cautioned her. She shouldn't be up here wandering the mountains alone.

He closed the distance between them. "Lavinia," he called.

She looked up in surprise.

"Yes? Did you want something?"

"Yesterday on my explorations, I came upon a campsite."

Her eyes grew round. "Oh? Where?" She glanced around.

He pointed across to the other side of the valley. "Over in those hills. Not that close, but definitely within reach of town. Just thought I'd let you know. Be watchful. I'd not want to have my sister or daughter up here alone. On the other hand, the campsite may mean nothing at all."

She glanced at her flowers and then up at him. "Was the camp old? From last year?"

He shook his head. "No, I'd guess two to three days, is all." He shrugged, feeling a bit embarrassed for having sought her out. She didn't need, or want, his help in any aspect of her life. "Just a little warning is all. You know, keep your eyes open. I'm going to mention it to the sheriff." He turned to go.

"I appreciate your thoughtfulness," she said, making him turn back. "I'm just about finished." She lifted the bouquet to his face and he took a long sniff, and then promptly sneezed.

When she laughed, her eyes lit up like the sun, and all the cares she was holding inside, it seemed, flew away like a flock of jittery sparrows. Embarrassed, he sniffed and wiped his arm across his nose at the exact time she withdrew a white hankie from her skirt pocket. She held the cloth out.

"Shouldn't I be offering you a handkerchief, not the other way around?"

"Not necessarily. Haven't you ever heard of the women's suffrage movement? Spend enough time around my family and you will."

She had a point.

"Rhett," she began, using his first name. "You're a mystery to us. We know you came from San Francisco and brought us word of the articles, but what you did in your past or where your home was, your family, and just about everything else is cloaked in shadows. Do you mean to be so secretive?"

He frowned and glanced at the sun in the clear blue sky. "Why're you curious?"

She blinked at his hardened tone, then bent over and picked one more stem. "Just wondering, I guess. You have become a part of our town . . ." She started back toward the trail.

There was no real reason he should be so curt, except his own shame. "I was a longshoreman back in San Francisco. I was born in California, where my father still lives."

She turned and studied him. Clarity shone in her coffee-colored eyes.

"That makes so much sense. When I first met you, in the hotel, I thought surgery with your hands might be difficult. They're much too large for tiny, intricate work. But for a laborer, they're perfect."

He felt like taking offense at her opinion of him, *a laborer,* but her comment had been said in innocence. She hadn't meant any offense. Warmth eased into his face. He'd never had anyone comment on his size before, unless he was about to go a few rounds with an opponent in a bar. The fact she'd actually been thinking about him was a compliment.

Lavinia Brinkman actually smiled. *Smiled!*

"I've embarrassed you," she said. "I'm sorry. Now, I really must get back. I told Karen I'd only be gone a few minutes, and here it's been far longer. She'll wonder where I am."

"As she should."

With her flowers held in one hand and the length of her skirt in the other, Lavinia strode away as businesslike as ever, not knowing the slip of a girl had wedged a crack in his armor.

She's been thinking about me? That can't be good. Maybe I was better off when she hated me . . .

"Can I ask you one more question?" he said, jogging to her side to catch up.

Dallas bounded up from his wanderings.

She lifted a brow. "Go on . . ."

"I was wondering about your suppliers."

She stopped, looking surprised. "You mean the foodstuffs I serve in *my* restaurant? Where I get them?"

He took a small step back, seeing that revealing the information might not be in her best interest. "Never mind, I shouldn't have asked." He didn't know the first thing about restaurants except what he liked to eat, when to pay, and to leave some coins if the service was satisfactory. But he did have Shawn's book of recipes. On his travels here, he'd gone over in his head how he'd practice cooking every day once he arrived, but that hadn't been the case at all. He needed to get busy. He smiled, releasing her from his question, and gestured for her to continue on with her return.

"Actually, I don't mind sharing. It's what we do with the provisions that will make our sumptuous fare stand out . . ."

"Or not."

"Now why would you say such a thing? I'm sure you'll do just fine. Just the talk of a new place in town has created quite a buzz. The Five Sisters supplies all our beef, and some of the chicken too since I brought in a few more laying hens. A ranch in Dove Creek, our lamb. If you're interested, I'll get you their name. Mr. Hoffman at the butcher shop does our butchering for a fee, as well as killing and preparing the chickens. The mercantile has a nice assortment of canned goods and staples, like flour and sugar, some spices. Others I have to send away for. Several local farmers bring me whatever fruit and vegetables they have in season that the bugs haven't devoured. They deliver milk and cream as well, when we need it. I'm never sure what we'll get, so we have to plan loosely. As a matter of fact, you ran into two farmers the other day coming out of my restaurant. Mel and Kelly Wilkerson. They're kind people and will give you the shirt off their backs if you need it. I'll send them over to your place, as well as other proprietors you may need to speak with, the next time they're in. How does that sound?"

A rush of gratitude filled Rhett. Lavinia was a wealth of knowledge. And generous as well. He'd best start a list and keep adding, if he was to remember everything that he needed to either gather, learn, or order. "Thank you. I'd appreciate that very much."

She gave him a funny look. "You have no experience with this? I'd think you'd have worked in or around an eatery for years if you wanted to open a place of your own."

"Well, some," he fibbed. To tell the truth now, he'd have to share about Shawn, and he wasn't ready to do that. Wasn't sure if he'd ever be ready.

"Good. Then I won't worry. I must be off . . ."

He watched her stride away, giving her ample time to get down the trail and back into the hotel before attempting his descent. He'd already caused her scandal enough.

The sound of a gunshot brought him up short. Off in the hills, in the direction where he'd discovered the cold campsite. Someone hunting? Most likely—*but then . . .*

He started down the trail himself, giving his rock sculpture a wayward glance. Since he had to wait on his lumber anyway, now was the right time to speak with Clint about his findings, especially since Lavinia seemed to venture to the meadow often for flowers. Even though strangers in the area was probably nothing, the sheriff might be interested. And he'd feel a lot better as well.

CHAPTER THIRTY-TWO

avinia!"

Lavinia turned. She'd just descended the long hill from the upper meadow, and she saw Emma heading her way at a brisk clip. "Where have you been? Karen is about to send out a search party. She's not only worried about you, but with the full hotel, she feels certain the lunch crowd will be as busy as breakfast. She's anxious for your return."

Lavinia held up the bouquet as her answer. "I'm sorry. When I get in the meadow, time slips away. Sometimes I wonder what it would be like not to be married to the café."

"Don't be silly. If you want to hire on someone to take the pressure off, do it. That's totally up to you." Emma tipped her head. "I can't figure you out. Sometimes you sing the restaurant's praises and other times . . ."

"I know. I better get moving. Karen needs me. And I want to get these into water before they wilt." She lifted the bunch of colorful flowers to her nose.

Emma's eyebrow jetted up. "Look! There's

Jeremy Gannon, the new doctor. I met him earlier today."

Lavinia glanced over her shoulder and across the road. The doctor had changed out of his nice clothes and into work attire. His sleeves, rolled to the elbow, exposed his strong arms, carrying two paint cans. A paintbrush was tucked under his arm, along with a roll of paper.

"I met him this morning in the café."

Emma's eyes bulged, the expression she got when she was enthralled by a subject. "Tell me more. Why didn't he show up on time?" She grasped Lavinia by the arm and drew her closer. "And what is he doing? His office and house were recently repainted."

Lavinia sighed. "I guess he thinks the place needs another coat."

Emma had been on the planning and welcoming committee and was sure to take offense.

"You can't be serious! I made the final check myself. What did he expect in Eden?" A thoughtful pout replaced her pretty smile. "I don't understand."

"Maybe you should go ask him. Right now I have to get back to the restaurant and Karen, before she takes a broom to me. I'm already going to be in enough hot water without making things worse."

"Perhaps I will," Emma said, hurrying off to catch the man.

"Hello, Miss Brinkman!"

Lavinia turned.

The telegraph operator and owner of the drug-store leaned out his door, a piece of paper in his hand. "I saw you pass the window and thought you might come in. You've had a reply to your telegram to Philadelphia."

Lavinia stopped and stared. Had she heard him correctly? Mr. Hansberry had finally replied? She thought she'd made her peace with losing her chance at the millinery apprenticeship. She'd thought she could be content here in Eden. And yet . . .

She slowly retraced her steps and took the telegram from his hand.

"Thank you so much," she whispered through a tight throat. She couldn't stop the tremor that moved her hands, so she clasped them together, along with the flowers.

He nodded and disappeared back inside.

She opened the folded paper and gazed down at the few words that would either bring great happiness or overwhelming despair.

Other person did not work out. STOP
The apprentice spot has reopened. STOP
Reply if you are still interested. STOP
Mr. Hansberry

Lavinia gasped and crushed the note to her chest. A thousand thoughts tumbled through her mind at once. Her dreams weren't dead. The signing for the ranch was in two weeks. She couldn't leave a moment before. Would that be soon enough for Mr. Hansberry? She thought of the hat factory, the many cute Hansberry boutiques across the city, Mr. Hansberry's deep, almost frightening voice, speaking about one of his latest creations. *I'll be returning to Philadelphia. But how will my sisters feel when I tell them?*

Euphoria swirling within, she refolded the telegram and placed it into her pocket. When she entered the hotel, she found people she didn't know milling about and sitting in the lobby.

Karen pulled to a stop in front of her. "My! What's put that light in your eyes? Did you find a buried treasure?"

"I did," she replied, holding out the flowers. "When Father called us back to Eden—and changed all our lives." And that was true. Even if she left now, she realized just how much she loved the place. How much she'd grown in the last few months. What she'd learned about life and about herself. She owed so much to her father. Now she could return to the city without any regrets.

"I'm glad your walk has revived you." Karen set the coffee cups she was holding on a clean table. "Lara hasn't come down from her room. Do you think we should send something up?"

Why did she feel so guilty when she thought of her friend? Lavinia wasn't the one who'd perpetrated such a double cross. And not just against her, but all her sisters.

"Yes, that's a good idea. I'll make a tray right away."

Karen's head tipped. "I can do that." She nodded and hurried toward the kitchen door and Lavinia followed, intent on putting the flowers into water and then dividing them up among the tables.

Pounding began across the street. *Rhett's lumber must have arrived sometime when he was in the meadow—with me.* How soon would his restaurant open? She had no idea. Actually, this morning, she wouldn't have minded a little help in the way of fewer customers.

She needed to reply to Mr. Hansberry right away. Tell him she wanted the position and could set out, but not for two weeks. Her sisters would be thrilled, wouldn't they? She'd be for them if the tables were turned. But there *were* issues. Katie, and what to do about her and Santiago. The strange way Mavis and Clint were acting. Belle wasn't with child yet, but surely she would be soon. That thought brought a moment of sadness. She'd like to be around for a new niece or nephew—and the excitement a baby would bring. Emma had several of Lavinia's hats stocked in the Toggery. Although none had sold at this point, what if they caught on once more women came to town? She'd need to be able to ship some new creations every few months. Would that be possible once she was an apprentice? And of course, the articles were never far from her thoughts—which brought to mind Lara, and everything Lavinia stood to lose when her friend went home.

Her hands stilled as she trimmed the stems lying on the cutting board. Until she'd listed all her concerns, she hadn't realized how busy—and complicated—her life had grown.

And Rhett . . . ? She worked the water pump and caught the splashing, crisp water in the large vase. After this afternoon, she had no idea what to feel about him.

CHAPTER THIRTY-THREE

With a good portion of the construction completed that afternoon, Rhett stood before his woodstove, his face shiny with sweat and his brain about ready to explode. After his conversation with Lavinia that morning, he realized the time had long since passed that he should be getting acquainted with the kitchen and how things were done. He made a quick trip to the mercantile and then the butcher shop, fending off knowing smiles, as well as a hundred questions from both proprietors about what he was about to create. As soon as he was back, he flipped the lock on the front door. He didn't need to be interrupted.

Dallas, watching from his spot by the door, whined loudly and then rested his chin on his outstretched leg.

Rhett glanced at Shawn's notebook open on the counter, flour and cornmeal strewn everywhere. He should have skipped the fritters, a delicacy Shawn had been exceptionally good at, and gone straight to the chicken parts. The recipe had said the lard should be boiling hot so the fritters would rise to the top quickly. They'd all sunk and then disintegrated at the bottom of the pot and were now turning black. He reached out to remove the pot from the heat and jerked back as pain seared through his hand, his work-toughened skin sizzling like butter.

He cursed.

Dallas jumped up and ran out of the room.

"Fine!" he bit out. "Just wonderful!" Shaking away the pain, he stalked to the sink. Working the pump, he held his palm under the cold water, feeling worse than a fool. He was attempting the impossible. "How stupid can I be?"

Taking hold of his irritation, Rhett went back to the stove. He wiped his sweaty, unburned palm down his filthy apron and scowled at the bubbling pot of goo staring back at him. So much for starting with something easy. He glanced at the paper-wrapped chicken. Why should he dirty two pans? Nothing wrong with the lard that was already boiling. He'd just drop the poultry in with the sunken fritters and see what conspired.

That night before supper, Lavinia made her way to Katie's room. She'd put off the confrontation long enough. Whether they were in Philadelphia or Eden, visiting Santiago at his saloon, unchaperoned, was not appropriate. And now the situation with Lara . . . When Lavinia had taken her a tray, they'd exchanged a few terse words, but that was all. Lara could use the information about Katie if she was inclined to exact revenge.

She knocked on Katie's door.

Katie opened the door, still working with her blond tresses. The moment she realized her caller was Lavinia—alone—her eyes shuttered.

Lavinia smiled. "May I come in?"

Katie glanced at the clock on her fireplace mantel. "It's almost time to go down for dinner, and my hair is being stubborn. I don't want to be late."

"We have a little time. There's something I'd like to discuss with you."

Katie stepped back, let Lavinia enter, and then shut the door. "I only wonder what took you so long," she said briskly, her lips pulled down. "I expected you last night and again this morning."

"Let's not be cross with each other," Lavinia replied. Katie could be prickly, and sometimes sharp-tongued, but she didn't mean any harm. She was frightened. Lavinia guessed she had tender feelings for Santiago. She just wondered what the man felt for her sister. And about the hours she'd spent at the cantina and what could have transpired. She'd not like to see Katie hurt in any way.

Lavinia held out a hand in supplication. "After this horrible thing that's happened with Lara, I have no desire to spar with you. I feel like I've been through a war and come out on the losing end. I just want to talk, Katie. That's all. Can we do that?"

Katie nodded, the anger giving way to worry, which made her look ten years old. She went to the mirror, finished pinning her hair, and then turned to face Lavinia.

"Why were you at the cantina? And you appeared at ease there, like that wasn't your first time stopping in. Nor your fifth or tenth. You've gone there often, if I had to guess. Does anyone else know? That you visit Santiago, a suitor much too old for you, in his home?"

A blush rose up her cheeks, but she held Lavinia's gaze. "Why should they know? I'm the only one with a business on that side of town. Everyone is busy with their own lives, running their own shops. And, if you've forgotten, I am an adult."

"Yes, you are. That's true. But you didn't answer my question."

"No. No one but you and Lara knows."

"And Rhetten Laughlin, Santiago, and his father. And whoever else might have noticed your buggy parked behind the saloon all those number of times."

Her eyes opened wider.

"Have you considered your reputation? What going there looks like to others? And I have to wonder about Santiago as well, and if he has any sense at all. Does he not think of you and your future? If he cares for you, he'd not put you in a spot for ridicule."

Katie and she were closest in age, and yet Lavinia felt vastly older now, looking down into her sister's anxious face. It was clear Katie hadn't given any of those questions much thought. Lavinia wondered what it would feel like to be involved romantically with a man. Rhett popped into her mind for a moment, a man seven years her senior. Her cheeks heated.

"Leave Santiago out of this," Katie sputtered defensively. "Visiting him was my idea and decision. He had nothing to do with it."

"How can I leave him out? You and he are involved. Way back when we first came to town, he had eyes for you, but I didn't know you felt the same. How long has your romance been going on?"

This might be worse than I think. I better prepare myself.

"We're just friends."

"I wish that were true, because you're only eighteen. You have your whole life ahead of you. I've never seen the two of you together, so you've not had that much time to get to know him."

"Why're you trying to marry me off to Santiago? I told you we're only friends."

Why don't I believe that?

"Katie, if the town finds out, it could be your ruin."

"Ruin for what? I love Santiago. What do I care what others think?"

"You just told me you and he were only friends. Is there more to tell, Katie? Please trust me."

Katie's face had turned white and her hands trembled. "What in the world are you implying?"

"I'm not implying anything except I'm worried you'll be hurt in one way or the other."

Instead of responding, Katie went to the mirror and blotted her face, took several deep breaths, and pinched her cheeks. "It's six o'clock," she said. "We need to go downstairs or someone will come looking for us."

"Yes, you're right." She reached out and caught Katie as she tried to pass to the door. "I like Santiago," she said softly. "But you're young. Please be careful. Your secret is safe with me. But I do worry about what Lara might say."

"I'll be careful. Guard my heart, as Mother used to say. But I love him, Lavinia. And it's such a wonderful feeling. I never want to live without him. He makes me want to sing, to fly . . . and his kisses . . ."

Kisses! Where was Katie headed? If not toward heartbreak, then something else entirely.

A bomb exploded at Clint's side, flinging mud and dirt into his face. He gasped, spun in the other direction, his rifle heavy in his arms. He hunkered down, took aim, pulled the trigger. A soldier on the next rise clutched his chest and fell. Clint didn't have time for guilt as fear and necessity pushed him forward. Where were his men? His unit? Was he all alone here holding back Confederate forces from taking the area?

Feeling warmth on his temple, he reached up and swiped away a streak of blood caused by a rock when the cannonball exploded. His regiment had scattered. The few remaining men couldn't hold out much longer. In the distance, lines and lines of tan uniforms marched steadily toward his position.

War was hell!

Glancing around, he saw two of his comrades taking aim at the enemy. Clint took another shot, quickly reloading.

With an expression as unbreakable as stonework, Colonel Hayes, a tall, dignified fellow, one he knew had been a lawyer before joining a volunteer unit, galloped by, shouting encouragement to the terrified men. His words bolstered Clint. He took a deep breath, letting it settle his runaway heart.

The shooting and confusion continued. Hayes's horse, shot out from under him, went down hard. The enemy marched on and would arrive on their knoll soon. If Clint didn't do something, the colonel would be lost.

Clint dived for the reins of a riderless horse as the frightened animal clambered by. Unmindful of the danger, he tugged the wide-eyed horse forward, its hide quivering in fear.

"Colonel, a horse!"

Colonel Hayes, just now coming to after being knocked out, blinked groggily. The enemy wasn't but a few moments away. They had to move now or be killed.

"Get up!" Clint shouted, taking his arm while keeping a grasp on the frightened gelding.

The colonel shook his head, still bleary from being briefly knocked unconscious. Clint yanked him off the ground and hefted his large body up into the saddle. He gathered the reins and stuck them in the officer's fist.

"Ride west, the way should be clear for a little longer," Clint yelled. "Go now, before it's too late."

Right then, Hayes took a ricochet to the head, but kept his seat. "Thank you, soldier!" he gritted through the pain. "You're a credit to your country. What's your name?"

With the sound of another cannonball exploding by his side, Clint's feet dropped from the top of his sheriff's desk, and he sat bolt upright, his heart pounding in his chest. Sweat dripped down both temples.

Quivering like he'd been locked out in a snowstorm, Clint tried to stop the feeling of doom that pervaded his thoughts. He took in the sight of his office, thankful to be alive. Thankful for having survived that long-ago battle. *War was hell!* Brother against brother. Something he never wanted to experience again.

When he finally felt able, he stood, crossed his office to a small stand where he kept a pitcher of water, poured himself a glass, and gulped it down as if it were his last. Afternoon sunshine pervaded his office. He didn't see much trouble in Eden. And thank God for that.

A small sketch of a mountain scene hung on the wall behind his desk. Mavis had come by one day last month and tacked it up, not even asking permission. They'd smiled at each other and chatted. "I guess those days are over," he said aloud. "All things come to an end sooner or later." He thought of Ella, his late wife. And his pa, the memory of his mother. "That's life. Get over it."

Clint wiped his mouth, then paced over to the window. Imagine, Colonel Hayes had gone on to run for president of the United States and win. The little Clint knew of the man, he respected. Did Hayes recall that long-ago day? The battle from hell? After Clint had made sure the colonel wouldn't fall from the saddle, he'd turned the flighty gelding around and slapped his rump, sending the two off in the right direction. By the time the retreat bugle had sounded, a quarter hour had passed, and he never saw the colonel again. But he'd followed his career, always amazed, always remembering those few moments in time.

Cash careened through the door; his rumpled appearance said he'd come straight from the livery and had worked hard all day. Pride pushed all memory of the recurring dream from Clint's mind.

"You ready for supper?"

"Sure am, Pa. Seemed like today would never end."

Clint lifted his nose. "What's that strange smell?"

"It's coming from the Hungry Lizard. I tried the door, but it was locked. I knocked several times, but Rhett's not answering. I peered in the window. Couldn't see nothin'."

"Well, it's none of our business." Clint stepped outside where the flighty palomino mare he'd borrowed from Maverick while Alibi healed was tied. She tossed her head, and Clint tipped an eyebrow at his son.

Cash chuckled. "She'll settle down. Give her a little time."

The question was, would Mavis? Clint couldn't imagine living in the same town with her if she never forgave his stupid blunder. A little over twenty-four hours felt like twenty-four years.

Cash, so good with horses, stepped off the boardwalk and rubbed the mare's nose. She calmed and dropped her head. "See. She just needs a little undivided attention."

Feeling discouraged, Clint lifted a worn-out shoulder. "I'm not so sure about that. She about pitched me off when I went to check out a campfire Laughlin found." *Just like Mavis.* "Don't know if it was the same one Henry and I saw, but was in the same vicinity. Let me know if you spot any suspicious strangers around, will you?" He slung his arm over his son's shoulder. "Now let's get some grub. I'm tired of thinking . . ."

CHAPTER THIRTY-FOUR

~✄✄~

I n the warm corner of what would be his dining room, Rhett shook the nightmare from his thoughts, rose from his bedroll, and strode into the kitchen, the essence of burned cornmeal and chicken still heavy on the air. At the sink, he splashed his face and torso, cool water calming his ragged nerves. He toweled off and tossed the cloth back to the counter. This room was better put to use for bathing than cooking. He was in trouble.

He'd dreamed of Shawn. The day he'd died. And again, the day of his funeral.

He went through the room and opened the front door. The coolness of the Eden night rushed in, blessedly softening his thoughts. Outside, the street was quiet. He tried to get used to the clearness of the sky and stars when fog and cold were his usual impression of nightfall. Two doors down at Poor Fred's saloon, he could hear the hum of men still awake and wasting their money.

Shame filled him. Still, after all this time, and the death of his brother, he was tempted to go for a drink. The taste of whiskey called him, and he ran a steadying hand over his face. Taking a deep breath, he looked the other way, to the moon shining off the face of the stone wall beside the hotel. If he'd not been three sheets to the wind the night before Shawn had been killed, he would have worked his own shift, and Shawn would be alive.

Pulling on an undershirt and boots over his socks, he ambled outside. Still some work to be done on his building to make it into a restaurant. He had to stretch his dollars. He glanced back at the saloon. In a few easy wins at poker, he could double or triple his net worth. But he wouldn't. That's what he'd been doing the night before everything changed. Gambling and drinking . . .

"Let it go," he mumbled to himself. "When I finish doesn't matter. This isn't a race. As long as I finish."

He walked out into the street and turned back to gaze at his place. At the moment, the building was looking better. He'd replaced much of the front, replaced the window casings and glass, and given the place a new porch. A modicum of pride filled him. He'd done a fine job so far.

Men came out of the saloon to the boardwalk, leaning against the post. They didn't see him standing in the street. One he recognized as one of the men who'd ridden into town a few days past. The other was Cash.

"We just might have something for you when

we get set up," the older fellow said. "Keep close, and keep your mouth closed."

"Sure," Cash answered in his boyish voice. Did the men know how young Clint's son was? And did Clint know where his boy was?

"You're a big, strapping kid. Just the kind we like." He slapped Cash on the back. He pointed to several horses tied at the hitching rail. "My cayuse is about on his last legs. If I stop by the livery to see about a new one, act like you don't know me."

Cayuse was the term a lumberman called his horse. Suspicion eased its way through Rhett's veins. He'd met more than a few at the lumber-yards and up and down the coast of California.

Cash didn't answer for a few long moments. "Why? I don't see why not."

"Just do as I say, if you want a good-paying job. I'm not ready to let the cat out of the bag just yet." His tone had turned hard. "Don't worry. We aren't doing anything illegal."

Yeah, I bet. Cash was involved with the wrong men.

Still, Rhett wasn't going to get mixed up in anyone else's business. He had enough worries of his own. He walked toward the tall rock face that had captured his interest since the day he'd stepped off the stagecoach. He placed his hand against the cool, stalwart rock. Amazing. And beautiful, especially with the moonlight reflecting the tiny particles of granite. They sparkled like stars.

Slow steps came out of the darkness.

Unarmed, he waited silently.

Soon he made out the shape of a cow, being led slowly his way. At the sight of the long robe of the woman holding the lead rope, he wondered if he was seeing things.

"Mr. Laughlin," she said in a soft voice. The cow halted beside her, its large eyes blinking in the darkness. It let out a long, lonesome moo.

He stepped closer. "Have we met?"

"Not officially. I'm Sister Cecilia Nushbell, from the Mother of Mercy Orphanage." She gestured down the road leading out of town toward the Five Sisters Ranch. "We're just a little ways out of town."

He'd heard about the place but hadn't given it much thought. He wondered how she'd heard about him. The sleepy-eyed cow looked in no hurry to be off.

"I'm pleased to make your acquaintance, ma'am. But how do you know me? That's a mystery."

She gave a small laugh and affectionately rubbed the cow's broad forehead. "Not a mystery at all. Our dear Lavinia works at the orphanage whenever she can spare a few hours. The children love her. She told me about how the two of you met."

"I see."

"Not really," Sister Cecilia replied.

He wondered at her comment. He'd not ask, because he didn't really want to know. "You're out walking your cow?"

Another humorous laugh. He figured she wasn't frightened of anything.

"No, our sweet cow, Sister Clover, likes to break out of her stall and take midnight walks. Most times she ends up in Saint Rose's garden patch. I think she likes Father Francisco and tries to gain his attention."

Okay . . .

"Good night," she said, stroking the bovine's face as they ambled away. "Milking time isn't far off."

Rhett realized he was watching her retreat with a wide grin. He liked her. Very much. And after such a short conversation. If only his life could be as easy as retrieving a cow from a church garden.

CHAPTER THIRTY-FIVE

Four days came and went without much incident. After pushing out the side wall as well as finishing the upstairs living quarters, Rhett felt a huge measure of accomplishment— toward the building, but not the cooking. He'd helped his father often, building new and remodeling old. If he had to choose a life away from the docks, construction fit him well.

Taking a break, he leaned against his front wall and wiped an arm over his moist brow. He hadn't been a resident here long enough to know who were townspeople and who were new, but the traffic in the street was steady, and seemed like more than when he'd arrived. The sooner he was able to get his doors open, the better. Rumor had it, a fella who'd recently arrived was an actual dentist, with equipment and a drill. Rhett steeled himself at the thought of a stranger putting a drill to his teeth. Back in San Francisco, there'd been several dentists, and he'd heard more than enough horror stories to stay away from those places at all costs. He clamped his jaws firmly together. He'd been blessed with straight, healthy ivories, and he'd not let anyone near them.

Rhett untied the kerchief around his neck and swabbed the sweat from his face. The day was warm for just eleven o'clock. But how much warmer was the hot kitchen with the oven cooking? He'd had several disastrous attempts at making biscuits, too black for even Dallas to consider. But he'd persevered until he had three batches in a row come out soft and golden brown.

Across the road, several people stepped out of the hotel, followed a moment later by Lara Marsh. He'd have to be blind not to notice she'd been around the last few days. Why had she left the ranch? He could understand if Lavinia were staying in town in her room, as she often did, but that wasn't the case. She came in early by buggy and left in the afternoon.

Lara spotted him and raised a hand to wave.

He waved back.

Soon she lifted her skirt and, being careful of riders, a wagon or two, and a man herding a half dozen cattle up the street, came his way.

"Good day, Miss Marsh," he said. She was nicely dressed, as she'd been the day he'd met her under the tall cottonwood next to the livery. Her hair, drawn back at her nape with a wide, royal-blue ribbon, looked freshly washed, catching the sunlight whenever she turned. There was a sadness in her eyes that hadn't been there before.

"Miss Marsh, how are you faring? I couldn't

help but notice, since my building is right across the street from the hotel, that you've moved from the ranch." It wasn't his business and he usually didn't talk so much, but they had spent that afternoon walk together, and they both held Katie Brinkman's secret. He supposed they did have quite a bit in common.

The new doctor came out of the mercantile, his arms full of purchases. He glanced about and nodded when their gazes connected. A moment later he started away.

"Good day to you, Mr. Laughlin," Lara said. "How's your restaurant coming along?" She gave the boards, which still needed several coats of paint, an appraising assessment.

She'd not answered his question.

"I'm getting closer. I have no real rush, except to get some cash coming in to offset the cash going out. This place has turned into a money-eating monster."

"I'm sure that'll take care of itself the moment your 'Open' sign goes up. People are curious. We've noticed all sorts of aromas wafting over." She waggled her eyebrows.

I bet.

"Everyone has forgiven you for your inauspicious beginnings with Lavinia. You should feel exceedingly happy about that."

And Lavinia? Has she forgiven me as well? "I hope you're right about that."

"What is your specialty, if you don't mind me asking?"

Again, an inquisitive smile lit up her face in a way that made him chuckle. "Just simple fare." *I wish.* "Stews." *I hope.* "A hearty chicken and dumplings, and robust breakfasts—the kind a man would enjoy and come away full."

"So you'll be open for all meals?"

"Someday. When I round up help. I believe I may open in stages."

Her eyebrow slowly inched up her face, and finally a smile appeared.

She pointed to the large "Help Wanted" sign he'd tacked up next to the door. "If you're still looking, I'd like to apply."

Surprise rocked him back on his heels. What exactly was going on with Miss Marsh? She didn't seem like the type that had to work. Or would *want* to work. Or knew anything about restaurants. Shouldn't he get someone with some experience, since he didn't have any? He'd been under the impression her stay was only so long and she'd be on her way. "I don't understand," he finally said. "Aren't you a guest at the Five Sisters? Why would you want a job in town?"

"I've moved into the hotel for now and plan to stay in Eden. But, you should know, before you make any decisions, the sisters and I have had a falling-out. They think I'm waiting for the stagecoach to take me to the train, but I'm not.

I've never been a quitter, and I don't aim to begin now."

The articles? It has to be. The timing was too much of a coincidence otherwise. Caution rushed through him. Hiring her would solve one of his problems, but he didn't want to alienate the whole Brinkman clan.

Lara waited patiently as a hundred thoughts ran through his mind. Looking into her face, he didn't see duplicity or malice, just youth, curiosity, and determination. He had to give her credit for backbone.

Right then a Conestoga wagon rounded the corner, driven by an eager-faced man. He looked Rhett over and drew back the lines to his weary team. "Howdy," he said. He doffed his hat. "Morning, Miss Brinkman."

Scowling, Rhett stepped forward. He wasn't Lara's keeper, but he didn't much like this fellow mentioning the Brinkmans the moment he'd pulled into town. "Who're you and what do you want? And this is Miss Marsh—not Brinkman."

The man's smile faded.

"That's not a very friendly tone," he said. "Just tell me where I can park this rig so I can get a decent meal. I'm starving." He turned to the hotel. "The hotel café any good?"

Next, the man eyeballed Rhett's building none too nicely. He needed a bath and shave but didn't look disreputable or like an outlaw. Actually, he had kind eyes, and a smile before Rhett had chased it away.

"Sure is." He'd better soften up. "For the livery, turn around and head down Falcon Haven a couple of blocks. It's easy to spot."

"Much obliged." The fella flexed his leg on the brake and slapped the lines over the backs of his team. The wagon jerked forward.

"All right, Miss Marsh, I'll give you a try, but I'm not exactly sure when I'm going to open. Hopefully by the end of the week, if not sooner. Will you be available then?"

She nodded.

"And I can't pay much."

"I understand."

"I guess we have a deal, then," he said, and stuck out his hand to shake.

"Deal!" She grasped his hand firmly and gave him her first real smile.

Was he crazy? He had to be. But not one other person, man or woman, had inquired about the job. Rhett wasn't sure if the reason was that they were already gainfully employed or if they didn't want to work for him. He had to have at least one employee to get started. And here she was, staring him in the face.

CHAPTER THIRTY-SIX

L avinia gazed out her hotel room window, enjoying a little time off. She'd been a jumble of nerves since receiving the telegram, but she couldn't tell anyone why. The same day, she'd replied, telling Mr. Hansberry to expect her in approximately three weeks. That would give her time to sign the paperwork for the ranch and then take the stage to catch the train in Pueblo.

It was Karen who'd suggested she take Wednesday off and stay in bed all day if she wanted—that feat was impossible. But Lavinia had acquiesced and asked Nicole to fill in. She planned to hire the girl full-time to take her place when she left.

To calm her runaway excitement, she'd been working on a new creation for the last hour. The little beauty had a curved, brown-felt brim that was edged with lace. Her good feelings disappeared when she noticed Lara cross the street and go directly toward the Hungry Lizard. She stopped on the front porch to speak with Rhett, who'd been working on the face of his restaurant—her *competition.* Lavinia set the hat on the dresser.

Seeing Lara brought an ache to her heart. How could she have sold their secrets? And worse than that, how could she fib about it? And even *worse* than *that,* the six of them hadn't yet made up. Three times when Lavinia had gone to her room during the week, Lara had refused to speak with her. The problem had mushroomed into something that might never be healed.

Outside on Eden's Main Street, she noticed Clint in a tug-of-war with the palomino mare he was using until his gelding was sound. She smiled. And here came kind Mr. Hoffman, the butcher. When he spotted a woman Lavinia didn't recognize, he doffed his fine, brown, beaver-pelt bowler in a most extravagant way. Knowing she was a hatmaker of sorts, the butcher showed the headpiece to Lavinia each time they met, which she thought very touching. Then Belle and Blake rode in, their love for each other apparent. Whirling, Lavinia turned away. Of course she was thrilled to be leaving, but that didn't mean she wouldn't miss her family and friends. Or the life she'd come to know in Eden. She'd fulfilled her father's desire by staying the six months—there was no reason whatsoever for a heavy heart.

Before she could go forward with anything, though, she had to mend fences with Lara. Everyone made mistakes. They'd been friends far too long to just let the relationship fall away. Going to the mirror, Lavinia checked her reflection, smiling at her cute yellow hat, and went out the door. She needed to catch her friend before she disappeared.

By the time she hurried down the stairs, both Lara and Rhett were nowhere in sight. The busy street held many new faces. Where were all these people staying? The boardinghouse must also be full. Heaving a sigh at missing her chance with Lara, she started for the path to the upper plateau. She'd lift her spirits by gathering new blooms for the restaurant.

Stretching her muscles felt good. Only a few strides up the steep trail and her breathing increased. She crested the top to see Rhett's rock watcher still standing. A swirl of emotion lifted her chest. Rhett was a mystery. The more she tried to learn about him, the more he kept his real self hidden.

Crossing the meadow to the stand of rainbow-colored grand buckwheat, as well as the plentiful supply of alyssum, she began to carefully snap off stems of both. Within the forest, a ray of sun glimmered on a deer trail she'd not noticed before. Blake had talked about hidden falls somewhere up this way, and how much their father had loved spending time there, thinking about his girls, praying they'd return.

Compelled, she moved forward, the flowers

forgotten in her grasp. Coolness surrounded her, and the way grew dark. The path was narrow, and at some places her dress snagged. She wished she'd worn her riding pants, the garments she used out at the ranch. A startled chipmunk darted out of her way. The call of a hawk shattered the silence.

Excitement filled her. None of her sisters had been out this far, she was sure. If they had, they would have said something. Crossing the trail was a stream, not much wider than the ranch buckboard. Anyone who wanted to continue would have to take large steps between the rocks. On a large slab of granite close to the shore was a small, three-rock tower.

Rhett!

She couldn't stop her smile. He'd been here as well. Walked this path, discovered this clear mountain stream. Being a newcomer hadn't held him back. Had he sat on the granite slab to watch the water, or was it the trees that drew him here? So many things she didn't know about him, except the gentleness of his hands.

On a whim, she set her handful of flowers down and went about looking for rocks of her own. She'd do as he'd done. Leave a marker. A sign that she'd been here for all to see.

Being careful not to wet her hem, she went to the shore and peered through the rushing water to the pebble-strewn bed below. She reached into the freezing water and tried to remember what Rhett had told her about size and shape. She fingered a few different rocks, but tossed them back, their irregular shape much too difficult for her. She fished out three more.

Placing the first took one second, but it took a good four minutes to balance the next. The third was an utter failure, and they all tumbled down, almost upsetting Rhett's creation. She tried again. Finally, her small formation stood close to his, less than half the height, but still, pride filled her heart. He was right. There was something satisfying about the challenge. She appreciated his efforts all the more now that she'd tried her hand. She marveled again at his larger, pointier, gravity-defying formation. That took talent.

Suddenly, a small gust of wind swept through the tops of the tall trees and ruffled her dress. Her yellow hat tumbled off, and she ran to retrieve it. The coolness of the air under the trees made her shiver.

The area was so quiet. The peacefulness she'd felt before dissipated, giving way to a niggle of uneasiness. What was wrong? Was that a warning? She held her breath, listening.

The sound of voices carried her way.

Rhett? On his way back? Proof that he'd come this way was right before her eyes. But she was pretty certain he'd come by himself. And she'd seen him working today. She again heard voices.

Several. Rhett's warning about the campfire sprang into her mind.

Suddenly, Lavinia wished she hadn't come so far into the woods by herself. Glancing around, she darted for the trees. She'd hide until whoever it was emerged. And once they'd gone, she'd make her way home. Could she find a hiding place before they arrived? If she was correct, they were coming up the trail the way she'd come herself, so perhaps they'd pass her by without even noticing.

CHAPTER THIRTY-SEVEN

C rouching behind several large pine trees that completely hid her person but weren't that far from the stream, Lavinia watched the trail, her breaths coming fast. She reached out with a shaking hand to balance herself against a chunk of granite that protruded up between the trees. Seeing the shadowy trail from her vantage was difficult.

Four riders rounded the corner and made their way toward the stream. A pack mule, laden with what looked like surveyor's equipment, brought up the rear. She recognized them as men she'd seen around town—mostly around the saloon— starting from the day of the wedding. A few of them had dined in her café the first time Rhett had come in. They'd introduced themselves as brothers looking to settle a section of farmland, but that had always felt like a lie to her. The oldest, a seemingly decent fellow, had done the talking for the group. A younger one with a large beard and shifty eyes made her wary. When their gazes connected, she'd always look away, but not before she saw something ugly behind his thoughts.

They weren't the sorts she'd want to find herself alone in a forest with, and yet she'd done exactly that. Huddling closer to the rock, she held her breath. As long as she remained quiet, she was sure they'd pass by in seconds, and then she could make her way back to Eden.

Unfortunately, they pulled up at the stream to water their horses.

"No one suspects anything," one said, splashing water from his canteen on his face and then drying it with a handkerchief. "Boss will be pleased."

He glanced around and then laughed, bringing a chill up Lavinia's spine. She didn't know what they were plotting, but by his tone alone, she knew it couldn't be good.

"Be quiet," the leader snapped, and tilted his head.

Lavinia followed his line of sight to the rock sculptures and the handful of flowers she'd forgotten on the granite slab. There was no doubt they knew someone had been there recently, for the petals weren't yet wilted.

"Should we take a look around?" the bearded fella asked. "We don't want anyone squealing to the sheriff before it's too late for him to do anything."

"Naw. Doesn't matter anyway. By the time they find our camp, there won't be anything they can do. The road will be cleared and we'll be embedded. Let's go."

Although their words confused her, Lavinia felt a rush of relief. She waited for them to clear out and then came out of hiding, her crouched muscles screaming for release. She didn't have time to lose. She should get back to town right away, but the leader's words rang in her head. If someone didn't discover them, something would be too late. There was only one thing to do, and that was to follow them without being seen. And if she didn't hurry, she'd lose their trail.

Lavinia rushed out, picked up her flowers, and hurried onward. Anxiety grew with each step she took. The forest loomed darker. She had to hurry not to lose the riders, who moved much more easily. Each time she came to a fork in the path, she left a sprig of alyssum to mark her way, so she could find the trail back. A half hour passed in the blink of an eye.

Finally Lavinia came to a crest. The men, without so much as a backward glance, went over the top and disappeared out of sight. She waited for a few minutes, and then edged forward. Below was an encampment of men, wagons, and large workhorses contained in a rope corral. Beyond that, the rushing Dolores River. She hadn't seen the tributary before, but she knew it wasn't supposed to be jammed with logs, all floating south.

She was no expert, but appearances seemed

they were cutting in a road from the river toward Eden. Only a large lumber operation would do that. Something much more substantial than Katie's small mill that supplied the ranchers around Eden, as well as silver and gold mines and the town.

Were they logging illegally on federal land? Would they cut down all the trees without a thought for the residents who lived in Eden? Anger and protection rose up inside. The views in Eden were one of the things that made the place so special. She needed to get word back just as soon as she could.

With a start, she realized just how low the sun had dipped in the sky. She had no lantern, and the woods would be much murkier than this open mountainside. And what if she got lost in the darkness? Her sisters, out at the ranch, would believe she'd stayed in town at the hotel. No one would send out a search party tonight.

A half hour later she stopped to catch her breath. The trees opened for a spell, and she glanced up at the moon. She was cold. Many nights since arriving in Eden, she'd heard the howl of wolves. She felt small, and alone. She prayed she'd be able to see the alyssum markers she'd left. Sometimes the trail narrowed peril-ously, and there were steep cliffs on either side. If she missed her step in the dark and fell, she wouldn't see the light of another morning.

Why had she been so foolish and impulsive as to set off like this alone? *Dear Lord, guide me,* she thought as she pushed on.

CHAPTER THIRTY-EIGHT

~✦~

Cupping his mouth, Rhett called out into the near darkness. "Lavinia! Lavinia, are you here?" Almost to the stream, he surged forward. Dallas ran ahead, nose down on the trail. It wouldn't be long before what little light there was vanished, making his search that much more difficult. He should have brought a lantern, or come sooner, before she'd had a chance to get herself lost.

"Darn foolish girl!" he said aloud, irritation heating his blood. From the trading post telegram office, he'd seen her leave the hotel and make her way to the trail they both shared when going to the upper meadow. He'd given her plenty of time to collect the flowers she was so fond of, and then more time to think over the situation she and her sisters were confronting because of the articles he'd brought to town. It was easy to imagine why she'd like to get away and think. All the personal family business that had been exposed couldn't be easy to ignore.

Even when he'd gotten impatient for her return, he'd given her another span of time for any other reason a female might want to be alone. But now, she'd had more than enough time to think over anything and everything. He was alarmed. And when he'd reached the plateau in the waning light to find the area empty, he'd panicked.

She'd get more than the stern talking-to she deserved, he thought, his worry fueling his anger. She'd get a tongue-lashing. Probably the first of her life. Living in Eden wasn't living in Philadelphia. Dangers were about.

"Lavinia!" he shouted again, one hundred depraved situations popping into his head. "Lavinia, answer me!"

Was she hidden away with a lover? A secret rendezvous? It was possible. Look at her younger sister, Katie. Maybe Lavinia had an admirer no one, *including him,* knew about.

That was an asinine thought. Couldn't be true. He didn't like to think of the other, more plausible, possibility. Like the men he'd warned her about.

Hearing the sound of the water, he stopped and glanced around. Had she come this way, gone this far?

In the last vestiges of light, he spotted the rock sculpture he'd completed yesterday still standing, and another much smaller alongside.

She's been here!

His mind surged at the same time a smile tried

to peek out. She'd taken to heart what she'd seen him do. Affection stirred inside.

Dallas stood in the stream, his mouth dripping from the drink he'd just taken.

Rhett glanced around. She'd been here, but he hadn't met her on her way back. That meant she must have continued on. Surely she wouldn't leave the path. She'd gone farther over the mountain. Was she aware of the bears and cougars?

Night would be here in a matter of minutes.

He crossed the stream in three bounding steps and hurried forward. Urgency pushed him onward. She'd been here but was now gone. What did that mean? Had she been taken against her will?

He slowed his steps with the fading light. No mountain trail was without danger. He had to stay alert.

A fork in the path brought indecision. Which way had she gone? Frustration sizzled inside. Tracking her at this late hour, with the tiny bit of light filtering through the trees, would be chancy. His anger grew with his concern.

Then he saw a few sprigs of the alyssum she liked so much placed purposefully on the right side of the fork. She'd left a trail! He glanced down. Another at his feet.

"Lavinia!" he shouted again between cupped palms, hope warring with his distress. "Lavinia!"

When had she become so important to him? When had the memory of her eyes gazing into his own gained the power to create such emotion? "Call out if you can."

CHAPTER THIRTY-NINE

L avinia snapped up straight and turned her head, listening intently. Earlier, in the waning light, she'd slipped on the bank of another small brook and fallen. Her dress was wet past her knees, and she'd cut the fleshy part of her left palm, her warm blood flowing freely. Her hand ached as she held it tightly with the folds of her skirt. Her head hurt, and fear swirled in her mind. She hadn't known how strong the mountains were. Or how dangerous they could be.

Was someone out there? Calling her name?

She desperately wanted to believe that was the case. She wanted to get warm and be safe. She'd also like to eat a large bowl of hot stew.

"Hello?" she called back softly, her arms and lips shaking from the cold. Since the temperature dropped considerably, gooseflesh had risen on her arms and legs. What if more men from the lumber camp were approaching? Should she call out and bring them to her as easy as pie?

But it might also be Clint. Or Blake or Henry. Maybe they'd come looking for her when she wasn't in her hotel room.

She didn't want to pass the night alone in the forest. Had the sound been her imagination playing her for a fool?

"Lavinia!"

Closer now and laced with anger.

Rhett!

A rush of happiness and relief made her light-headed. Or was that just the cold and her empty stomach? The darkness kept her rooted to the spot as hope blossomed. She hadn't thought of him as her rescuer, but suddenly, filled with excitement, she knew he was the only one she wanted to find her. She willed herself to stand, pushing away from the group of trees where she huddled.

"Rhett? I'm here! I'm here!" If it wasn't Rhett, she was in bigger trouble than she'd ever thought.

And then he was there. Without permission, he wrapped her in his arms and pulled her tight against his chest.

Dallas bounded around them, sniffing and whining.

Rhett was large and warm. His heartbeat pounded against her ear, and his strong arms created a new light-headedness that she fully enjoyed. She inhaled his familiar scent and pulled him closer. "You found me," she said against his chest. "You found me, Rhett. Thank you. Thank you from the bottom of my heart. I was frightened. This forest is much darker than out at the ranch, where the land is open, the horizon easy to—"

"You hurt?" he asked against her hair, cutting her off. A layer of gruffness to his voice spurred a wave of emotion.

In no hurry to leave his warm embrace, she shook her head. "No, no. Just so relieved you showed up. I'm amazed. Twice now, you've come to my rescue. I wonder what that means?" His hands on her back produced a flurry of tingles.

"What happened? I saw you leave town and climb the path to the meadow. When you didn't return, I got worried."

"Thank God you saw me. And thank God you followed. I've been preparing myself for the thought of spending the night out here alone." She drew in a deep, calming breath. "I heard coyotes that sounded very near."

"There's a lot more than coyotes out here. There're wolves, bears, and cougars—to name only a few of the dangers. You were foolish to run off like that. Why did you leave the meadow?"

Unwilling to let his warm body pull even an inch away, she kept her arms clasped tightly around his waist and drew him even closer, if that were possible. "Please don't scold me right now. I'm cold and I've cut my hand. I still fear you might be a fantasy. A dream I'm having while lying alone on the forest floor." She shivered. "You are real, aren't you?" She thought she heard a quiet chuckle but wasn't sure over the sound of Dallas crashing around in the woods.

He pulled back as if to try to see into her face. "Yes, I'm real."

The hardness of his chest muscles under her uninjured hand made her mouth go dry.

"I thought you said you weren't hurt. Let me see your hand."

"It's too dark."

At that moment, a silvery beam of moonlight shimmered through the pines, illuminating his eyes, his concerned gaze wrapping around her heart like magic. He lifted her palm and softly felt around.

"Ouch." She whimpered and tried to pull away. "There's nothing to be done until we get back to town."

He was doing something, fumbling around in his pocket. "Here."

Carefully, he wound what felt like his handkerchief around her palm. His fingers, warm to her chilled skin, sent tingles firing up her wrist. She sucked in a shaky breath, unnerved and on tilting ground in the darkness. Rhett's large form felt enormous before her in the blackness, so solid. She'd never been so aware of a man before, and the feeling almost swept her off her feet. She knew since he'd arrived she had nothing to fear.

"At least my bandanna can keep the injury from any more damage. How does that feel?"

His breath touched her face, making her shiver. "Better. Thank you."

He placed his warm palm over her ice-cold hands. "You're chilled to the bone." He removed his light coat and laid the garment over her shoulders. "It'll have to do until we get you back to town."

He rubbed his hands up and down her arms.

"That feels wonderful."

"Good."

He stilled, and she slipped back into his warm embrace. "Rhett, I have something important to tell you." *I may as well do it while I'm warm in your arms.* "I was at the stream and I heard some horses coming up the trail. I hid behind the trees, but they saw some flowers I had left on the rocks, so they knew someone was about. They had surveying equipment and have been in the café several times. They talked about something they were doing that sounded bad for Eden. That by the time anyone discovered them, it would be too late to stop them. When they started away, I followed."

He made a sound in his throat. "Of course you did."

She wouldn't scold him for the reproachful tone. He'd searched her out when he didn't have to. Out of concern for her safety. That meant so much.

He took a deep breath, and she felt his chest rise and fall.

"Loggers?" he asked. "I overheard a conversation outside the saloon last night that made me suspicious. They're probably planning to strip these mountains. The silver and gold mines around need lumber for their tunnels, and New Mexico is growing and has little timber of its own. The demand for lumber down South is pretty great."

"Yes! And they're using the Dolores River to float the logs downstream. They must have a mill somewhere. As we speak, they're working on a road to bring them closer to Eden. And you should see the tree stumps along the river they've already cut. It looks like something out of a nightmare."

He bit out a curse.

"Can they do that, Rhett? Use government land on a whim? Or maybe they have a permit." Several moments passed without a reply. "Rhett?"

"They'd need a permit to do what you suggested. But sometimes dishonest businessmen use any land they want. Just like you heard, by the time an alarm is sounded, and if the town is able to get rid of them, they've already made a fistful of money. If the operation is large enough, they function by paying fines."

"That's horrible! You sound like you know a lot about the lumber business."

"Some."

By his tone, she had the idea he didn't want to

talk about the reasons why he knew, or perhaps the timing wasn't right. "How can we stop them?"

"I don't know that we can without bloodshed. Money moves many men to do things they wouldn't do normally." A burst of wind made aspen leaves clatter and pine boughs sway. "I hate to see such destruction come to Eden."

"Bloodshed?" she whispered, the word conjuring up a horrible vision in her mind. How could she leave Eden with such danger hanging over her sisters' heads, and their father's beloved town under threat? Her heart pounded, and she laid her cheek on Rhett's chest a moment longer, trying to pretend her world hadn't just taken a dangerous turn.

CHAPTER FORTY

Rhett and Lavinia moved carefully, picking their way along the dark trail. Rhett didn't know what to think of the way she had stood in his arms, feeling almost like a lover. Her hand on his chest had felt intimate, and sweet, and he'd had a strong urge to kiss her.

He shook his head and kept walking. She was young and scared. He shouldn't read something into her actions that wasn't there. Still, he'd better be careful. He'd been in love before, he thought, thinking of the heartbreak Margery had caused him. He knew the signs when they were shoved in his face. A swooning Lavinia Brinkman was the last thing he'd expected after the start they'd had on her sister's wedding day. Still, tenderness welled up inside him when he listened to her footfalls behind him. The warmth of her hand in his felt right.

He mentally chastised himself. He had one job to do, and that was to open Shawn's restaurant, not get involved and lose his heart. *Shawn will never have the chance to fall in love! Why should I?*

She tugged on his hand. "Rhett?"

A breeze had intensified the low temperatures in the higher altitude. The sound of the swaying treetops reminded him of waves, waves covering his younger brother.

"Yes?" He stopped and waited for her to continue, shutting out his brother's memory.

"Are you angry?"

"That you went off and got yourself lost—yes. That was foolish."

She squeezed his hand. "I hoped we were past you being mad."

He wished there was at least some moonlight coming through the trees so he could see her face. If he could, the softness he imagined was in her eyes would be replaced with reality. Unfortunately, there wasn't.

"We'll be past it when we're back in town and you're safe. I'm unarmed. I feel responsible for you. I don't like that feeling."

He heard her huff in the darkness. *There, that's better.*

"You're certainly *not* responsible for me."

Yeah, right. Tell that to your sisters if something happens.

"I just wanted to ask . . . I saw you speaking with Lara this afternoon. Did she tell you what happened?"

Has Lavinia been spying on me? Do I have more to worry about than I think?

"No, she didn't. But her moving into town was a red flag. You all have a falling-out?"

The misery in her voice stirred his compassion. She seemed honestly moved by what had happened with Lara. He wanted—no, needed—to push her away. Make all the warm concern stop. Against his better judgment he asked, "Do you want to talk about it?"

Why in the world am I getting involved? I need to keep a distance.

"I think I'm going to explode if I don't get some of this pain off my chest. I didn't sleep a wink last night. Lara is the only person who knew so much about our personal lives. All the things that were written about us in the articles. It hurts to think she could betray us and then deny it. But accusing her also hurts. I'm mixed-up. I don't know what to think from one moment to the next."

"I see."

"Yes, we believe she sold the information to the editor and then didn't own up to the fact when we confronted her. Her parents are quite well-off. Lara has so much, I can't imagine her being jealous of us, but maybe she is. Maybe when we inherited what we did from our father, the enormity of it all was just too much for her. And she wanted to strike us in some way."

He felt her shiver in the darkness.

"But even as I say the words, that doesn't feel right either."

"Maybe she *is* innocent, Lavinia. Sometimes the truth can be staring a person in the face so closely, reality is difficult to see." He supposed he'd feel the same if someone wrote about him and his brother, how Shawn had taken Rhett's shift so his older brother wouldn't lose his job, which ultimately led to his death. "Even if all the evidence does point to her, maybe you should follow your instincts."

"My heart says she's not responsible, but I'm the one who brought up her name. I'm the one who suspected her first."

The hoot of a nearby owl brought her closer.

"Lara's asked me for the job opening I'll have when the restaurant opens," he said. "I hired her."

Lavinia sucked in a breath.

"Is that a problem for you?"

"Not at all. Actually, it's a blessing. I'm just surprised. We all thought she'd be on her way home. I guess she changed her mind. And the reason her staying makes me happy is because we'll have more time to work through this complication. We love Lara, but if she won't speak with me . . ."

He couldn't see her face, but by her tone, it sounded like she was calm. "I'm glad to hear that. I didn't want to upset you or your family any more than I already have, but when she asked, it was impossible to say no. Besides, I think she may be a good draw for the unattached men of Eden. I'll need all the help I can get to launch the place off the ground. I'm sure its success won't be as a result of my cooking."

He thought he heard Lavinia straighten.

"Don't be upset," he went on. "Your café has you as a lure. I'll need something to encourage the men to give my place a try. You wouldn't begrudge me that, I hope."

She stood silently in the darkness. Maybe he'd surprised the words and questions out of her. He'd have to remember that tactic for the future. "Don't you agree?"

"I think you're being silly. But I'm sure she'll be a good employee—or at least try to be. She enjoyed helping out in my place, but that was just for fun. She'll need quite a bit of training. Restaurant work can be tricky when all the tables fill with hungry, impatient patrons. You'll have to show her the ropes, Rhett."

He chuckled nervously and rubbed his free hand over his face. He was dreading opening night.

"Rhett? You do have experience working in a café or eatery, don't you?"

"A little more since a couple of your suppliers paid me a visit last week, thanks to you. I now know how to put in an order. And I've been practicing. Other than that, not much. Just some light cooking from helping out at home. But I'm sure I'll catch on quick enough. Either that or sink and lose the place. I have no intention of doing that. I'll be fine, you'll see."

"Rhett, I'm shocked! Will the opening be soon? In the next few days . . . You've never said."

Her tone seemed to wobble, and he wondered why.

"Not sure, but hoping for a week. I'm pretty much ready anytime—with the construction, that is. That's the part I like." The wind, now picking up, whispered in the treetops. It felt like there was something she wasn't saying. "Do you think you might help train Lara?"

She squeezed his hand ever so lightly. Was there something wrong?

"Lavinia?"

"Yes—if I'm still here."

What is she talking about? It felt as if his heart dropped to his boots. It was easy to deny his feelings as long as he knew she'd always be around to see and talk to. But was she planning on going somewhere?

"What do you mean?" he asked softly. "Are you planning a visit back to Philadelphia?" *A visit's not so bad. A few weeks to a month . . .*

"Not a visit," she whispered almost reverently. "I'm leaving."

Heat sprang to his face, and the air no longer felt cold. "For good?"

"Yes. I've accepted an apprenticeship in a prestigious hat-making company. It's something I've wanted for my whole life. A dream come true. I won the spot before coming to Eden and then lost it by staying too long. But I've been given a second chance." She let out a deep breath. "I'm ecstatic."

Then why don't you sound happy?

"I didn't tell my sisters before, because Mavis had just lost Darvid, and then we got the telegram about Father and we had to come to Colorado. I'd appreciate it if you keep what I've said to yourself until I have the chance. I just got the telegram last Saturday."

And she still hadn't told everyone?

A loud roar sounded somewhere off in the trees. Lavinia gasped and wrapped her arms around him, making it difficult for him to keep in the front of his mind his resolve not to fall for her. He gently stepped back and pried off her arms. "That was a long way off."

"What kind of animal made that growl?"

She was trying to be brave, but her shaky voice gave her away. There wasn't a woman he knew who wouldn't be frightened if placed in her shoes.

"Cougar, maybe. But lest it's cornered, they rarely attack a human unless provoked. We should be going, though."

Dallas growled deeply and then bounded away

from them into the darkness, crashing off the trail and through the brush.

"Dallas!" Rhett shouted. The thought of losing the last thing he had left of his brother's was unthinkable. He turned and shouted several more times, the desperation in his voice sounding strange to his own ears.

In the distance, Dallas barked several times, growled, and then let out a loud *yip yip yip.* After that, all was quiet.

"Dallas!" Lavinia shouted at the same time he did. She had a death grip on his shirtsleeve. Again, he wished he'd brought along a lantern.

"Here, Dallas! Here, boy!"

Dallas reappeared at their side, breathing hard and whining loudly. Rhett hunkered down to the dog's level only to quickly pull back.

Lavinia, standing close to his back, gasped. "What's wrong?" she asked. "Is he hurt?"

"Yeah. Has a mouthful of porcupine quills, some on his face . . ." He ran his hand over Dallas's body. "Neck, chest . . ."

"Oh, poor boy!"

"Exactly. Now, I need to get you both back as soon as possible. Let's go. Dallas is everything to me." His voice broke. "The only reminder of . . ." He snapped his mouth closed, knowing he'd gone and said too much if he was to truly start over. When he started off, Lavinia stayed back, making him return to her side.

"Rhett, you've avoided sharing any of your past with me or anyone else." Her hand on his arm was affirming. "Who does Dallas remind you of? Please tell me . . ."

He was thankful for the darkness. The thought of something happening to Dallas had rocked him to his core. He might butt heads with the animal, but he never wanted to lose him. Sometimes it seemed he saw Shawn's expression on Dallas's face, as outrageous as that sounded. Dallas was Rhett's link to his past.

"Please, Rhett. Maybe I can help?"

He didn't know if the sincerity in her voice was his turning point, or perhaps the darkness that kept her probing gaze at bay was to blame, but suddenly, he wanted to share. For a moment he squatted down again and carefully petted Dallas on his back and hindquarters where there were few quills. Then he stood.

"All right. Dallas belonged to my brother. Shawn saved him from some drunken sailors. Dallas was thin and had mange. He followed the heels of one sailor who appeared at our docking shed."

"Is Shawn your brother?"

"Yes. We worked together on the San Francisco docks for years. He bought Dallas for a huge amount of money to get him away from the cruelty. More than a month's pay.

"The ship was from Australia. They said he's

part dingo, a wild dog that runs free in that country." Rhett chuckled, thinking how Dallas's mood determined if he'd be obedient. "Dingoes are smart and cunning. I believe what they claimed. Dallas is usually one step ahead of me, whatever I'm doing. All that considered, he's a good dog, well trained by my brother and getting better all the time for me."

"Why do you have him now?" she asked in a small voice, almost carried away by the sound of the wind.

"My brother, Shawn . . ."

"Rhett?" She rubbed his arm. "You can trust me. I can hear the emotion in your voice. Did something happen to Shawn?"

He swallowed down a lump of regret. "He stayed behind . . ." *In his grave.* Taking a firm grip of her hand, he moved forward, finished spilling his guts for the night. He'd said more than he'd wanted to. "Let's get the two of you to Eden. You're near frozen and now Dallas'll have hours of pain once I begin removing the quills. It's not an easy job." He didn't wait for her next question but continued down the path, hoping they wouldn't meet any more obstacles. His heart felt about as battered as poor Dallas.

CHAPTER FORTY-ONE

❧

It was past ten o'clock when Rhett finally led Lavinia down the trail from the upper meadow, a firm hold on her hand so she wouldn't stumble. Plenty of lanterns still burned in windows above shops and even below, belonging to owners who'd not yet retired. They would be foolish to believe they wouldn't be seen coming into town. He chanced a glance back at Lavinia, her skirt damp and marred with dirt and smudges. Her hair had long since fallen around her shoulders, and her eyelids drooped. She'd sleep well tonight, if she didn't allow her imagination to run wild, worrying about what others might think about them. If his appearance in town hadn't caused enough of a stir already, sneaking back into town after dark together, looking as if they'd enjoyed a good roll in the hay, certainly would. No doubt about that.

"Miss Brinkman?"

The voice was deep, one Rhett didn't recognize. They had almost arrived at the hotel, where Lavinia could slip inside using the back door. Now there was no escaping.

They turned.

Jeremy Gannon, Eden's new doctor, stood before them in the lantern light from the drugstore and telegraph office. His eyes widened at the untidy condition of Lavinia's dress and mussed hair, but he didn't ask any questions.

"I owe you an apology, Miss Brinkman," he said, his tone contrite. "I'm sorry for my rude behavior when we first met in the café the other day. I suffer from serious headaches called migraines. The only thing that seems to help is lying down in a dark room and staying completely still, or, sometimes, strong coffee, and plenty of it. I'd been suffering on the stagecoach for three days, and I let that affect my manners. I hope we can begin anew."

Lavinia's mouth dropped open. "Doctor, I'm so sorry to hear that. Of course. And I'm sorry for being impolite to you."

"I hadn't noticed."

They smiled.

At that moment, Dallas came trotting out of the darkness, seemingly unaffected by the porcupine quills sticking out of him at all angles. It was the first good look he and Lavinia had of the dog.

"Dallas!" Lavinia cried. "I can't stand to look!" Her hands encircled her throat, and her large eyes filled with tears.

"My dog encountered a porcupine while I was out searching for Miss Brinkman," Rhett said, wanting to explain right away about her tousled appearance. "She was lost above the meadow in the woods." He hoped the doctor wouldn't spread any rumors. "I was lucky to find her in the dark and get her home. Dallas wasn't so lucky."

The doctor knelt and inspected the horrible sight more carefully. Dallas couldn't close his mouth for the quantity of quills stuck in his tongue and gums. Dr. Gannon looked up at them.

"Do you know how to extract the quills?" he asked, his voice all seriousness. "They don't just pull straight out the way they go in. It takes some finessing. Backward-facing barbs grip the skin, making extraction extremely difficult and painful. The dog is liable to get ferocious when you try."

"I don't." But it sounded like the doctor did.

"Why don't you bring him to my place? I'll give him some laudanum to make him sleepy. I have instruments." He stood and waited for Rhett's reply. "There must be three or four hundred quills, if I had to guess, and the chore of removing them will take all night."

Dallas was staring at the doctor, as if to say *yes!*

"Thank you, Doctor," Lavinia gushed, her face still twisted in sympathy. She glanced at Rhett. "Let the doctor do it. He knows what he's doing."

Rhett nodded, and a grin appeared on Dr. Gannon's face. "I grew up on a farm in Kentucky.

Our hounds tangled with the porcupines a few times a year. You'd think they'd learn. My father was a surgeon before me and taught me all he knew—*about animals.*" He gave a hearty laugh. "I think he made more money tending horses, cattle, and hogs than humans. Anyway, I'll do what needs to be done and keep him until you come for him sometime tomorrow." He glanced down at Dallas. "How does that sound, Dallas? You want to be my first patient?"

Relief washed through Rhett. "Let's get him to your place, then. We have business with Henry Glass that won't wait until morning."

What Lavinia had said about the tree stumps she'd seen and the log-clogged river was still fresh in his mind. They needed to get the word out about the lumber outfit and what they were doing on the Dolores.

Henry stared at them over tented fingers from his side of the desk as Rhett and Lavinia relayed all they'd heard and seen. His rumpled hair was out of character. "That must have been the campfire Clint and I saw on our way back from the ranch the other night. Surveyors scouting the lay of the land. And the Dolores River is perfect. Wide of bank and fast flowing. Katie should have something to say about this. They'll be scabbing away her business."

What a bedraggled group he and Lavinia made,

Rhett thought as he let out a long sigh. He was thankful Dallas was in capable hands. It did his heart good to see the caring way Dr. Gannon had treated him, as gentle as if the dog were a person. Rhett and Lavinia had waited around until Dr. Gannon had drizzled a healthy dose of laudanum down a sputtering Dallas's throat, fearlessly holding the dog around the neck as if he had a wrestler in a choke hold. It only took a few minutes before the dingo mix blinked sleepily and then sank to the floor, resting his quill-covered nose between his paws, still unable to close his mouth. Then Rhett and Gannon hefted him onto the clean examination table, but not until the doctor took care of the slice on Lavinia's palm. Dallas hadn't been Dr. Gannon's first patient; Lavinia had.

"Warmer, Lavinia?" Henry asked, looking at her huddled in his thick winter coat, over the top of Rhett's. Her lips were still blue, and Rhett was anxious to get her back to the hotel where she could change out of the sodden dress and be tucked into bed—not by him, of course, but herself. Her free-flowing hair was a delight, shrouding her shoulders, the color reminding him of a soft beaver pelt, dark brown with golden highlights, and making her look very young. He needed to remember that.

And poor Henry. He'd been sound asleep when they'd knocked on his back door. Now, sitting behind his desk in his nightshirt and slippers, as well as a robe, he looked the oldest Rhett had ever seen him.

"Just thought you ought to know right away. Also about Lavinia being lost, in case you hear some wild stories about us sneaking down the trail from the meadow after dark. Now you know we had good cause."

"I'll say you had cause. Clint will be mighty perturbed when he hears about this lumber crew, whoever they are. As will Blake and everyone else. I'll be sure to pass on the information to Clint first thing in the morning. I don't doubt he'll be riding out there immediately."

Rhett sat forward. "He better not go alone. We may never see him again, and they'll claim ignorance that he ever arrived."

"Sounds like you have some experience with loggers." His eyes narrowed a bit, but his expression stayed neutral. He was interested, just like everybody else. People here just wouldn't give up until he told them his past. Dammit. Couldn't a man start over with a clean slate?

"You've already told me, Rhett," Lavinia said sleepily. "Go ahead. You can trust Henry."

Henry frowned. "Is there something I should know about?"

"Rhett?" Lavinia said softly. "Henry's just being friendly. He doesn't mean any harm."

Rhett bristled. "I'm from San Francisco, as

you already know. I worked on the dock with my brother, Shawn. My life took a different turn, and I decided to move to Eden. I have experience with the lumbermen along the California coast. Nothing more. Anything else you'd like to know?"

Henry sat back from the force of the statement flung in his face. If he didn't expect an honest response, he shouldn't have asked.

The attorney, whom he now considered a friend, put up a placating hand. Disappointment was on Lavinia's face.

"We all have pasts, Rhett," she said softly, reaching out and touching his hand. "Yours isn't so bad. Why're you so sensitive? I'm the one who should be sensitive." She gave a soft laugh. "From the articles you brought to Eden about me and my sisters, you know the countless things we have to be ashamed of or embarrassed by, but now that they're out for all the world to know, I've been thinking that it's sort of a good feeling. Nothing left to hide. If anyone's going to like me, it won't be because of any preconceived notions. I had a lot of time to think, creeping down that dark and lonely trail before you found me. Who cares if someone knows Mavis and I got tipsy sneaking into a stranger's wedding when we were twelve and eight, pretending to be long-lost relatives of the bride? It was fun. We took our punishment from Velma and moved on.

Now that I think about it, we were looking for attention—whether good or bad didn't matter a whit. Something was better than nothing."

She gave Henry a wide smile, as proud as a peacock, as if she'd just made some important discovery. "Perhaps Lara did us a big favor and we owe her a thank-you. I'm going to speak with my sisters about that as soon as I have a chance."

Maybe Lavinia was happy her past was an open book, but she'd certainly think differently if she knew he was the reason his younger brother was dead. He'd let women, whiskey, and song overrule his better thinking. A real man would never have behaved so irresponsibly. He wasn't proud of his actions and was sure Lavinia would feel the same.

But what she'd said, about owning up to the past and releasing its hold over you. And about second chances. Maybe he'd have to give that some thought.

CHAPTER FORTY-TWO

~⚔~

At the livery the next morning, Clint saddled the skittish palomino mare he had on loan from Maverick, while Blake, already mounted, waited for him to finish. Maverick slid a Winchester into his scabbard in the front of his saddle and then took the reins of another mount that Rhett would use as soon as he arrived.

Blake leaned forward in the saddle. "Like I said, we were surprised when Lavinia came out to the ranch this morning with her story of a lumber company pillaging the forest. I can't believe she actually hiked into the timberland alone. That has me nervous. That's a big land out there. If she'd gotten really lost, there's a chance we'd never have found her."

Clint knew the feeling. "I was just as surprised as you," he said, tightening his cinch and looping the supple strap into the leather keep. "Henry came by last night, even though it was late. Filled me in. I guess I've been a day late with finding 'em each time they had a camp. We'll see what's up soon enough." He gave Blake a long look. "You really don't need to bother riding out with me. I can handle this myself. I know you have work to do."

"The way Laughlin told it," Blake said, "these scabbing practices aren't all that uncommon. Neither is a man losing his life over trying to stop it. We'll go together. What threatens Eden threatens us all."

Maverick ambled in and tied two more saddled horses to the hitching rail.

Blake had a point. Better to show a strong hand right from the get-go. "Getting answers won't take long if the fella in charge is there." If what Henry and Laughlin said was true, who knew where they'd stop their timber felling? He didn't want Eden to lose its forests. Even a few miles away, where the clearing didn't show. Once a big-time lumber outfit got a toehold, there'd be no stopping 'em.

At the sound of approaching hoofbeats, the men turned to see all five Brinkman sisters, led by Belle on Strider, the horse that had been the girls' father's until he'd died.

"What're you doing here, Belle?" Blake called. He rode forward to meet them a few feet from the livery doors. Of the sisters, Belle was the most accomplished rider. The rest of the girls had been given horses and had ridden a fair amount, but they didn't spend most of their days working the ranch like Belle did.

At the sight of Mavis, sitting tall in her saddle

with determination on her face, Clint's heart warmed. She'd been avoiding him, but he had hope of rectifying things.

"What do you *think* we're doin', cowboy?" Belle teasingly answered. "We're going with you. This town means everything to us—as it did to our father. We'll not sit back and leave all the work to the men. We're just as capable as the rest of you."

Katie and Emma didn't look quite as confident as their married sister, but Mavis and Lavinia did.

Mavis glanced around. "Is this all of us?"

"You're not going." Blake removed his hat and scratched his head. "Taking on a camp of angry men is no place for a woman. Or five of them. Be reasonable."

"Blake," Lavinia began.

Blake narrowed his eyes, cutting her off. "There could be trouble."

"That's why we're coming," Emma replied.

Blake laid a hand on Belle's leg, seeking her gaze. "Please listen to me on this, Belle," he said, less forcefully. "I don't want anyone to get hurt."

"We won't be hurt, Blake," Belle responded. "But we won't be kept back from helping Eden, the ranch, or the men we love."

She has a point, Clint thought.

Henry was staying back. If they didn't return by the specified time, he was to gather a group of men and come out. They needed someone in town who knew what was happening. Rhett arrived on foot. Maverick handed Laughlin the reins of a horse he'd saddled, and the newcomer mounted up as if he'd been riding all his life. Wouldn't take long to get out to the Dolores.

CHAPTER FORTY-THREE

As Lavinia rode her horse along in the group, she couldn't, for some reason, keep her mind off the telegram she'd received five days ago and the one she'd sent back to Philadelphia. Her excited feelings were like a jumble of gooey Christmas candy. She recalled telling Rhett about her plans in the darkness of the trees, and the warmth of his hand in hers. How close he'd stood to her when he'd found her huddled in the forest. She tried to recall his reaction, but could only remember how her tingling nerves made her light-headed.

She let go a long sigh. *I should tell my sisters today, get the good news off my chest, so I have plenty of time to prepare properly for the journey.* She glanced ahead at Rhett's back, riding close to Blake and Clint. She really should, but the contract signing for the ranch felt like the right time. Not yet, not today. What would a few more days matter?

Belle's been walking on air since her wedding. I'll be doing the same, only in Philadelphia.

313

My life couldn't be better if I wrote the script myself . . .

Mr. Hoffman, wearing his brown bowler hat, stepped out of the butcher shop and waved to the party of nine as they rode past and up the road from the livery toward the telegraph office, where they'd catch the trail to the meadow. When he smiled broadly at Lavinia, a warm goodness filled her. The butcher, like just about everyone else in Eden, was kind and thoughtful. She would miss the townspeople, the children at the orphanage, and the nuns, she realized. They'd become more like family than friends.

They started up the narrow trail. After today, the mostly hidden path would be much larger and easy to spot once the horses had stomped it down, as Maverick's mount, directly ahead of hers in the single file, was doing at the moment. More people might venture up to the meadows, which made Lavinia a tiny bit sad. She'd thought of the private place as hers alone, and maybe now Rhett's as well.

"Have you heard Lara is staying in town?" Lavinia said over her shoulder to Mavis. Intermittently, she could see Emma behind Mavis, and then Katie and Belle. She spoke up so the rest of her sisters would hear. "I'm thankful she's not rushing back to Philadelphia. Perhaps we can mend the rift between us. She's taken the job at Rhett's restaurant."

All her sisters looked surprised.

"No, I hadn't heard," Mavis replied, sitting her saddle with the grace of a dancer. "But I think that's wonderful. As upset as I felt before, now I'm just sad. I wish she'd say why she did what she did. It couldn't be for the money. Her parents are well-off, and she is too."

"I'm surprised!" Emma called forward. "She has no experience waiting tables. I can't really see her cooking or cleaning up, but I applaud her for her bravery. And I'm glad she changed her mind about leaving right away. Who knows, perhaps she'll decide to stay for good."

Lavinia nodded. "Something hit me yesterday that I'd like to share." She was enjoying Tidbit's easy stride and the back-and-forth rocking of her saddle. The climb up the path was relaxed, especially on horseback. She thought of all the times she'd made the journey on foot. The warm morning sunshine felt good as well, especially after being so cold last night. "This might sound strange, but I'm not that troubled anymore about everyone knowing all the things that were written about us. I say, so what! If people get enjoyment knowing all our private matters, who cares. I think we should go to Lara and tell her she's forgiven. Make that the end of it. She doesn't even have to admit her deed. It's like our hurt, or perhaps even our pride, has driven us apart and ruined a beautiful, dear friendship we've all held special for years. The only thing that will bring us back together, back into unity, is our love. But only if we *really* forgive—and then *forget*."

She glanced back to see the effect of her words. Her four sisters appeared deep in thought. She'd been happy when Belle chose to ride in the back with them instead of up front with Blake. She and Blake were together for most all the hours of the day and night. Sometimes, Lavinia felt like Belle had forgotten them. Their sisterly relationship was important too. A special bond that needed to be nurtured and cared for.

Katie, aboard her flea-bitten fourteen-year-old gray gelding, Spur, smiled. The horse had been pulled out of the retirement pasture along with Mavis's, Emma's, and Lavinia's mounts, and was gentle and well trained, having spent his younger years as a ranch horse, just like the rest. "I never considered that. I've always been nervous about someone hearing I failed my first test and asking, and how I would respond. Feels like the sting is gone." She shrugged and laughed in her lighthearted way. "If the subject ever does come up, I'll just tell the truth and that's that. No need to try to artfully change the subject or skirt the issue to keep my failure hidden. I'm only human—just like the rest of the world. And today, I'm feeling happy I am." She exhaled loudly. "What a difference a few days can make."

"That wasn't a failure, Katie!" Emma defended,

glancing back at the youngest. Dusty, Emma's mount, a leggy sorrel gelding with a small star—not much more than a few white hairs—between his eyes, trudged stoically along. "Taking the test twice was *allowed*—and nothing to be ashamed of. We're all so proud of your accomplishment. You'll be a fabulous teacher one day." She shrugged and turned back to the front of the trail.

"That's true!" Mavis agreed, clucking to Gem, her gentle strawberry roan. "And don't you ever think different. Getting a teaching certificate was no easy feat."

One fact Lavinia could always count on was the loyalty of her sisters. Their bond was unquestionable. Again she thought of Mr. Hansberry, but pushed him out of her thoughts. This day, they were on a mission for Eden. That's the only issue she'd allow in her mind and heart—except, maybe, a few thoughts of Rhett.

"I'm glad Lara's staying on as well," Belle said. "Her arrival for the wedding was icing on the cake. I agree with Lavinia about forgetting about the articles and forgiving Lara. The past is gone and not to be relived. It's best all around."

Lavinia heard a round of amenable sounds from behind, and she smiled to the sky.

"I can't tell you the feeling I get when I think of all us girls living here, marrying, and producing the next generation of Brinkmans," Belle went on loudly so everyone could hear. "Together forever. When Mavis married Darvid, we only got to see her on Sundays, if then. I never said anything, but I always felt like a part of me was missing. Family is so important and so much sweeter when we're living close. We can help raise each other's children. Father certainly knew what he was doing . . ."

Lavinia jerked her face forward, an invisible knife blade slicing deep in her chest. *How on earth will I break the news? I'll be a turncoat. The only one to run off for my own selfish satisfaction.*

She buried her hurt and forced a smile onto her face. "So far, this ride is wonderfully relaxing," she said. "I haven't been out on Tidbit much this month." She reached down and lovingly patted her horse's shoulder. "Poor boy. He's getting fat and lazy."

Belle laughed. "That's because he's barely over fourteen hands tall and roly-poly. I wonder who used to use him at the ranch. Did they tell you, Lavinia?"

She shook her head, not caring if Tidbit was little more than a pony, and thankful for the change in subject. When she needed speed, Tidbit gave generously, and mounting and dismounting was as easy as pie. She glanced around now as they crested the rise to the gorgeous meadow— her meadow, she thought. *Mine and Rhett's.*

On top, where the trail widened out, the sisters

rode side by side. "Look how lovely the morning is! I can't get enough of this fresh air."

Emma pointed at the stone tower. "What's that?"

Lavinia gave a small laugh.

Belle narrowed her eyes. "Lavinia?"

"The watcher. I wondered if anyone would notice him."

"The what?" Belle asked. "How do you know?"

Lavinia realized her mistake immediately. Katie, her brows raised, waited for her response, as did the others.

"Rhett is a rock sculptor. He made it last Saturday. I'm amazed some coyote hasn't knocked it over yet. Isn't it clever?"

"Interesting," Katie said. "You and Rhett, alone up here? I never would have guessed."

Even though her tone said those living in glass houses shouldn't throw stones, her smile was affectionate.

Lavinia, unruffled, lifted a shoulder and tightened her legs around Tidbit, making him step out. "What can I say? We both enjoy the outdoors." She pointed to the side of the meadow as they crossed. "I come up here almost every other day to hunt for early flowers for the restaurant. Where did you think my pretty blooms came from?"

"I hadn't realized," Emma commented.

Katie nodded. "I wonder what will happen

when we reach the loggers. It's quite exciting—and a little scary."

"Blake thinks there'll be a lot of talk, but he's also worried someone might try something stupid. He's asked that we stay back once we get there."

"Did I hear my name spoken?"

Blake had pulled up and was waiting for them to catch up. A light breeze played with Banjo's mane and tail as Blake sat relaxed in his saddle, his wide shoulders and square jaw looking quite manly. Lavinia glanced ahead to Rhett's retreating back, suddenly wishing he'd reined up as well. What would her father think of him?

Mavis laughed. "You have good hearing, brother-in-law! And yes, you did hear your name pass your bride's lips. Can't you go two minutes without your beloved wife at your side?"

"Is there a problem with that?"

Lavinia relaxed in the saddle, enjoying the easy banter. Whether they wanted to think it or not, they might have a fight on their hands. Confronting the lumber operation could be dangerous. She thought of the squinty-eyed younger man, and an uneasy shiver tickled up her spine. As if he'd felt her disquiet, up ahead, Rhett turned in his saddle and glanced back, catching her gaze. He stared for a moment and then turned forward and reined up with Clint and Maverick.

"Once we enter the timberland, the trail is quite

narrow," Rhett said when the women arrived. "You'll have to ride single file again. And I suggest keeping the noise to a minimum, just in case they have sentries."

He shifted in his saddle, looking as comfortable as Blake or Clint.

Clint nodded. "That's a good idea, Laughlin. We don't want to go looking for trouble we can avoid."

Reaching the creek on horseback took less time than it had on foot. When the group came to the stream, Katie, now riding in front of Lavinia, turned and stared. With a tip of her head, she gestured to Rhett's tall sculpture and Lavinia's small, simplistic one.

Tidbit splashed through the stream without a care. The forest was different this morning. The once dark, scary trees now moved gently in open invitation. Perhaps the fact she had her whole family around her, as well as four armed men, played a part in her boldness. It was the first time she'd seen Rhett with a gun instead of a hammer.

When they came to the first split, Katie, having heard the recounting, pointed out the wilted alyssum on the side of the trail. Lavinia smiled to herself, again remembering standing in Rhett's arms. Speaking about intimate things, the sound of his heart and the warmth of his chest. With the winding trail, she couldn't see the men anymore, but she knew he was there, leading the way.

They reached the knoll with no fanfare, no sentries to stop them, and no real expectations. What would the river look like in the light of the day? The men had dismounted and left their horses back where they wouldn't be spotted from below. They slowly approached the ridge.

Filled with dread, Lavinia dismounted and tied Tidbit's reins to a bush, hurrying forward. The men had pulled their rifles from the scabbards and remained out of sight, hunched forward on the edge of the ridge, forearm rested on bended knee as they took in the damage below. Seeing the encampment for the first time in light made Lavinia sick. Her sisters' murmured despair was lifted away on the breeze. Logs even now jammed the river. Between Rhett and the rest of the men, their expressions were a mixture of shock, devastation—and anger. Her heart trembled at the thought of what was to come.

CHAPTER FORTY-FOUR

Clint turned to Mavis and her sisters, barely able to contain a curse. "You'll remain up here with the horses. Out of sight. We don't want the camp to know that you're here. Is that clear?"

Blake and Rhett nodded their agreement. Lumberjacks weren't normally to be feared, any more than other hardworking men, but the fact that they were here without letting him know, despite that they'd been in town a handful of times, made Clint suspicious. He'd lay money on the fact they didn't have authorization to be cutting this timber.

"Is that clear?" he repeated, intentionally avoiding Mavis's gaze.

Lavinia nodded, her expression serious. "It is."

"Belle?" Blake said. "We won't be able to concentrate on what we're doing if we have to worry about you five. Are you going to do as Clint asks?"

Belle looked around at her sisters, and they all nodded. "We will."

"Good," Blake said. "We're just going down

to talk. Find out what's going on. We see the beginnings of a road and the trees they've already felled along the bank. Now we need to see their paperwork."

Clint heaved a sigh. They'd be spotted the moment they started down, but that couldn't be helped. "Let's get this done," he said, and glanced at Mavis. He still felt a connection. Her hurt and pride couldn't stop that. "Mavis, you're in charge, as if you didn't know that already." He wished for their easygoing camaraderie. "If something happens, you're to mount up and get the hell out—fast. Get back to Eden and let Henry know what's transpired."

For a flicker of a second, he thought he saw warmth deep in her eyes. She nodded. "We will. I still think we could be a help down in the camp, being John Brinkman was our father. His name carries clout. Maybe the foreman down there knew him. Maybe we'd have better luck with him than you."

That was her hurt talking, but he wouldn't take offense. "You may be right, but we're not going to chance it. We'll stick with my plan. Those were the terms you agreed upon when we allowed you to come along." He let his gaze slip around the group.

She nodded stiffly. "That's true. You have my word we won't interfere."

"Good." He turned, gathered up his horse,

and mounted, followed by Blake, Rhett, and Maverick.

Lavinia and the women watched from behind a grouping of rocks as the men rode down the hill. Just like Clint predicted, they were spotted immediately. Working stopped. One man ran over to a covered wagon and soon emerged with another, larger man. Nerves skittered up and down Lavinia's back. Armed and standing tall, they waited for their four men to reach the bottom of the hill. She couldn't imagine what Belle was feeling at this point, watching her new husband ride knowingly into danger.

"What do you think'll happen?" Katie whispered. As far as Lavinia knew, she hadn't seen Santiago since she, Lara, and Rhett had caught them in the cantina.

"That's a good question," Emma whispered back. "I wish Henry were here. The more men, the better. Look at all the lumberjacks. I wonder where they get all the food to feed this crowd."

Belle hadn't said a thing. Her troubled gaze stayed on the riders as she chewed her bottom lip. They'd reached the bottom and stayed mounted as the men in the group crowded around.

"I wish we could hear what they're saying," Mavis said softly. When her hands trembled, she clasped them together but never took her eyes off the men.

And Lavinia stared at Rhett, whose broad back was easy to spot on the end next to Blake. The only one of their men hatless. There was something about the way he sat his horse too. Different. She liked that.

The man in charge looked around at his camp and waved his arm, as if trying to explain something. Clint dismounted, and instead of dropping his reins to the ground as she'd seen him do many times with Alibi, he handed them right, to Maverick. The men stood face-to-face.

Lavinia felt a rush of panic.

Was something about to happen? Surely the loggers didn't think they could get away with harming a sheriff and three other men. That would be madness.

"Oh, Lord," Belle whispered. "Things look tense. Please don't let anything happen to the men. Please don't let violence break out. They're seriously outnumbered."

"Everything'll be fine," Lavinia said to calm her nerves. She reached over and placed her hand over Belle's, who was shivering even though the sun was gaining strength and Lavinia felt a sheen of perspiration on her forehead.

Shouts sounded from upstream on the riverbank. A tall tree, far from the camp, crashed to the ground. The distraction startled the men around the powwow. Confusion broke out. Did they think they were under attack?

Mavis held out her hands as if that would stop the confusion, soften rattled nerves. But like an anthill, men began moving, some running. The foreman, barely visible anymore, glanced around and shouted some orders. When Clint turned to go back to his horse, someone hit him over the head with something, and he crumpled to the ground.

CHAPTER FORTY-FIVE

~❧❦~

Mavis gasped and sprang to her feet, but her sisters pulled her back.

Lavinia watched in horror as a circle of men, tall and brawny, closed in around the horses. It was difficult to see. Turning, she gaped at her sisters crouched at her side, her heart thundering in her chest. Would they kill Blake and the others for asking questions? Fear for everyone threated to drop her. Fear for Rhett superseded all thought.

She corralled her fears. "What's happening down there? Will they hurt the men?" Blake, Clint, Maverick . . . *and Rhett.* The feel of his warm arms last night was ever present on her mind. His agitation when he'd thought her in danger, and then his kind and patient words when she'd told him about Lara. She didn't want him harmed. He meant something to her. But what?

"I don't know," Mavis whispered urgently, watching intently, her hands gripping the rock in front of her. "I have a very bad feeling about this."

The rest of the men dismounted.

Belle was already on her feet, running to the

horses. She withdrew the rifle from the scabbard on her saddle and raced back. It was almost like she didn't see her sisters anymore. Her expression, set in stone, was one of resolve.

Sinking back behind the stone, she raised the rifle and took aim, but Emma pushed the barrel down. "Belle! Be careful! You might kill someone!"

"That's what I intend to do if they touch Blake, or any of the others. What's happening? Can anyone see in the mess?"

The crowd had closed in, joined by the foreman that had come from the wagon. Lavinia couldn't distinguish much from this distance. The crowd swelled and moved. She thought she saw someone throw a punch, and then two. "A fight's broken out! They're outnumbered! They don't stand a chance!" Fear for their men raced up her arms.

"We have to do something before it's too late!" Mavis stated. "Emma!" she shouted. "Besides Belle, you're the best rider. Gallop back to town and tell Henry. Get men. Hurry!"

Emma ran to the horses. She ripped Dusty's reins from the bush where he was tied, shoved her foot in the stirrup, threw her leg over the saddle, and galloped away without a backward glance.

Lavinia prayed urgently for the men in the lumber camp, for her sister and the dangerous ride ahead, and for others to get here as fast as they could. They needed a miracle, and they needed one fast.

Belle took aim.

Crack! Crack!

Dirt kicked up at the feet of the men on the perimeter. Movement stopped. She still couldn't see Rhett and the others. The crowd turned and looked at the place the bullets landed, and then up the hill, seeking the shooter.

Lavinia sucked in a breath. "We have to spread out, and Belle needs to shoot from a different location so they think we have several gunmen watching."

Mavis and Katie nodded. Belle slunk back and hurried twenty feet over, edged out, and pointed down the hill.

Men had peeled away, making ready to come in search.

"Hurry!" Lavinia shouted. She stood, ran to Tidbit, and withdrew the gun she'd only shot twice, on Blake's insistence. All the sisters had taken part that day, but only begrudgingly, thinking they'd never need to shoot anything. Only Belle took marksmanship seriously and had been shooting since her first month. Blake bragged on her all the time, saying he'd never seen anyone, let alone a woman, take to the rifle as quickly as she had.

As two of the men hurried toward a couple of

horses, she placed perfect shots between their boots. They pulled up and looked back at the man in charge, whose attention was now on Belle's new location.

"Move again, Belle," Mavis softly called.

Lavinia ran to Strider. She wasn't all that well acquainted with their father's tall black horse. He turned to see who approached his side, then pinned his ears when she reached up to unbuckle the saddlebag where she knew Belle kept ammunition. Belle had fired four times. She'd soon need to reload.

"Easy, boy," Lavinia crooned. "I don't mean any harm. I just want a few bullets from your saddlebag." As fast as she could, she unbuckled the leather, just as she heard two more shots from Belle's rifle.

On tiptoe, Lavinia grasped two handfuls and ran to Belle's side, holding them out with shaky hands. She desperately wanted to see what was happening below.

"Thank you," Belle mumbled as she reloaded faster than Lavinia thought possible.

"What's going on down there? Can you see Blake or any of the men?"

"At times when the crowd shifts."

Lavinia glanced over to Katie and Mavis. Her older sister's face was ashen, and it looked like she wanted to bolt down the hill.

"What should we do now?" Lavinia asked,

close to Belle's ear. The men below seemed to be waiting for some kind of command or order. Would they kill Blake and the rest? That seemed far-fetched. Rhett's calm voice, when he'd been extracting the splinter from her eye, flitted through Lavinia's mind. She remembered the gentleness of his touch. His crooked smile as he'd helped her run to the church. So many memories in such a short amount of time.

Belle nudged her with an elbow. "How many do you think are down there?"

She had no idea, but for Belle, who was staying calm and collected well past the point that she'd have expected her to, she'd give a calculated guess.

"I don't know. Seventy-five, eighty, maybe."

"Exactly. With so many men, I'm surprised they haven't rushed us. With only one rifle, they could easily overpower us in no time."

Lavinia nodded. "I figure they're lumberjacks, not killers. Most probably have families and are good men."

"She's right," Mavis agreed, having slipped in beside them. Katie kept watch from her spot behind the large rock Mavis had just left. "They've come out here to work, not lose their lives. They may act loyal to the foreman, but I highly doubt they're cold-blooded killers."

Another shout went up, and another. Looked as

if someone was fighting again, although it didn't look like any of their men. They needed to act, do something to calm the tension. How could they help before all was lost?

CHAPTER FORTY-SIX

W e were stupid to let them go down alone," Lavinia whispered. "Money will make men—"

"Look!" Katie pointed, her breath coming fast. "Men are sneaking up the hill! If we're overtaken, what chance will Blake and the rest have?"

Aiming carefully, Belle squeezed off a shot that landed three feet in front of their boots.

The men, dressed in suspenders and tall black boots, with bandannas around their necks, jerked to a halt. The shortest one actually dropped to the ground, and the other two covered their heads with their arms. They turned questioningly to their foreman below.

"Stay where you are!" Belle bellowed in a deep voice. "Unless you want your ears shot off."

They ducked. Katie laughed. "Good shot, Belle. You scared the poo right out of 'em."

"Katie!" Mavis yelped. "Mind your tongue. You sound like a ranch hand."

"No, she doesn't," Belle replied. "The ranch hands don't talk like that!"

"That's what those scabbers get," Katie went

on. "Our men went down there with peaceful intent and were set upon. Clint's been hurt."

"Yes, yes, I know." Mavis wrung her hands. "I'm going down there myself to stall them until Emma returns with help. I can't stay put a moment longer."

"I'm the one who should go down," Belle said. "Because of Blake. I can't see the top of his head anymore or any of the others. I'm worried sick."

"You can't go down," Lavinia objected. Seemed none of her sisters were thinking clearly. "You're the sharpshooter who's keeping them honest." She glanced around at all her sisters' faces, dearer to her than her own heart. "Belle, you're staying here with Katie, and Mavis and I will find out what's happened to Clint."

Katie reached over and clutched Lavinia's sleeve. "No, it's too dangerous."

Mavis nodded to Katie. "We have to. If we say more men are about to arrive, they won't try anything stupid. If they think it's just us up here, that foreman may be even bolder. We have to try."

Lavinia stood, untied her cream bandanna from around her neck, and waved it back and forth. The three climbers on the side of the hill were still huddled in place.

"Hold your fire," Lavinia hollered.

More movement in the tightly compacted crowd below made Lavinia's throat tighten. Clint had told them specifically not to interfere, and here they were ready to march into the camp. *Are we doing the right thing?*

Mavis reached over and took Lavinia's hand as they descended. "Don't be frightened," she whispered. "Right and truth are on our side. They aren't going to kill all of us. Only fools would do that."

Mavis's words were justified, but that didn't stop the butterflies in Lavinia's stomach. She thought she might be sick. Her sturdy riding boots helped to keep her footing as they completed their descent. Would Henry show up soon? She wished him here now.

The sea of men parted.

Clint was sprawled on the ground, and Blake, Maverick, and Rhett stood guard by his side. Blake and Maverick's eyes narrowed. Rhett's hands fisted at his side, his mouth flattened, and one eyebrow tipped at Lavinia. Seemed nobody approved their decision.

"What the hell is going on?" Mavis demanded.

Lavinia gaped at Mavis, never having heard her sister speak so sharply. Her sister's gaze touched Clint only briefly and then cut to the head logger. "I asked you a question! Is this how you treat everyone who comes into your camp? You'll pay for this. And pay big!"

Just like the others, the foreman wore tall black boots, thick brown pants, a tight-fitting shirt with matching red suspenders, and a kerchief around his neck. He was middle-aged and well built. His shaggy brown hair was streaked with gray.

Lavinia disliked him instantly.

"We didn't intend for any violence to happen, Mrs. Applebee."

So he knows us, Lavinia thought. Amid all the new faces, she didn't see the four men who came often into Eden to eat at her café, the traitors. Liars, all of them.

"Just so you know," Mavis went on, "we have several sharpshooters on the hill. Don't try anything against the law."

"They can take out a fly on your nose without leaving a scratch," Lavinia added, hoping Belle was really that good. She hadn't known her sister had become so proficient with her Winchester, having seen no proof until today, just Blake's words. "As well as sharpshooters, an army of men is on its way here as we speak and will arrive any moment." She thought she saw Rhett smile. "You've all broken the law by attacking the sheriff."

The closest men around her mumbled with disquiet.

Mavis went to Clint and squatted at his side. Leaning over, she carefully examined the side of his head where he'd been struck. Her hands trembled as she tenderly brushed the hair back from his eyes. She glanced up at Blake. "Has he regained consciousness?"

Blake shook his head. "No."

That was all Blake said. Lavinia could tell he was steaming mad they'd disobeyed. They would all hear about this for months, she was sure.

The ring of men surrounding them backed up, making room. A cool whiff of air, with the scent of the river, was a welcome relief.

The foreman straightened. "When the tree by the bank fell, one of my men mistook the sound for a gunshot. He struck out. It was an accident."

The foreman touched Clint's boot with the toe of his own boot, and Lavinia thought Mavis was going to spring at his face and claw his eyes out.

"He'll come around soon enough. It's just a whack on the head. Men get hurt worse out here all the time. That's nothin'."

Mavis returned to Lavinia's side. "Doesn't look like nothing to me," she said angrily.

"Clint had asked for the paperwork giving you permission to cut," Rhett said, "when some fella stepped forward and hit him over the head with the butt end of his ax."

Thank God Rhett's all right. Blake and Maverick too. But poor Clint. He looked so helpless stretched out on the ground. "What do we do now?" she found herself asking. "Wait for help that's on the way, or try to take Clint back to Dr. Gannon's ourselves?"

Blake shook his head. "He can't ride."

"My men will carry him," the foreman said. "Stu, Bill, Sam, Clark, Mason, Hawk!" he shouted. "Get a stretcher and take the sheriff back to town and then get back here right away. We have work to do."

Six men stepped forward. Lavinia couldn't hold her curiosity any longer. "What will happen to the forest? Are you still going to be logging the trees?"

"We'll have the surrounding acres cleared before summer sets in," the foreman said. "If you're smart, you won't waste your time trying to stop us. By the time you even get a response from anyone in authority, we'll be finished and gone. More men are arriving soon. And now that you know that we're here, no more working under the darkness of night or trying to keep our operation hidden. We can come and go in Eden without problem. We always win, Miss Brinkman. Now, let us collect your man so you can be on your way. We have trees to fell."

Lavinia glanced at the river, her heart sinking. Logs floated down the waterway, their branches having been sheared off. She thought of her beautiful forest. Of Eden. Of their father's dream. They couldn't let this happen! Something had to be done, and quickly.

CHAPTER FORTY-SEVEN

C rowded around a still-unconscious Clint in the doctor's office, Rhett and the others talked in hushed voices. At Clint's side, Mavis dipped a washcloth in a bowl of cool water, wrung out the excess with bare hands, and placed the material back on Clint's forehead.

Rhett noticed her missing finger, and his gaze strayed to her face, so full of concern for the sheriff. He was sure she didn't hear the conversation going on around them. *So that's why she always wears gloves. There wasn't anything about her missing a finger in the articles. Now, for Clint's sake, she's putting her embarrassment aside.*

His gaze strayed to Lavinia, and thought about what she'd told him last night. She was leaving Eden. Perhaps, if given the chance, something could have grown between them. Her company always brightened his day, and she was more or less always in his thoughts. He swallowed and moved his attention to Cash and Nicole, Clint's young sister, on the other side of the bed.

The group had been halfway back to Eden,

riding behind the six lumberjacks carrying Clint on a stretcher, when Henry, Cash, Emma, and twenty more men galloped up to them. Cash had vaulted out of his saddle and run to his father's side. When the boy realized his father was still unconscious, he had let out a primeval howl of pain.

Dr. Gannon had been waiting when they arrived, and Dallas, now devoid of the quills, seemed back to his old self. Gannon examined Clint and made him comfortable.

Now they had to wait. Hope he'd awaken. As difficult as it was, the doctor said he didn't have a crystal ball to say when that might be.

Lavinia appeared totally worn-out. All the sisters did. But especially her. Rhett remembered the way she'd marched into the lumber camp, before all those men, holding her head high even though he could see the fear in her eyes. He respected her, and thought her brave. That must have cost her dearly.

"Knock, knock. May I come in?"

The group turned at the soft voice.

Lara stood in the doorway, her hands clasped before her.

"Yes, please do," Lavinia replied. All the sisters nodded in agreement. They stepped aside, making room between Lavinia and Katie for their friend.

"I saw you bring the sheriff in. Will he be all

right?" She directed her question to Dr. Gannon.

"It's too soon to know," the physician said, moving to Clint's side, where he lifted his wrist to take his pulse. "He seems to be gaining strength." He glanced at Cash, who was watching him closely. "I feel quite sure he'll be able to go home in a day or two. But he won't be chasing outlaws for a few weeks. Someone else will have to do that for him."

Cash nodded and then cut his gaze away. He might be built like a man, but he was still a boy, one in fear of losing his only parent.

Rhett swallowed down his hurt and guilt. He knew that look of desperation he saw on Cash's face. How helpless he felt. How angry.

"What will happen with the forest?" Lara asked Henry. "Do you know?"

When Emma had ridden into town, many citizens had taken notice. News traveled fast in Eden.

"You want to answer that, Blake?" Henry said. "You were there."

Blake and Belle stood shoulder to shoulder, Blake's hat brim crunched in his fingers. His drawn face looked beaten. "The lumber company scabbing on the Dolores River makes a practice of cutting on federal land. They have no right to be there, and the foreman more or less admitted that. Says there's nothing to be done to stop them. They come in quietly, work fast. Clear out everything they can. A good five acres have already been cleared."

"I was amazed at the number of logs in the river," Emma said, her tone sad. "It looked horrible. I'm surprised they don't jam up at the narrow turn."

Rhett nodded. He knew something about this. "They do, from time to time, but they have men called walkers who walk the logs to undam them. A dangerous job, but production stops when the river fills up and they can't float any of the logs away. Until they're cleared, progress is brought to a halt. Sometimes they have to use dynamite."

Blake shoved his hands in his pockets, almost looking like a little boy. "This outfit goes around cutting lumber that's not theirs to take, until they're either finished or thrown off. They float it down the river to a mill, where they'll cut boards and supply the mines and whoever else needs their product. By the time we get through the red tape to throw them off, just like he said, they'll most likely be finished and have moved on."

"Can't the sheriff just demand that they go?" Lavinia asked. "Stealing is a crime."

"Not with so many men as backup. There'd be a bloody war, and they know we don't want that."

"I'll send some telegrams," Henry said. "Starting with our congressmen. Someone should be able to tell me something. There must be a legal way to kick them out."

Rhett knew these kinds of men. He'd lived with just their type on the docks most of his life. Did any of the Brinkmans, Harding, or even Clint or Henry know what they were up against? He didn't think so. He'd best keep a sharp eye out for more than suspicious activity in town. He'd make sure that no one tried to take the loggers on alone.

CHAPTER FORTY-EIGHT

~❧❦~

A ll in all, Lavinia was surprised at how disconcerted Rhett seemed that the lumber
outfit was threatening their town. The stormy
look etched on his face since the six lumberjacks had laid Clint down in Dr. Gannon's office
and quietly filed out the door was something
she wasn't used to seeing. Before Lavinia had
a chance to look out the window, they'd disappeared, on the way to her café.

"What now?" Emma asked beside Clint's still
form. "How can we stop those men from clearing
Eden's trees?"

Katie, who'd been silent since arriving, looked
haggard. "I can't believe this is happening. Has
Eden ever had trouble like this, Blake? And look
at poor Clint. I'm worried sick about him. We all
are."

Blake stood behind Mavis, who, finished with
the washcloth, sat beside the bed, her hands, still
ungloved, gripped in her lap. Cash and Nicole sat
on the opposite side. The doctor had done all he
could for now, and it was a waiting game. Head
injuries could be tricky, he'd said. All could seem

fine until the patient regained consciousness, or not. Lavinia had thought he hadn't needed to be so forthcoming in his prognosis, especially in front of Clint's son and sister. Or *her* sister. She didn't miss that his words had made Mavis turn chalk white. Everyone understood a brain was fragile. One couldn't go around smacking it without repercussions.

"How dare they!" Katie stood and paced across the room. "You all know my first concern is Clint, and that he makes a full recovery, but that foreman galls me. With Clint out of commission, what can we do? I've learned a lot since taking over my mill. We choose carefully before we cut, where, and how much. We never take too many trees from one spot. Making room for the forest to grow is a good thing. The forest is healthier. The trees left behind have sunlight. Thinning also keeps back the danger of fire. I'd never really given much thought to the lumber business before, but it's like a science." A whisper of a smile curled her lips.

And does she enjoy being close to Santiago? With easy access to seeing him alone, anytime she wants?

Ashamed for her wayward unkindness, Lavinia immediately called back the thought. She'd been alone with Rhett in the woods for quite some time last night and other times in the meadow. Nothing had ever happened.

A small moan escaped Clint's lips.

Cash leaned forward, taking his father's hand in his own. The two looked so much alike, it was uncanny.

Nicole leaned in and gently placed her hand on her brother's head.

Mavis took up his other hand, as if in defiance, letting everyone know she didn't care a whit what they thought of her actions.

"Pa?" Cash said, when Lavinia could tell he couldn't wait a moment longer.

Cash's anguish tore at Lavinia. It would be unthinkable to lose Clint now. Her gaze sought out Rhett, who looked unsure. His chin dipped and one side of his mouth pulled, as if he knew what she was thinking.

"Pa, can you hear me?"

Nicole leaned close to her brother's face, holding back her thick, coffee-colored hair with one hand, her amber eyes brimming with worry. "Clint, please, speak to me." She glanced up and looked at Cash. "To us. Cash is here by your side, and Mavis. We all are." She swiped angrily at a tear that had slipped down her cheek. "You're not being nice, making us worry like this. I want you to open your eyes right now. Stop vying for attention."

The stark difference from Nicole's usual, more vibrant personality was not lost on Lavinia. Clint's sleeping form had brought out her vulnerability, a virtue she usually kept hidden. Lavinia knew Nicole didn't mean a word of what she'd said. Clint was the last one to ever draw attention to himself.

The look on Mavis's face broke Lavinia's heart.

Dr. Gannon came to the foot of the bed. "I think it's best if everyone cleared out. Let the sheriff get some rest. It's possible he can feel the tension in the room." He put out his hands to help usher everyone toward the door.

Cash stood defiantly. "I'm not leaving."

Nicole straightened and shook her head. "Me either."

Where did that leave Mavis? Would she put up a fight to stay as well? Lavinia recalled her earlier thoughts that something might have transpired recently between her oldest sister and the sheriff. Both had been exhibiting strange behavior. She hoped they'd be able to work through the situation and get back to their close friendship.

"The doctor's right," Henry said, his hat still grasped in his hands. "Our hovering won't help Clint. Dr. Gannon knows where to find us if Clint wakes up. Besides, I feel an urgency to stop those men. I can't do that here!"

Elizabeth, Johnny, and more than a handful of people had gathered out front, having seen the sheriff carried into town on a stretcher.

Blake nodded and held the door for Belle. "The

best thing we can do for Clint now is to make sure nothing more happens in Eden while he's recuperating. I, for one, will be staying in town, at the sheriff's office, until he's back on his feet."

"I'll keep an eye out as well," Rhett added, his deep voice drawing Lavinia's attention. "My place is right across the street from his office. Cash, Nicole, if you need anything, just let me know."

The more Lavinia came to know Rhett, the more she admired his forthrightness and conviction. Soon he'd have his restaurant open and she'd be gone. She hoped she'd be around for opening night. Would waiting a few extra days put her apprenticeship position in jeopardy?

"I'd like to stay as well, Doctor, if I may," Mavis said.

He nodded.

Lara turned to leave, but Lavinia gently took her arm. "Lara, may we speak with you for a moment outside?"

CHAPTER FORTY-NINE

Lavinia, Emma, Katie, and Belle approached Lara, standing on the edge of the boardwalk. Lavinia knew this was absolutely the right thing to do and would be so glad to close this chapter.

"Yes?" Lara said. Her hands were clasped together in front of her skirt. Her raised chin was a good sign, but her gaze was hard and confident. "It's dreadful about that lumber operation. Chopping away at Eden's forests. They must be stopped!"

Lavinia followed Emma's attention past the buildings to the thick forest on the mountains beyond. Letting someone destroy the beauty of Eden would be a sin. They had to try everything to stop the clear-cut logging.

"You're right. It's horrible. We have to think of something," Belle agreed. "Father would be appalled."

They had two blocks to walk back to the hotel. Lavinia's nerves had her antsy. "Want to walk as we talk?" Lavinia suggested. "Mavis has stayed back with Clint, but she's in full agreement with what we'd like to say."

"All right." Lara turned, and Lavinia and her sisters followed. "What's on your mind?"

"We're all in agreement that we miss you, Lara," Lavinia said. "We don't care what's transpired. We forgive you and would like you to forgive us. No infraction is important enough to lose you over."

Lara's sad gaze moved between them. "But I didn't sell your secrets, or do anything to be forgiven for. You still think I was the one."

Lavinia swallowed and looked at her sisters. She'd supposed Lara would be relieved to be forgiven. Lavinia had thought she'd either admit to the act or just let it go, like they wanted to do—but not deny it again. Lavinia glanced at the ground, struggling with what she should do—or how she should respond.

"I believe you, Lara," she found herself saying. And the strange thing was, she did. "Someone else is responsible. We may never know who, but that's all we can consider. Do you believe me?" She looked at her sisters. No one else seemed to want to say anything.

Tears filled Lara's eyes. "I want to. But . . ."

Lavinia's throat pinched tight. "But?"

"I'm afraid you're all just saying that. That you still think I'm to blame."

Katie rushed forward and took her hands. "I don't. You saying so is enough for me."

"Me too," Belle said, nodding.

351

Emma came closer as well. "And me."

"And me," Lavinia added. "I just hope you can forgive us. And especially me. I was the one to first suspect you."

Lara nodded slowly. "Thank you," she said, as if their statement was the last thing she'd been expecting and she wasn't quite sure how to react. She briefly glanced away. "I didn't sell or give your stories to anyone," she said softly, hefting a deep sigh.

For a moment, Lavinia felt she had more to say, that she was going to go on, but she didn't. Instead a bright smile appeared on Lara's face, one Lavinia knew well. Their friend opened her arms and the sisters piled in.

CHAPTER FIFTY

Midmorning the next day, Rhett surveyed his restaurant with a heavy heart. The construction was complete. His rooms upstairs were finished, and the bed even had sheets. There was only one thing left to do: practice a few dishes until they came out right. He'd perfected his biscuits and could make a batch without burning his hands. Now he just needed a nice soup, a chicken dish, and a dessert. That wasn't asking much.

With an apron tied around his waist that kept his shirttail tucked in, he pulled the pencil from behind his ear and stared at the pad of paper in his hands, struggling with what should be done next.

If only Eden's forests weren't under attack. Concentrating on anything else is near impossible. But I have no choice. Everything I have is invested in this business. I have no other option but to go forward.

He'd worked nonstop all night and then into the morning finishing the remainder of the chores that needed completion. As far as he knew, the kitchen was ready to be put to the test. He had enough plates and utensils to outfit all the tables. The room was clean and tidy. The walls were still bare, except for a mirror; a fancy, outdated calendar; and a sketching of the Pacific Ocean, all of which he'd found in the back room of the mercantile.

Who am I kidding? Without a cook, I'm sunk. Should I look to hire one until I develop the desire, like Shawn had?

Why on earth had he taken this on? Shawn should be here, not him.

The sign had been delivered yesterday while he and the rest had been circled around Clint's bed. In the dusky light of sunup, he'd hung the sign on the front of the building overtop the old painted "Hungry Lizard." Its carved two-foot-tall cursive letters proclaimed this "Shawn's Café."

He turned when the door opened.

"Knock, knock," Lavinia said, stepping inside. "I hope you don't mind me letting myself in." Dallas ran to her side, and she squatted down to love on him for several moments, her eyes shining. "I saw you through the window." She laughed when Dallas tried to lick her face. "I was on my way to the doctor's office to check on Clint and wondered if you might want to go with me." She glanced around. "And by the way, things look nice. You've been working hard."

And he had. To get her out of his thoughts. She

was leaving in a matter of days, he'd reminded himself with every breath. Her hair, haphazardly pulled back in a messy bun, was out of character, and even more shocking, her head was bare. "Only to keep my mind off the frustrating knowledge there isn't anything to be done to help Eden." He smacked his fist in his palm and stared at her.

A worried crease marred her normally smooth brow. "I know. I didn't sleep at all last night. There has to be a way to stop the logging. The sight of the Dolores River packed with trees, Eden's trees, makes me sick . . ."

Here she was again, sharing her heart. Making him feel like they were soul mates. Since the walk in the woods, when she'd opened up to him about her dreams of being a hatmaker and asked for his advice regarding Lara, something between them had changed, at least for him. This was the moment he wanted to share with her.

When he cleared his throat, she glanced up, questions in her eyes.

"I'd like to tell you something, Lavinia, if I can?"

"Of course. What is it?"

He shifted his weight from one leg to the other, almost wishing he hadn't brought the subject up. Finally, he said, "Growing up, I loved the water. I'm a strong swimmer and used to love to explore river bottoms, lakes, the ocean—where didn't matter as long as the sun above beat down and I had time off from work." He kept his gaze on the far wall. "But now, the water frightens me. Crossing the bridge to your sister's mill takes every ounce of power I have."

He felt her pull back, shocked at his proclamation. She searched his face, but didn't speak. "Because of Shawn," he whispered. "And the way he was killed."

Her brows slowly pulled down. "Shawn is dead?"

He nodded. "He took my work shift when I failed to come home. I'd been carousing. Because of my debauched behavior, he was hit on the head by some crates and knocked into the water. If not for me, Shawn would be alive today." Suddenly he felt embarrassed. "I dream of a watery grave for myself sometimes and wake up in a sweat." He rubbed an unsteady hand across his mouth, wondering what had possessed him to say so much. "I guess I wanted to share with you since you shared your dreams with me."

Her gaze slowly searched his face. "I'm so sorry about your brother, Rhett. That's horrible." She reached out and took his hand, gently squeezing. "I'm sure you must miss him deeply. Still, the guilt for his death does not rest on your shoulders, as much as you like to think so. If nothing else, the last six months have taught me that. Unfortunate things happen in life, they just do. Look at my father pining for his daughters to return to him for eighteen long years, while we were led to believe he was a monster who didn't want us. I've had my days of feeling guilty for not searching him out anyway." She shook her head and dropped his hand. "We can't control our destiny. And we aren't responsible for ill-fated circumstances that befall us—or the ones we love." She went up on tiptoe and kissed his cheek. "Yes, I shared my dreams with you in the forest, and I'm happy I did. No one else knows . . ."

He gazed into her eyes. "Thank you," he whispered. Her pardon meant so much.

Untying the apron, he tossed the garment onto a table and grasped Lavinia's hand, reminding him of their night in the forest.

"Yeah, I'd like to go check on Clint," he said as they went through the door. "Nothing feels right until we get this clear-cutting travesty taken care of."

Dallas jumped to his feet and followed behind.

When Rhett and Lavinia walked into the doctor's office, the wounded sheriff looked up from a sitting position in his bed, a white bandage still wrapped around his head. A fluffy pillow was propped behind his back, and he looked comfortable. Henry sat at his side, the creases around his eyes and mouth deep and disturbing. He must not have had any more luck than Rhett in coming up with a solution. He stood when he saw Lavinia.

Dr. Gannon worked at his desk in the back of the room, and Dallas bounded over to greet the physician.

"Clint!" Lavinia exclaimed, rushing forward. "Thank God you're awake." She reached toward his bandage but didn't touch his head. "How do you feel?"

He chuckled and lifted a brow. "Like I'm back in the war."

"You're looking better," Rhett said, thankful Cash wasn't going to lose his father. Clint looked almost as good as new.

"And I'm feeling pretty darn popular. Cash and Nicole just left, and Mavis sat with me all night. At least, that's what the good doctor tells me. I wasn't yet awake. Henry is here, and now the two of you . . ."

Lavinia looked to Henry, who gestured to the chair. She shook her head.

"No good news here," Henry said. "I've sent out almost ten telegrams with no responses at all. As much as I don't want to admit the fact, that lumber outfit might be correct. By the time we get any answers, or any help from a higher source, they'll be ready to move on." His mouth tightened. "I've racked my brain and have gone through my resources three times over. I hate this as much as everybody else. I'm afraid that unless we can come up with someone of great influence, we're done."

Silence filled the room.

Dallas walked over and laid his head on Clint's bed.

It was a moment before Clint's eyes brightened and a smile tugged the corners of his lips. "I may be pulling at straws, but what about the former president of the United States? Would he do?"

Rhett couldn't tell if he was joking.

Clint's cheeks turned a dark scarlet.

Henry took a step closer to the bed. "What're you saying?"

"I'm saying, I know the former president. He was Colonel Rutherford B. Hayes when I briefly served with him in the war. I was just a kid. It was the battle at Cedar Creek in sixty-four. His horse took a bullet and went down. Colonel Hayes was knocked out. Just as the enemy was cresting the hill, I caught a riderless horse and helped him remount. Don't know if he'll remember me from Jack."

Henry's shoulders snapped back. "I'd remember if someone saved my life!"

"I certainly would," Rhett said, nodding at Lavinia.

Dr. Gannon stood and came close.

"Most importantly, did he ask your name, Clint?" Lavinia blurted.

"He asked, and I told him . . ."

Henry clapped his hands together. "This is great news! Even though he's been out of office now for only a few days, I'd imagine he'd have the ear of President Garfield, if anyone would. Perhaps Hayes will convince the new president to send the army, stop the cutting. I'll go get to work."

Lavinia reached out. "But the trees now . . ."

"The army could take weeks—and that's *if* President Garfield takes action," Rhett said. He paced to the window and stared out. The view of the school playground, and beyond that, his restaurant, Shawn's Café, stirred his insides.

He spun on his heel. "What if we could slow down the cutting until the army arrives?"

Dr. Gannon rubbed his chin. "If they arrive, you mean?"

"We're thinking positive, Doctor," Lavinia said. "What have you come up with, Rhett? That expression has me curious."

Rhett stared at the doctor. "That elixir you dosed Dallas with to make him fall asleep. What was that, laudanum? How much do you have?"

"Several cases, as a matter of fact. I brought many supplies with me. What do you have in mind?"

Rhett waved them closer and lowered his voice. "Clint's boy, Cash, is on friendly terms with several of those men over in the camp. We'll send him with a message—an invitation, actually, something especially for the lumberjacks. Once they get here for my grand opening, this is what we're going to do . . ."

CHAPTER FIFTY-ONE

~✦~

With excitement thrumming through her veins, Lavinia did another sweep around the dining room of Shawn's Café, anxious for six o'clock to arrive. She fingered her small purple hat, which looked nice with her purple-and-white apron, and stifled a satisfied grin. The invitation had been delivered three days ago, the same day they'd hatched the plan and sent a telegram to Washington. The lumbermen, having spent time in town, had no reason to be suspicious of Cash's invitation. Since their arrival in Eden, the same day Rhett had arrived, they'd seen his efforts taking place. The construction, the building. They knew he wasn't a hometown boy—no real stake in Eden *yet*. A pre–grand opening for the lumbermen was logical, as the invitation stated Rhett Laughlin, a San Francisco transplant, needed to try out his new recipes, and extended his offer to thirty-two lucky men. They would have to choose who, with a lottery, would get to attend. Cash had done a fabulous job selling the idea, explaining Rhett had little to do with the town, and that the sheriff, Cash's father, was no fool to try to take on such a large outfit. They wanted to live and let live until the day the lumberjacks moved on . . .

Oh, how sweet the victory will taste.

She gave a small laugh.

Rhett, wearing his apron like a master chef, came into the room, a long, stew-covered wooden spoon in his hand. Wide shoulders were covered with the new shirt from Emma, and his slacks fit him better than any glove she'd ever seen. His glorious brown hair, thick and shiny, made her fingers itch to touch. But it was his gorgeous blue eyes, sparkling with mischief, that made butterflies career inside her belly as if playing in a whirlwind.

"Did I hear something out here?"

"You did. And you might again, many times throughout the night. I'm so excited. I know your plan will work like clockwork. I just pray we have a response to Henry's telegram to President Hayes soon!"

The thought of walking over and surprising him with a long, sultry kiss crossed her mind— *several times.* Last night she'd dreamed of their first encounter, but the whole thing played out much differently after she'd thrown herself onto the bed and demanded his help. The memory of his warm fingers brushing her flesh, as he'd buttoned her dress, was a slow torture. And this time his gaze gobbled her up when he watched her step out of her robe and stand before him in her corset and stockings.

Had they really done that?

Her breath came quick. She needed to banish all thoughts of Rhett's touch, gaze, lips . . . None of that was possible.

She flushed and broke his gaze. "Only five more days until we sign the document that will make us partners in the Five Sisters," she blurted to remind herself that these thoughts torturing her were impossible.

"So true." With a swipe of his finger, he tasted the remnants on the spoon, taking his time to slowly lick a drop off his lips. "This is very good, Lavinia. I can't thank you enough for the lesson."

"It was my pleasure," she responded teasingly.

"And as soon as you sign the papers, you can tell your sisters of your apprenticeship with Mr. Hansberry. You'll soon be on your way."

She tipped her head, surprised he'd remembered Mr. Hansberry's name. Also at the unfamiliar silkiness in his tone. *But what about my other desires? The ones that grow stronger every day, especially now, drawn by your eyes?*

He came forward, so close she thought he planned to kiss her.

He held out the spoon. "Take a taste yourself." His warm gaze kept her transfixed. "See if it needs more salt."

Was he speaking about the stew? She couldn't pull her eyes from his. He'd hypnotized her. Everything around them fell away, and all she could see was Rhett's eyes and lips. She wanted him desperately. Still holding the spoon, he opened his arms.

Lavinia wrapped her arms around his middle, and his lips found hers. They were strong, and confident, and slowly cherished her mouth, sending a searing excitement racing to her toes. His free arm pulled her tighter, flat against his solid chest and strong body, making her feel tiny in his arms.

At the sound of footsteps on the boardwalk, they jerked apart.

Lara, dressed for work, stepped inside and stopped. Her eyes went wide.

Gathering her senses, Lavinia took the spoon from Rhett and tasted the stew with her fingertip, trying to keep her hands from shaking. "I don't think it needs a thing."

"Agreed."

Lara passed by as if she were the only one in the room and went into the kitchen. "We all ready?" she called from behind the wall.

Feeling Rhett's stare, Lavinia met his gaze once more. She didn't see any answers there.

"We are," she answered, feeling jittery. "Set to serve some delicious meals. Is Dr. Gannon ready?"

Lara peeked around the kitchen corner and smiled. "Absolutely."

Less than ten minutes later, thirty-two hungry men appeared at their door, washed up and wearing wide smiles.

"Welcome, men," Rhett said, opening the door wide so they could file inside. "Thank you for accepting my invitation."

Lavinia, still unsettled by Rhett's kiss, greeted them with a smile and walked them to the eight tables of four, set with red-checked tablecloths and white napkins. She and Lara would do the serving, and Rhett would appear to have done the cooking on his own. One of the fellows was the bearded lumberjack Lavinia didn't care for.

Rhett watched with pride. "Men, please get comfortable. I appreciate you taking the time to be my tasters at my preopening. That way, next week, for the townsfolk, I'll have worked out my kinks—if I have any." He glanced at her and Lara waiting by the kitchen door and smiled, the gesture warming her insides.

"What's she doing here?" the bearded lumberjack asked boldly. "She's your competition. Across the street."

"Lavinia was the first person I met when I moved to Eden. She's graciously offered to help out tonight. If you have a problem with that, you're free to leave anytime."

Although his words were strong, he smiled and

used a nice tone. The man mumbled under his breath and looked down at his hands.

"Don't make trouble, Jim," another lumberjack said. "We're honored we were invited. I, for one, am hungry enough to eat a whole steer. I hope you made plenty of food."

Rhett smiled and nodded. "Plenty." He signaled to the girls to take out the glasses of wine they had in the kitchen. The town had donated all the food, wine, and supplies, since this was a joint effort to save Eden's forests.

He met them in the kitchen. Taking the bottle of laudanum, he spiked one glass of wine, using the minimum amount the doctor had instructed. "Remember who you give this to," he whispered.

Lavinia nodded and placed the glasses on her tray. She and Lara delivered the wine as well as baskets stuffed with fresh bread from the oven and crocks of butter. The warm room, alive in the lamplight, felt festive. Lavinia prayed their plan would work. If it didn't, she didn't like to think of the repercussions.

She met Lara in the kitchen. "So far, so good," she said. Three extra-large kettles of thick stew simmered on the stove, the contents bubbling gently.

"I just glanced out the window," Lara said. "Your sisters are watching from your hotel room window. And Clint and Henry are on the hotel porch." Her smile was impish. "I'm glad I got to play a role."

"You're an employee," Rhett replied. "Of course you would." He glanced at Lavinia and then back at the stew he was stirring. "This ready? Take a look."

Lavinia touched his arm for support. "I think it was ready an hour ago. I say we get down to business. They're clamoring for food."

He raised a brow. "Is our man sleepy yet?"

"Difficult to tell. Seems they're all excited for a night away from the camp. And they're awfully large. Perhaps we should have dosed the wine more heavily."

Rhett rubbed his chin. "And now with the glasses on the tables, too late to do anything about it."

"Maybe, maybe not." Lavinia bolted out the door with the wine bottle.

"Who would like more wine?" she asked, liberally filling the men's glasses. When she came to the empty glass of tainted wine, she withdrew the bottle before pouring a drop. "I'm sorry, that glass has a smudge along the lip. Let me get you a new one." Before the man could protest, she'd grasped the glass and hurried away.

"You're talented," Rhett said softly. "I'll have to remember that." With his hand covering most of the bottle, he poured in more laudanum, being careful with the amount. "That should do it. And if not . . ." He shrugged. "We'll have to think of something else. Doc wouldn't help us on this part, just let us raid his supplies. We can't give them so much they kick the bucket. You take that out and I'll dish up the stew and ipecac."

Lavinia topped the goblet off with wine and delivered it to the table. Only the one man had been given laudanum. And another one would get ipecac. "Supper is coming right up, fellas. Thanks for being patient."

After everyone was served, the three stood in the kitchen doorway watching. Spoons clanked as the men shoveled in their meals as fast as they could.

"Be sure to save room for dried-apple pie," Rhett said over the clatter.

"Two o'clock," Lavinia whispered. "He's nodding off."

"Hey, what's wrong?" the man beside Lavinia's victim said. "Sam?"

The man's head hit the table with a thud, directly beside his bowl. The other three at his table jumped up in surprise.

Rhett, Lavinia, and Lara hurried over.

Rhett looked around, alarmed. "What happened?"

"Don't know. He just passed out."

"Oh!" Lara's eyes were large. She took a step back. "Has he been sick?" She said the lines she'd been given with flourish.

The bearded man named Jim narrowed his eyes at Lavinia. "Did you put something in our food?"

"What a thing to ask!" Rhett answered, his voice hard and steely. "I'm trying to start a restaurant here. Look around. Is anyone else sick?"

"Should we take him to the doctor's?" Lara asked, wide-eyed.

"Maybe he's just tired," Lavinia replied. "We could lay him on the floor."

Rhett took a small step back as well. "What if he's got something?" He looked up at the gaping men.

Jim scowled. "He was fine two seconds ago."

"Maybe he *should* go to the doctor's," his table partner said. "He's a good man. Has a wife and boy. Regularly sends his pay home. I'd not want him to perish."

Lavinia pointed. "The place is one street over. Easy to find."

The occupants at his table carried him away.

The other man who'd been served the ipecac chose that moment to groan loudly. His spoon clattered to the table one moment before he gripped his stomach. Wide-eyed, he looked around in a panic. "I'm gonna be sick!"

The room erupted with worried voices.

Rhett ran over and handed him a glass of laudanum-dosed water. "Drink the whole thing. Maybe it'll help settle your stomach."

The man complied.

Rhett took the empty glass. "You better get to the doctor's too." He needn't have spoken, because the lumberjack was already stumbling out the door, followed by a few friends. "We don't know what we're dealing with . . ."

Jim stepped up threateningly. "If you've done something to these men, you'll pay!" He glanced at his own bowl on his table.

Others wiped their mouths and pushed away from their seats, as if waiting for the next victim to fall.

With a hand to his forehead, Rhett looked dubious. "I guess I'm getting off on the wrong foot here. I hope this isn't the end for me and my restaurant." He turned and gave Lavinia a secretive wink. "Any way you men could keep this under your hats? I'm already battling the rumor that this place is haunted. I'd not like to add fuel to the fire . . ."

Men rushed for the door faster than fleas off a drowning cat.

"I better go check on those men," Rhett said to the few left behind. "I feel responsible since they were in my establishment when their ailments hit. You're welcome to partake in dessert, if you'd like," he said to the near-empty room.

"I'm staying in town with the men," Jim said in the doorway. "The others can tell the foreman what's up." He narrowed his gaze at Rhett and the two women. "I don't put nothin' past you . . ."

CHAPTER FIFTY-TWO

Pounding on Dr. Gannon's locked infirmary door brought Rhett around. He'd stayed all night with the physician, looking after the two sleeping lumberjacks. After all, the crazy idea had been his, and as the hours passed, the possibility of the plan actually working felt more and more far-fetched. Lavinia had begged to stay, to help, but that wasn't going to happen as long as he had breath to send her away. He remembered the kiss, and their walk, and the fact that she'd tell her sisters about her plans in only four more days. After that, her leaving would be set in stone. Until then, anything was possible, not that he deserved a chance at love . . .

He wiped a hand across his gritty face and nodded to Jeremy Gannon. The two had become fast friends.

"Open up!"

The bearded lumberjack called Jim.

As Gannon went to unlock the door, Rhett glanced down at their two victims, not yet awake from their long sleep. The night before, after the second man had emptied his gut into a bowl, the good doctor had helped him onto a cot by his sleeping friend. On a third cot, Cash lay, feigning sleep. At the side of his bed was a vomit bowl containing a mixture of rotten eggs and other offensive foodstuffs they'd collected from the butcher.

Jim barreled into the room, stopped when he spotted Cash's form in the dark corner, and then went straight to his two comrades' beds. He reached out and was about to touch the first man's shoulder, but Rhett caught his arm.

"I wouldn't do that if I were you," Rhett warned. "Not yet, anyway. Not until we know what we're dealing with here."

"Why?" he barked.

Very carefully, with only the barest touch, Rhett peeled back the light sheet covering the fellow, and then pulled down the neckline of the man's undershirt. A sprinkling of black dots showed on his chest. He quickly replaced the fabric.

Jim stepped back several feet. "What's that?"

Dr. Gannon shrugged. "I've never seen the like, but I can't say it's not contagious." He felt one sleeping lumberjack's forehead and then made a show of thoroughly washing his hands. He briskly rubbed them dry. "We'll know more in the next few days. Have you spoken with any of the other fellows yet?"

Jim shook his head.

"How do *you* feel?" Rhett asked, rubbing his stomach. "I'm not feeling too great myself. Come here and look at this." He lifted a lantern and went to the far wall, where Cash slept in the shadows.

Jim stayed where he was, watching from his side of the room.

Lowering the lantern, the light illuminated Cash's face—they'd darkened his skin with red dye and then marked his neck and lower face with good-size black splotches, much larger and darker than on the lumberjack's chest.

Dr. Gannon straightened. "I believe this case is a couple days farther along."

Jim began to shake. "But that boy's been out to the lumber camp. He's talked with everyone." His head jerked around to the doctor. "What can we do?" he asked in a quivering voice.

"I'm sorry, I really don't know, but I'd warn everybody to lie low until we know the threat has passed. Don't tax your constitutions. Drink lots—"

"Our what?"

"The balance inside your body that keeps you healthy. Just rest for a good week . . . No work at all."

"I saw something like this in San Francisco," Rhett whispered in a tortured voice. "Ten years back. Wiped out the whole dock. The doctors there called it the sleeping speckled plague." He shook his head and walked to the window, a low moan slipping from his lips. "The city looked like a ghost town for months afterward . . ."

He didn't have to say another word before Jim was backing out the door. He turned and raced toward the path that led to the meadow, and as soon as he was out of sight, Gannon, Rhett, and Cash burst into laughter.

CHAPTER FIFTY-THREE

~~~

"C ongratulations, everyone," Henry chortled, popping the top to an expensive bottle of champagne and filling eight glasses on his office desk. Blake and Clint, both wearing wide smiles, passed Lavinia and her sisters each a glass. Without another word they softly touched together their glasses, the clink a beautiful sound to Lavinia. So much had happened in six months. Life had gone from a day-to-day existence to living fully each breath she took.

"To John's daughters. Brave and filled with fortitude. Your six months has passed without incident, or anyone leaving, and as soon as you sign this contract, you'll be equal owners in the Five Sisters Ranch! And on top of that, we've successfully shut down the illicit cutting of Eden's trees." He smiled at Clint and raised his glass. "Thank God President Hayes remembered you. He lost no time in dispatching a battalion of soldiers from Fort Garland, only two hundred and forty miles away, the day the telegram arrived in his hands. Eight days later, the loggers have been apprehended. Congratulations on many jobs well done! You've saved Eden's forests. John Brinkman would be very proud of you all."

Lavinia stood shoulder to shoulder with her sisters, oldest to youngest. Blake flanked Belle. Clint stood apart by the window, but Lavinia didn't miss all the tender looks he and Mavis had exchanged within only the last few minutes, making her ache for Rhett. She'd have liked him to be permitted to be here, but today was a family affair, though it included the sheriff too, since he'd been as close as family to their father.

In a moment of quiet auspiciousness, Mavis took the pen Henry offered and signed her name. She handed the pen to Belle, who carefully dipped the tip in the inkwell and put her new name on the line below. As soon as Emma signed the contract, she handed the pen to Lavinia, who judiciously wrote out her name, wanting her signature to be pretty. She placed the pen in Katie's hand. Blake signed last.

Henry raised his glass once more and then downed the whole thing. "It's done," he said proudly. He immediately plopped into his chair and rubbed his forehead, bringing a round of laughs. He glanced up. "From the inception, I'd thought the idea far-fetched, but your father never wavered. His faith was firm, and now I can rest easy."

With a cheer, everyone drained their glasses.

Henry stood. "And here's to that ingenious

young man Rhett Laughlin, who hatched the plan to slow the loggers. If not for him, eight days could have been disastrous. As it was, those fellas were afraid to lift a finger for fear of coming down with the sleeping speckled plague."

Clint joined in with a chuckle. "I was out on the Dolores this morning. It's quiet and lonely, but a good reminder for us to protect what we have. Just because something is strong doesn't mean it can't be lost." His gaze touched Mavis. "Those men had families to think of. They wouldn't risk their lives for a greedy foreman."

Henry's office had never felt so confining before. Was that because Lavinia intended to tell her sisters about her plans to return to Philadelphia? She imagined they'd be delighted, but Belle had, more times than not, stated how happy she was that they all lived together in Eden, as their father had hoped. Mavis was content here, as was Emma. Katie had the look of love in her eyes, and Lavinia figured she'd share her own news when the time was right. Lavinia adored Eden as much as any of her sisters, but she also had a dream. *What about Rhett? Where does he fit into my life?* That thought was silly. He had become her dearest friend, her confidant. The notion sent a painful slice through her heart. When his lips had been on hers, he'd felt like a lot more than that. She kicked away a warm surge of desire, as well as her confusing thoughts . . .

"Yes, congratulations, everyone," she said. "The opposition felt impenetrable, but they were no match for us!"

Opening another bottle, Henry refilled their glasses.

They clinked glasses again, and Lavinia took a sip, the bubbles going straight up her nose. Her courage was waning. She needed to act quickly. "Excuse me, I have an announcement," she said.

Belle's and Katie's blue gazes anchored onto her face, as did Emma's emerald. Mavis, smartly dressed and wearing one of Lavinia's creations on her head, responded, "Yes, Lavinia? Go ahead, we're all listening."

She blinked. Would everyone's smiles disappear as soon as the words were out of her mouth? Why did it feel like she had a five-pound horseshoe stuck in her throat?

"Wait!" Emma sang out, excitement dancing in her eyes. "Before you go on, Lavinia, you must know both tulip-shaped hats you have on consignment sold! This morning! Sisters came into the store and had to have them. I knew you'd be excited to hear. They're opening a shop of their own close to Mademoiselle de Sells. I guess Rhett is right. More men *and* more women! Congratulations, Lavinia. As soon as you can, I'd like you to design a few more for the shop."

Jolted, Lavinia digested Emma's words. At the looks of pride and sincere love on everyone's faces, any thought that she was invisible, or didn't belong in Eden, fled out the window. How absurd! She'd been silly thinking that, utterly silly. Leaving Eden now felt like a prison sentence, not a dream come true.

I'm allowed to change my mind. Circumstances have changed. I've changed. And not just because of Rhett either. The first moment I have I'll telegraph Mr. Hansberry my apologies. My future lies here in Eden.

"Go on, sister-in-law—and now partner," Blake joked. "We're all listening. What's the big news?"

What should she tell them? Suddenly, an idea struck her. One that had been waiting for her to embrace all along. She took a deep breath. "Lara has an idea she's asked me to share. I believe it has merit. She thinks we should make the Five Sisters into a travel destination where Easterners come to get a taste of the West. The clean air and mountain walks are healthy. She says one ranch, and perhaps more by now, have already opened their homes. Money is being made hand over fist." Everyone stared at her blankly. "It might be a great way to make our mark, a different mark, on the country."

Blake broke out laughing, as if the idea were absurd.

Henry looked as if he couldn't contain a smile of disbelief.

Clint's eyebrow had crested so high, his thoughts were obvious.

But Belle, and the rest of her sisters, had a dreamy light in their eyes. *Men and women really do think differently.*

"We'd fix up the old ranch house—not too much, mind you—and that's where guests would pay to stay," she rushed on. "We'd take them on trail rides, campouts, and maybe even a cattle drive."

Blake stepped forward, his palms raised. "Just hold on there! The Five Sisters is a working cattle ranch, and that's what she'll stay."

"Says who?" Belle asked softly. "Don't forget, we're fifty-fifty partners now."

Blake cut a look to Henry, who shrugged.

Mavis sipped from her glass and then sent Lavinia a smile. "I believe we have the topic for our first official ranch meeting next month."

Blake groaned loudly. "And so it begins . . ."

CHAPTER FIFTY-FOUR

⚬⚬⚬

The morning of Lavinia's birthday arrived quickly, but not so fast that Lavinia didn't notice Rhett's absence or miss his company. The prior week, with plotting the lumberjacks' preopening supper, convincing them the whole lumber operation might be at risk of falling ill, and then making sure they took the warning to heart, was a whirlwind of excitement. The entire affair had been so much fun. She and Rhett had schemed about every aspect of the plot. He was smart, funny—and *charming* too. Actually, the most fascinating man she'd ever known. But for the last six days, including the contract signing, he'd stayed locked up in his restaurant as if he were avoiding her on purpose. Or maybe he was afraid she'd give *him* the sleeping speckled plague! She supposed he was practicing his menu, but still, that felt suspicious. Aromas floated over now and then, but she'd not gone to investigate. In truth, she felt more than a little hurt. But then she'd remember the kiss, the one she'd initiated by stepping willingly into his open arms. Maybe he was putting space between them so parting wouldn't be so difficult when the time arrived. If he would ever show his face, she could tell him otherwise . . .

Did everyone in love feel so confused and agitated?

In love! That was impossible. She and Rhett were friends, nothing more.

She shrugged off her irritation as she drove the buggy toward the ranch. The weather was nice, mild. A cloud of sparrows swept down toward her horse's head and then playfully darted away. Later tonight, her sisters were throwing a small gathering for her birthday at her café. *I'm twenty today, but I don't feel a bit different.* Quite possibly, she'd receive a letter from their father like Belle had last year. The prospect was exciting. When questioned, though, Henry was evasive and wouldn't let on. She should prepare herself if it wasn't to be. Maybe, toward the end, Father had been too weak to write to them all.

Approaching a dip in the road where the lane to the orphanage branched off, Lavinia slowed the buggy. Taking this part of the road too fast was hard on the buggy's undercarriage. The gelding slowed to a walk, and she maneuvered him through the less rugged area.

"Lavinia!"

She snapped her head around.

Sister Agatha ran toward her, waving her hands. The young nun's flushed face and disheveled brown habit robbed Lavinia of breath. A thousand horrible possibilities flashed through her mind.

"What is it? What's wrong?" Lavinia called when Sister Agatha was within hearing distance. Fear for the nuns and children sparked up her spine.

"It's Jackie! We can't find her. We returned from a picnic at the river, and she's nowhere to be found. Sister Cecilia is doing another search of the grounds and house, but she asked me to go back to the river and hunt for her there."

Lavinia reached out and helped the nun into the buggy. The gelding, who'd been headed to home and hay, was reluctant to turn around, but Lavinia got the job done. Jackie's dear face, her red curls, and the way she always made Lavinia feel so special moved through her mind. "Where?" she asked once they were headed back. "What direction on the river?" She slapped the lines across the gelding's back. The rig took off.

"Just down from the bridge that crosses Aspen Creek to the lumber mill," Sister Agatha shouted. "Sister Cecilia likes the clearing by the alders. Do you know the spot?"

"I do. Hold on. I don't like to think of Jackie alone by the water, or in that part of the town. It's close to the Old Spanish Trail that comes up from Santa Fe. Where strangers arrive."

She gave the nun a meaningful look and coaxed the horse into a canter, a gait that was normally too fast for the buggy. They careened around the corner at the sheriff's office and kept moving. If Clint hadn't so recently suffered a head injury, she'd stop for his help, but then she realized he probably wasn't even there.

She didn't have a second to waste.

Rhett stepped out his back door, the charred remains of a chocolate cake crusted on the side of the pan and ready to be dumped. He'd gotten a craving for something sweet.

Dallas raced out the door, barked once, and bounded away.

Rhett looked up. Lavinia, with one of the nuns clutching the buggy seat beside her, flew by his place in a cloud of dust, traveling much too fast for safety.

"Hey! Lavinia!"

Too late, she was gone. He watched the buggy speed around the next corner and head down the road toward the Spanish Trail Cantina. Dropping the whole pan into the trash can, he bolted away, running across town, intending to cut her off. Whatever was happening wasn't good.

Darting through the area between the boarding-house and the livery, Rhett was just in time to see dust in the road where the buggy had passed but was already out of sight, with Dallas hot on their heels. Rhett dug deeper for energy and raced on. Up ahead, the haphazardly parked buggy came into sight. But there was no sign of Lavinia or the nun. What were they up to?

He stopped beside the horse, pain cramping his side. Since their kiss a week ago, he'd been mightily mixed-up. Why did he have to have feelings for a woman who was determined to leave? Just as well. He was still paying his debt to Shawn. That would never be over.

"Lavinia!" he called, glancing around. The horse pranced in his harness, the brake keeping him from running off. "Lavinia, where are you?"

The sound of the rushing river entered his thoughts. His breathing picked up. His gaze slid to the water's edge. A clearing with soft green grass had probably drawn the women, but the riverbank was right there. Memories of Shawn, in his watery grave, made his feet heavy and his lungs catch fire. Just the thought of being on the shoreline had his heart thundering in his chest. He clenched his fists to keep them from shaking.

"Lavinia! Can you hear me?" Furious at himself for his cowardice, he took one tiny step forward, and then another. He had to get down by the water, where the brush, trees, and rocks hid what was beyond.

The nun who had been in the buggy ran forward

from the brush line. Her habit was soaked up to her knees, a panic-stricken glint in her eyes.

"What's happened?" he asked. "I saw you race by." The woman's face was awash with grief.

"We've lost one of our girls. Lavinia is searching by the water's edge, past the scrub oaks and bushes, places where a little girl could hide, or get lost. I'm retracing our steps to the hanging footbridge past the mill, in case she's gone that way."

This was a nightmare he'd rather not be living. "I'll go back the way you've come and take up the search."

"Bless you, sir."

Here the river turned and started away from the trail. The channel narrowed, and the current grew swift. The roaring of the water kept his thoughts scattered.

A strange prickling on the back of his neck made him turn his head and glance farther down-stream.

Lavinia crawled on a narrow ledge of a rock surface that dropped twenty feet to the rushing water. A young girl, with hair the color of tomato sauce, was before her, crouched on the ledge, unable to go any farther. Her face was contorted and wet from tears.

Lavinia inched along on hands and knees.

Rhett sucked in a breath but kept walking, fearing that she'd somehow slip and fall. She'd stripped her skirt away and only wore panta-loons—once again.

Dallas bounded out of the brush and barked.

Her head jerked up a moment before she tumbled into the icy cold.

CHAPTER FIFTY-FIVE

Right before Rhett's eyes, Lavinia disappeared. Without missing a beat, he ran forward and dived headfirst into the dark blue where the water looked deepest. He pulled with his arms against the freezing cold that stung his face. He mentally battled the pounding, black fear scorching his mind and screaming for him to swim to the surface before it was too late. His boots were like anchors, snagging him back, slowing his progress, and trying to sink him to the riverbed.

Beneath the surface, he searched through the murky gray, trying to see. His hand struck a boulder, which then battered his side. With great effort, he flipped around feet first; the current was an iron grip. *Where is she? Where's Lavinia? Has she already drowned? Will she meet the same fate as Shawn?* Rhett forcefully shoved the thoughts away. *I won't let that happen.*

Diving below, he tried to see the bottom, but the water was too fast, too deep. He swam for as long as he could, then broke the surface, gasping for air.

A fork split the water ahead. Which way to go? He stopped kicking and put out his hands, letting the current take him. He shot down the left side, praying like never before that he'd gone the correct way. Where was she? He had to find her soon.

A sound caught his ear.

He turned.

On a steep bank, Lavinia grasped a root as she fought the current. Just beyond her, the water disappeared over the edge of the riverbed. A waterfall.

"Lavinia!"

Her shoulder tensed, but she didn't look around.

Diving under, Rhett kicked forward. Reaching her side, he grasped the root as well but felt their anchor wobble. Their combined weight would soon pull their tether away from the bank, sending them both over the falls.

"Hang on!"

Lavinia gasped. "The branch! It's pulling away."

He could barely understand what she said through her clacking teeth. Her purple lips looked painful, and a red splotch on her temple made him think she'd struck her head. He was astonished and thankful she was still alive. But he understood the danger; he could feel their lifeline easing away. She was right; they had only a few more seconds. His gaze cut back and forth, desperate to find a way out, something else to grasp, a possible—

"Rhett!"

The branch released.

Sucking in a deep breath, he lunged forward and wrapped her in his arms. If they were going over the falls, they'd go over together.

It felt like they fell for an eternity. Her chest pressed against his was warm, and he could feel the strong beat of her heart amid her shivers. They hit and sank several feet. His back struck something hard, knocking his breath from his lungs. Pain coursed through his body. He kicked with everything he had, bringing them to the surface.

With his arm locked around her middle, he dragged her to the edge. They flopped onto the dank-smelling sand, too exhausted to speak.

After a few moments, he raised up onto an elbow. "Lavinia," he said softly, through his own rattling teeth. He wiped the excess water from his face and pushed his hair out of his eyes. "Lavinia, please, open your eyes." Placing his palm on her cheek, he stared into her face, gasping deep breaths of air.

This couldn't be happening again!

Not to Lavinia.

"Open your eyes, honey," he whispered. Fear flashed through his body. Had she sustained a hit on the head or snapped her neck?

"Uhhh . . ."

Groggily, Lavinia's soaked eyelashes fluttered, and then she opened her eyes, the sun-colored flecks with tiny sparkles of emerald making her light brown eyes look almost green. Their incredible beauty was something he'd never forget.

"Rhett? Is that you?"

Relief washed away his fear. "Who else would be saving your life?" he said next to her lips, unable to stop himself from giving her a soft kiss. "I thought I'd lost you." He ran his hand over her head, feeling for lumps, and then down her shoulders and arms. Seemed the splash of red on her temple was her only injury.

"Wh-what happened?"

"We went over the falls." *You in my arms. Heart to heart.* He lifted his head and tried to look over his shoulder, but the pain in his side was too great. He stifled a groan. "And almost went over another one right over there. How do you feel? I believe you hit your temple on something. Do you remember?"

She lifted her arm and felt around her head with blue fingers. "N-no. I only remember swimming for my life, the ice-cold water, and a devastating sadness that I wouldn't see any of the people I love ever again." Struggling, she suddenly tried to sit up. "Jackie! On the ledge!"

"We'll get to her next."

"There was a bear. And she ran to get away. She didn't know the ledge was a dead end and was too frightened to try to come back."

"We've only been gone minutes. I'm sure she's still there."

Her eyes went wide. "But, Rhett, your fear of the water? How—"

"Some things are more powerful than fear."

He grimaced as she squeezed him tighter. "Can you walk?" he asked, changing the subject.

With a crashing sound, Dallas lunged through the bushes and immediately pushed his cold nose into their faces, whining loudly. His happiness at finding them brought a sentimental lump to Rhett's throat.

"You and me both, boy," Rhett said. "You and me both."

CHAPTER FIFTY-SIX

Now dry and warm after a long, hot bath, Lavinia reclined on her hotel room bed, fading in and out of slumber. Her hair smelled of lilac and her skin was soft and creamed. For the last half hour, she'd been gazing out her window at the town, thankful to be alive.

If Rhett hadn't shown up, she could very well be dead, having drowned or gone over the second waterfall, breaking her neck in the process. A multitude of emotions swirled inside. She felt like the whirlpool just off the side of the suspension bridge. When she'd been carried along by the swift current, all she'd wanted was another day with her sisters. The only thought that had outweighed that was seeing Rhett's face, hearing his voice, or seeing him smiling before her right after they'd kissed. There was no Mr. Hansberry, or thoughts of Philadelphia. Just Eden and the ones she loved.

Imagine. Rhett dived into that water for me! Facing his most ardent fear! I'm humbled, and more . . .

Knock. Knock. Knock.

She straightened on the bed and sat farther up on the pillow. "Yes?"

"It's Lara."

Lavinia smiled. They'd made up. All was good. "Please, come in."

"I'm sorry to intrude on you after your harrowing ordeal," Lara said, stepping inside. She closed the door and clasped her hands. "But I just couldn't keep this to myself a day longer. Not with you almost . . ." Her face darkened with emotion. "It wouldn't be right."

Knock. Knock. Knock.

"Lavinia, it's Mavis. Are you decent?"

"Yes, come in," Lavinia called. The contrite look on Lara's face knotted her stomach.

Mavis stepped inside but pulled up when she saw Lara. "I'm sorry. I didn't know you had company."

"Don't be silly." Lara twisted her hands. "I'm hardly company. I have something to say to Lavinia, and I'm glad you're here, Mavis. I haven't been completely honest with any of you. This pain in my heart is too heavy to carry a day longer. I must confess, come what may."

Mavis exchanged a long glance with Lavinia.

"You're responsible for the articles?" Lavinia whispered, praying it wasn't true.

Lara nodded her bowed head. "In a way . . . yes."

Lavinia stood and went to Lara's side. Mavis was already there.

Lavinia touched her arm. "In a way? I don't understand."

A deep sigh escaped Lara. "I wanted to tell you when you came to me the first night, but I was deeply hurt that you'd think me capable of such a treachery. Then my hurt changed to anger."

"Tell us," Mavis whispered.

"I was running late for my music lesson. I came from the library with my diary, intending to put the small book safely away in my bedroom, as I've done for years. But my father appeared. I set my things on the side table as we spoke and promptly was involved with other things. Running quite late now, I scooped up my belongings and rushed down the street. After my lesson, I had several other errands to attend to before returning home. The next evening, when I went to retrieve my diary, I was horrified to remember I'd not properly put it away. I have no idea if it was lost or taken. I retraced my steps ten times, to no avail." She looked up with watery eyes. "I can't tell you how sorry I am. And for not admitting my responsibility right away." She sniffed and wiped her nose with her handkerchief. "Yesterday I received a post from Mother. Whoever had my property has sent it back to our home, no return address . . ."

Stunned, Lavinia didn't know how to respond.

The loss had been an accident, but Lara should have said as much at the time. "Do you think your older brother, Calvin, could be Harlow Lennington, the San Francisco author?"

A tear slipped from Lara's eye. "The thought has crossed my mind. He was home for a visit at the time. I felt so horrible when you came to forgive me. Again, I wanted to tell you, but I was frightened you wouldn't understand. And that the whole mess would begin all over."

"At last the mystery is solved—at least partially," Lavinia said. Since she'd almost died today, Lara's withholding the truth at an emotional time didn't feel all that horrible an infraction. "Your love of writing has helped Eden grow, Lara. That's how we should look at this, and nothing more." *And it brought me Rhett. For that, I'd shout all my past silliness to the moon.*

When Lavinia smiled, a mountain of sorrow fled Lara's face.

Mavis nodded. "Thank you for telling us the truth."

Lara blinked away more tears.

"With that taken care of, I come bearing gifts." Mavis stepped forward, a bright smile on her face. "It's your turn, Lavinia." She took an envelope from her reticule and held it out.

The moment Lavinia saw the post, she knew it was her birthday letter. *Oh, Father. Thank you.* She took the letter with shaky fingers.

Mavis stepped forward and gave her a warm hug. "We're so blessed Father thought to write to each of us." She looked at the letter quivering in Lavinia's hands. "Well, aren't you going to open it?"

She shook her head. "Not until I dress and walk up to my meadow. That seems like the perfect place to speak with Father in person."

CHAPTER FIFTY-SEVEN

Lavinia dressed, slipped on a yellow bonnet whose colorful ribbons would make any birthday girl happy, and left the hotel, keeping her gaze trained far away from Shawn's Café. She wanted to read Father's letter with an open heart, not one pining for Rhett.

Walking with determination, she passed the stage office, noticing the arrival times on the blackboard. She turned at the drugstore and took the path slowly, seeing the manure left behind from their ride out to the lumber camp. So much had happened. She and Rhett had kissed, and, more, he'd saved her life.

Her heart pinched. Maybe after she read the letter, she'd look for flowers, see if any of April's had bloomed yet. Something pretty for the restaurant, she thought, her heart warming. Slowing, she paused on the trail and turned, taking in the view of Eden below.

My home. Now and forever. The thought gave her a tremendous amount of happiness. She'd been mixed-up, but now her vision of her future was razor sharp. And for that, she was grateful.

At the crest, she pulled up. Rhett was sitting beside the watcher with Dallas asleep at his side. He stood. Was he thinking about Shawn? Or someone else entirely? She came forward without an invitation. "How're your ribs?"

He tipped his head. "Sore. And your head? How do you feel?"

"Better, thank you." Was the kiss forever on his mind as well? The feel of his lips on hers? Or the plunge in the freezing torrent? He'd faced his most powerful fear for her. That fact was not lost when she gazed in his eyes.

"I saw you coming up the path," he said, as if he wanted to disclose he'd been observing her.

She smiled. So cautious. "You and the watcher, huh? What about Dallas?"

He looked at the dog, who hadn't budged a muscle. "No, not him. I think he's worn-out. And I don't blame him." Rhett shook his head. "This is a birthday you'll not soon forget. Have you told your family?"

So much had happened in these past few days that she was startled to realize she hadn't told him she'd decided to stay. She shook her head, pulled the letter from her pocket, and held up the envelope. "Not yet. I've received my birthday letter from my late father, though." A smile worked its way out. "I'm excited."

"I've heard about the letters. Pretty amazing

when you consider . . ." He pointed to the area where she always hunted for blossoms. "Go ahead and read it. Don't let me intrude. By the way, I like your bonnet." A true smile finally appeared on his face, although his eyes stayed somber.

Turning, she hurried off, wondering if Rhett got light-headed when he spoke with her, like she did with him. Seated on a large speckled boulder next to where the wild alyssum grew, she opened the envelope with trembling fingers. Thoughts of her dying father, writing when he was so weak, brought a lump to her throat. She'd been given so much by coming to Eden. She took a deep breath and began to read.

My dearest Lavinia,
Happy birthday, sweet child. I remember the day of your birth as if it were yesterday. How time plays tricks on us. Can you really be twenty years old? That does not seem possible. Without exception, I've loved you deeply every day we've been apart. By now, if you're in Eden as you read this letter, it means you've stayed. Inherited the ranch. That makes me happy. Both of your parents had pioneer blood. You're not meant to waste your life away in a city where nobody knows you.

Lavinia discreetly wiped away a tear that had escaped her eye.

On this day twenty years ago, I'd been breaking colts. The day was chilly and I remember being exceedingly hungry. After I washed up and came in for supper, I noticed your mother moving more slowly than usual. Mavis was playing with Belle and Emma, three little moppets—my children. Your mother finally admitted labor had begun. I was perturbed she hadn't alerted me sooner, because I needed to ride for the doctor but didn't want to leave her alone. The midwife who delivered your sisters had died the month before. As much as I pleaded for her to let me get Dr. Dodge, she was adamant in her refusal. The orphanage was only two miles away. I prayed someone there would know what to do. I returned with Sister Cecilia.

In wonder, Lavinia recalled all the time she'd spent at the orphanage with Sister Cecilia. *Imagine that.* The soft-spoken nun had never let on. Lavinia looked up from the wavering lines to gaze at Rhett's broad back where he stood overlooking the town. With his hands in his pockets and boots planted wide apart, he resembled a pirate. The meadow's ever-present breeze moved the grass as well as his hair. What was he thinking? His posture seemed so sad. Lost, almost . . .

You were about five pounds at birth, delicate, with porcelain skin. Once a few days had passed, always smiling. Celeste and I had to be careful because your sisters believed you a doll, a plaything. With all the attention you received, you grew like a weed the first two months, and then you began to have problems with your ears. Any hint of wind would bring on an earache. You'd pull on your ears and cry most piteously, upsetting us greatly. Your mother would cry with you. She tried herbal teas, homemade tinctures, powders from the mercantile, hot oil, but nothing helped. At her wit's end, and to keep the wind from starting any more problems for her precious girl, she took to keeping a warm, knitted cap on you at all times that covered your ears. Morning or night didn't matter. You even wore it to bed. As you grew, your cap turned into bonnets, or scarves, always something. You were such a good baby, and never pulled them off, as if you knew they were important. And it worked. Your troubles eased away. I used to call you Little Bo Peep, for your wide-brimmed hat resembled the illustrations in a book of nursery rhymes.

Lavinia gasped. The papers fluttered as she dropped her hands into her lap and gazed off into the distance. *My dreams of becoming a milliner actually began here in Eden! Because of all the caps Mother made. How sweet. I'm so thankful I've come to the decision to stay. And now I have confirmation my thinking is right.*

She gazed down lovingly at her father's script, her heart swelling as she read his salutation. How much they'd lost. A warm tingle of awareness began in her breast and moved into her chest and throughout her body and mind. When something you've believed in for your whole life is upended, the world tilts. Placing the cherished correspondence back into the envelope, she stood and started for Rhett. She'd been shy about telling him she'd changed her mind. What would he think of her? Wishy-washy? A silly woman? And now she couldn't wait. Halfway there, she shouted his name, and then started to run.

He turned just in time to catch her when she flung herself into his arms.

"What?"

"I'm so happy. So happy! My life, everything I've ever thought has been focused on something

I thought I wanted. But I was wrong. My heart belongs here! And so does my millinery business. I don't need Philadelphia when I have this." She pulled away for one moment to gaze down at the town, and then up into his face, so close to hers. "And you. I wasn't invisible, as I'd thought. Not at all. And here is where I'll make my mark, here in Eden."

Despite his bound ribs, he tightened his hold around her. "Why? What's happened?"

"It doesn't matter. All that matters is I'm not leaving! I'm staying in Eden. I hope that makes you happy."

His mouth found hers. They kissed, sweetly, hungrily, madly. Nothing had ever felt this right.

He pulled away, but only slightly. "More than you could ever know. But . . . are you sure?"

She tenderly cupped his cheek as she memorized his face. "I've never been surer of anything in my life. You make my heart sing, Rhetten Laughlin. Why would I ever want to be anywhere else?"

CHAPTER FIFTY-EIGHT

F our days later, with a lively spring in her step,
Lavinia made her way from the livery, where
she'd just dropped off a lunch basket for Maverick
and Mavis, toward the new lumber office located
in the touristy area of Eden and close to
Mademoiselle de Sells. With Rhett and Cash on
the job, the interior of the building shell was completed quickly. Half for Katie and the mill and
the other half for Rhett Laughlin Construction.
With all the people migrating to town, the lumber
business was booming. All that was really needed
was someone with the knowledge of what to do
with the lumber. Rhett was that man.

She switched the second heavy basket from one
arm to the other as she entered the cobblestoned
area, smiling at the new fabric store, the new
miners' supply, and the new ladies' fashions
boutique. A little competition for Emma, and a
new outlet for her bonnets.

Smiling, as she did every time she saw the two
shingles, Lavinia marveled at how her life had
changed. With her hand on the knob, she stepped
inside.

Katie looked up from her desk, a pretty bow in her hair and a pencil behind her ear.

"Lunch has arrived," Lavinia announced, disappointed Rhett wasn't around.

The room was split down the middle with a half-wall divider. Each space had a desk, a large flat counter to lay out plans, and a window on opposite walls. Howard, Katie's foreman, retained his office at the mill, where he kept an eye on production, and where Katie usually visited at least once a day. Her side of the building had a few feminine knickknacks set around, but Rhett's was stark, with only a wall calendar. The first day of April was crossed out.

"Fiddlesticks," Lavinia said, setting the basket on Katie's desk. "I thought Rhett would be here. Cash as well." She gestured to the food. "I packed for all three."

Katie's knowing brow crept upward. "They're here, around back. Showing some samples to *another* new fella. I think he's considering building a hotel or boardinghouse. I'm amazed. Whichever, if his plans go through, the project will be substantial." She leaned in and lowered her voice. "And I heard him ask about the Brinkman sisters. And if they were still unmarried." She gave a small laugh. "You might want to go say hello."

Lavinia waved off her little sister's suggestion, knowing she was teasing. "I think he'd be more interested in you, with the lumber mill, Katie. He could save a lot of money if the two of you married. He'd get the lumber for free—and then some."

Katie smiled mischievously. She lifted the cotton covering to peek inside the basket. They'd never spoken further about Santiago. When Katie looked inside, a real smile appeared. "Thank you again for lunch. You spoil us."

The last few days in Eden had been hopping. And there was no reason to believe the influx would stop anytime soon. "I guess we have Lara to thank for losing her diary. Those articles have proven to be a boon for our quaint little town." She began unpacking the fare and taking the men's portions over to the other desk. "They brought Rhett Laughlin." She looked off dreamily. "Hmm, Lavinia Laughlin. The name sounds nice."

It's true! A soft flutter in her tummy reminded her of the butterflies she'd felt when his mouth had hungrily covered hers in the meadow only a few days before. She'd always imagined what true love would feel like, but she really hadn't understood at all. *Now I do . . .*

The door opened as boisterous voices sounded out front. Rhett stepped in, followed by a tall fellow who looked to be close to Clint's age. Cash ambled in next. The day after she'd told Rhett she was staying, he'd gone straight to Cash with his idea. If she was changing her dream, he was changing his as well. The restaurant had been Shawn's desire, not Rhett's. He wanted to build, and he wanted to build here in Eden. With Cash at his side, they both would make a much better living than what they'd been doing before.

Rhett smiled when he saw her, causing a new round of flutters.

"I brought you and Cash some lunch."

The new fella brightened. Glimmers of gray salted his dark hair, which was nicely trimmed around his ears. His eyes seemed perceptive as they took in Lavinia and then Katie. Before he was able to say a thing, or Rhett was able to introduce them, Clint stepped inside holding his hat.

He pulled up short. "Well, we're having a party, I see." He put out his hand to the new man. "Clint Dawson, sheriff of Eden."

"Darrell Wells." They shook. "Pleased to make your acquaintance," Mr. Wells said. He quickly nodded at Lavinia and then at Katie, who was still sitting at her desk. "And you two beautiful women must be Brinkmans, if I had to guess?"

Lavinia wanted to laugh, especially when Rhett and Clint exchanged a meaningful glance.

"Yes, they are," Rhett said, stepping next to Lavinia. His finger discreetly brushed her arm. "They're our national treasure here in Eden. We watch over them carefully."

Mr. Wells's brows rose amusingly. "And I aim to help."

Embarrassed, Lavinia made a soft sound in her throat. "I won't keep you, Rhett. I just delivered some fried chicken and warm biscuits." She wished Clint and Mr. Wells weren't here. Rhett had taken to kissing her cheek each time she came to visit, which kept her dreaming up reasons to make the short walk. Her gaze darted to Katie. She understood her little sister better these days as well. Love was a potent drug.

"I won't keep you," Clint said. "And I'll walk you back to the restaurant, Lavinia. But first, I thought you'd all like to know, President Hayes has sent me a letter."

His chest actually puffed out.

"He plans on visiting Eden sometime in the future. Him and the missus."

Mr. Wells looked duly impressed.

"Why, that's wonderful, Clint!" Lavinia exclaimed.

Katie beamed. "You're famous."

Rhett and Cash nodded happily and exclaimed their good feelings.

Clint, proud as a peacock, nodded and stepped out the door. That was her cue to leave as well. Tonight, Rhett would come by the restaurant for supper and to return her basket. They'd sit for an hour on the hotel porch talking and watch people go by—or perhaps take a walk to the meadow, where they could steal a few kisses. He hadn't yet decided what he was going to do with Shawn's Café, and she wasn't pushing. That decision had to be his alone. Whether he decided to keep and open the place or put the ready-to-go restaurant on the market, she'd support him all the way.

Stepping outside into the brisk April day, expectation filled her. Life in Eden was an adventure.

Rhett surprised her, and stepped out too.

Clint dipped his chin and peeled off back toward the livery.

"What about your customer?" Lavinia asked. "Won't he wonder where you've run off to?" Rhett's smile gave her warm tingles.

"He knows. And he's willing to wait."

"Katie says Mr. Wells wants to build something substantial. Congratulations, Rhett. Before long you'll be booked a year out." They passed the butcher shop and turned onto Main Street. He reached down and took her hand. She glanced sideways, to find him smiling into her face.

"You sure are something, Miss Brinkman."

"Rhett?"

"I guess I'm finally realizing what a gift God has dropped into my arms. I feel like I've been forgiven for Shawn's death and only have happiness on my horizon."

She pulled him to a stop, gazing into his eyes. "You've never been blamed. And yes, only goodness and love from this day forward."

She leaned in close. "I wish we were up in our meadow, so I could show my true heart's desire how much he means to me." She laughed softly and then glanced up the knoll, where the watcher stood tall and strong. "But the watcher knows. Our life is only beginning."

He squeezed her hands and then placed a chaste kiss on her cheek. His dazzling smile warmed her heart and soul. "That's just what I needed to hear," he whispered. "Now and always."

ACKNOWLEDGMENTS

Heartfelt thanks to Megan Mulder, my wonderful Montlake editor, for her thoughtful guidance with this book. Working with her has been a joy. Thanks also to Jessica Poore and all the fabulous staff at Montlake Romance. I'm humbled and privileged to be one of your authors.

With each project I complete with my developmental editor, Caitlin Alexander, my esteem for her grows. She's magnificent. Thank you!

As always, thank you to my family, for their love and support through the months of writing and editing. Also to my friends and readers! You are the frosting on the cake.

And to God, for raining His love down in abundance. I feel greatly blessed.

ABOUT THE AUTHOR

Caroline Fyffe was born in Waco, Texas, the first of many towns she would call home during her father's career with the US Air Force. A horse aficionado from an early age, she earned a bachelor of arts in communications from California State University, Chico, before launching what would become a twenty-year career as an equine photographer. She began writing fiction to pass the time during long days in the show arena, channeling her love of horses and the Old West into a series of Western historicals. Her debut novel, *Where the Wind Blows*, won the Romance Writers of America's prestigious Golden Heart Award as well as the Wisconsin RWA's Write Touch Readers' Award. She and her husband have two grown sons and live in the Pacific Northwest.

Center Point Large Print
600 Brooks Road / PO Box 1
Thorndike, ME 04986-0001 USA

(207) 568-3717

US & Canada:
1 800 929-9108
www.centerpointlargeprint.com